GUCCI GIRLS DON'T DATE COWBOYS

O'SULLIVAN SISTERS BOOK 2

SOPHIA QUINN

FLP

Cover art (copyright) by Tugboat Design
www.tugboatdesign.net

ISBN: 978-1-99-115933-5 (Paperback)
ISBN: 978-1-99-115934-2 (Kindle)

Forever Love Publishing Ltd
www.foreverlovepublishing.com
2022 - USA

1

Even in her worst nightmares, Lizzy's wedding gown was a work of art. She'd spent hours designing it, poring over fashion magazines and websites until she found a Gucci inspiration to work with. She crafted the dress as if she were painting a masterpiece, then made sure the seamstress strove for perfection with every stitch and button.

Lizzy let out a sleepy sigh, the familiar music swelling in her barely lucid mind as she linked her arm through her stepfather Derek's. Ed Sheeran's "Perfect" was being played by the string quartet she'd booked months ago, the romantic tones swirling into the air and making her feel radiant—ethereal.

Every night it was the same. The dream started off so beautifully…

The walk down the aisle. All eyes on her—admiring her stunning dress, her perfectly styled hair and makeup. She was the belle of the ball.

And it was perfect.

Until the nightmare part kicked in.

Like always, her flawless wedding dream turned into a surreal nightmare.

This time she tried to wake herself up, rolling over with a groan. She was conscious enough to know it was a dream, but no amount of writhing in her bed would end the torment. So, once again, she was forced to finish the walk down the aisle—only to falter to a stop in front of a perfect stranger.

Who was this woman?

And why was she standing opposite the man she was about to marry?

"Get out of my spot," Lizzy said.

The stranger didn't hear her. She was too busy gazing up at Lizzy's fiancé with an adoring look on her face.

"Connor?" Lizzy tried to get his attention, but he was too enamored with this strange lady to even notice the woman he was *supposed* to marry.

"Hey!" Lizzy moaned the word out loud, her brain reaching for light, consciousness, anything to wake up and end the worst part.

The guests in the crowded pews behind her started to whisper.

She glanced over her shoulder, trying to silence them, but her pointed look did nothing. The whispers increased. Lizzy whipped back, and finally Connor noticed her standing there. He frowned, like he didn't know who she was, and then recognition dawned.

His lips parted a little, and he looked confused. "What are you doing here?"

Lizzy lifted her bouquet and wanted to scream, but she didn't have time to say anything, because his eyes bulged, and then he started laughing.

He laughed!

He pointed.

And then the entire church full of guests joined him.

The stunning brick building echoed with a chorus of mockery. The stained glass windows shook with Lizzy's humiliation.

"Stop," she whimpered, wishing she could raise her voice and shut them all up, but the laughter continued to rise around her until she was shaking.

The vibrations coursed up her arm, buzzing inside her head.

Wait, no.

Buzzing?

That wasn't a dream.

That was her phone!

She sat up with a jolt, scrambling for the device. It was instinctual, and in her sleepy state, she didn't stop to think.

She answered without looking. "Hello?"

"Lizzy?" The male voice on the other end of the line had dread pooling in her stomach as she grew more alert with each passing second.

She knew that voice.

Oh no. What had she done?

She pulled the phone away from her ear to see the name on her screen.

"Lizzy, it's Justin."

"Justin," she whispered, horror sweeping through her. She'd been successfully avoiding her manager's calls for weeks now.

Why, oh why, had she answered her phone?

She squeezed her eyes shut. Of course it was Justin. She should have known.

Biting her lips together, she sniffed in a sharp breath,

then tried to sound bright and alert. It was a joke. She'd barely spoken more than two sentences in a row since she arrived in Aspire, and her voice sounded like it needed oiling.

"Oh, hi, Justin." She opened her eyes and blinked, forcing her sludgy brain to cooperate.

"How are you feeling?" Her manager's voice was hesitant and soft. "Are you… are you sick?"

She sniffed and wondered if heart-sickness could count as an illness. "Um…" She licked her lips. "No. My voice is a little croaky. I've only just woken up." She looked at the clock and winced. It was nearly noon.

"I see." All sympathy dropped from his voice, and he was back to the prim, proper, clipped tone he always loved to use on her. "Lizzy, I thought you were only intending on taking a short break."

She plucked at the seam of the thick duvet she was still half buried under. "Um, yes?"

"Well, it's been four weeks."

A brief silence had her heart slamming against her rib cage. "Yes."

Justin sighed. "So, you've used up all your leave. You have none left."

"Oh. Okay." She swallowed hard. That dread in her belly was a ball of despair. But she would *not* cry. She dug her fingers into the duvet and made a fist. She would *not* cry over the phone to Justin-the-Smug-MBA-Student.

He'd been condescending to her before the wedding disaster because he 'had plans' to rise up the corporate ladder, and she'd been content to stay on the sales floor.

"In fact, you had none left two weeks ago." He sighed, and the sound of patronizing disappointment coming from this pompous little twentysomething made her want to spit.

And cry.

Ugh. She would *not* let Justin-the-Brown-Noser hear her cry.

"Lizzy, are you planning on coming back?"

"Of course." The moment she said the words, she knew they were a lie. She didn't want them to be, but how could she go back? "Um…I just need some more time."

"I don't have any more time to give you. I'm sorry, but I'm going to have to let you go."

Her heart sank to the floor as her stomach churned. The shock was a sharp slap across the face. "You're firing me? But I'm one of the best saleswomen Nordstrom has!"

Justin sighed again. "Lizzy, you haven't shown up to work in over a month."

"But…but…" She looked around the dimly lit bedroom like the perfect words might be lying around amid the mass of crumpled tissues and discarded mugs. "But I'm on bereavement leave," she finally finished.

Justin's silence stretched too long. And when he spoke, his voice wasn't smug, and it wasn't patronizing. It was filled with something far worse—pity. "Lizzy… As far as I'm aware, no one in your family has passed away in the last four weeks."

"Justin, I—" Oh crap. She was crying. The tears filled her eyes and clogged her throat. She sniffed. "I lost *everything*. You know I did. I had to end my engagement and call off my wedding, and if that's not a reason to mourn, I don't know what is."

It would have been a much more powerful speech if her voice hadn't broken with a pathetic sob at the end.

Justin sighed.

She hated his sighs.

"Lizzy, this couldn't have come as a surprise." He sounded tired. And old. Way older than his twenty-four years. "I've been emailing you, leaving you messages on your voice mail..."

"I haven't been checking my messages," she muttered. "I'm kind of going through a crisis right now, in case you hadn't noticed."

"Look, I'm really sorry about what happened to you. I really am. But I need employees I can count on. Lizzy, I'm sorry, but you're fired."

Panic surged through her, hot and terrifying, and with a sharp inhale, she...hung up.

A quick gasp popped out of her as she gaped at her phone. That had been rude. And immature.

She shook her head. Didn't matter. He'd just fired her; he could deal with a little rudeness. And besides, she was the one she ought to be worried about. She'd just lost her job!

The silence in the bedroom was suffocating—one of many things she hated about this ranch house her biological father had left them. It was always quiet. Too quiet.

She could barely sleep at night without the soothing background sounds of traffic and voices and sirens. Oh, all right, maybe sirens weren't soothing. But they were familiar, and right now she missed her apartment in Chicago.

She sniffed. She missed her old *life.*

A fresh wave of tears swelled, and this time she made no attempt to stop them. What was the point? She'd just been fired. After having been cheated on.

She was allowed to wallow.

She fell back against the pillow with a moan.

Nordstrom's was her second home in the city. She'd

been working there as a sales associate ever since she'd graduated college, and she was good at it. What was she supposed to do now?

The question crushed her like a weight. She sank into the bed as it settled over her.

What was she supposed to do now?

She sank further into the soft mattress, the cushy pillow, and burrowed under the thick duvet. She could just go back to sleep. Turning her head slightly, she sighed at the sight of sunlight peeking in through the crack in her blue flower-patterned curtains.

Lizzy wrinkled her nose. Whoever decorated this place had been a big Laura Ashley fan. So not her style.

She threw off the duvet with a sigh. Tempting as it might be, she couldn't stay in bed forever. She had to come up with a plan.

Frowning, she sat up and stared at the dirty dishes that cluttered her bedside table. Planning had never been her forte. Her older sister Emma was the practical sister—she basically lived by pros-and-cons lists and kanban boards.

She'd know what to do.

Lizzy crawled out of bed and hurried into the adjoining bathroom. Emma's room was on the other side, and Lizzy could guarantee it was a darn sight tidier than hers was.

She groaned and shut the door on the mess, splashing water on her face in an attempt to feel better.

It wasn't like she'd hit rock bottom or anything just because she'd gone from being a happily engaged, gainfully employed style icon in one of the best cities in the world to...*this.*

Reaching for a towel to dry off her face, she stared at her reflection.

Familiar green eyes and long blonde hair told her who she was—but nothing felt the same. Who was this person gazing back at her?

It definitely didn't feel like Lizzy O'Sullivan.

She leaned her elbows on the counter and dropped her head into her hands.

Nope. Nothing at all depressing about this.

Drawing in a deep breath, she lifted her head, met her own gaze in the mirror, and tried not to cringe. No makeup and puffy eyes was not a good look. And her normally blown-out locks were a matted mess around her shoulders.

She couldn't go on like this.

A calendar by the door caught her eye—an idyllic country landscape. Obviously. Because apparently the people in these parts weren't content to just live in the middle of nowhere. They liked to be reminded that they lived in Podunk even when they used the bathroom.

Her gaze ran over the dates on the calendar as she tried to figure out what day it was.

Had it really been four weeks since she'd fled Chicago to find her sister in Montana?

Her gaze stopped on the little box that she knew was the right day.

Oof.

The air rushed from her lungs like she'd been sucker punched.

Tomorrow was her wedding day.

A sob caught in her throat as she threw open the door and snagged a sundress from her closet.

She needed Emma. Her sister was the only person who could help her figure this out. It was why she'd come here in the first place…four weeks ago.

She winced. *Crap.* Turned out time didn't just fly when you were having fun. It flew by when you were wallowing in despair too.

She opened the bedroom door and padded to the kitchen.

"Emma?"

No answer.

The house was absurdly quiet. She took a quick tour of the main level, but there was no sign of her sister.

There was no sign of her sister's boyfriend, Nash, either, thank goodness.

She had nothing against Nash. In fact, Lizzy actually liked the ranch foreman. She'd have liked him based solely on the fact that he looked at her sister like she hung the moon. Emma deserved someone who appreciated her.

But on top of that, he was kind and easygoing, and never pried when she randomly burst into tears on those nights Emma forced her to come out of her room to join them for dinner.

So no, she had nothing against Nash. Except for the fact that he had a tendency to be too kind. Too understanding.

But at least he didn't laugh at her like Kit, his ranch hand and best friend.

Still, if Lizzy ran into Nash right now and he gave her that sympathetic look, she'd...she'd...

Well, she'd probably cry again.

And she was tired of crying. She was just tired. Period.

But there was no sign of Nash or her sister in the house. Lizzy frowned at the back door leading out to a porch that overlooked the stables and the giant stretch of nothing that lay beyond.

Emma found it awe-inspiring.

To Lizzy, it was depressing. It made her feel like a tiny

speck in an endless sea of oblivion. Give her skyscrapers and bustling pedestrians any day. But if she knew Emma, she'd likely be out there feeding the pigs or practicing her riding skills or something equally awful.

With a sigh of resignation, she headed toward the door. Like it or not, it was time to face the world.

2

Kit wasn't the only one who noticed when Lizzy pushed open the back screen door and stepped onto the porch.

"What's she doing out here?" Cody asked, pushing his shovel into the dirt as he stopped to watch this unusual sight. "I thought she was nocturnal."

Kit chuckled as his younger brother's brow creased in confusion.

They both stopped to stare up the hill. From this distance, he couldn't make out Lizzy's exact expression, but her movements were still clear.

Her blonde hair was piled high on her head, and she was holding a hand up to block the sun like she was stepping out of a dark cave.

Which, in a way, she sort of was. Kit didn't keep tabs on her, but from what Nash told them, she'd spent most of her time camped out in her room, bingeing on Netflix and eating ice cream.

JJ, their resident mountain man with an overgrown beard and a grease-stained T-shirt, pushed up the brim of his baseball cap to get a better look. "I thought she was a vampire."

Cody chuckled as Kit jokingly smacked JJ upside the head. "Give her a break." He tried to quell his laughter. "She's going through a tough time."

Kit couldn't hide his grin as he chided his friend. He couldn't help it. He'd always been quick to laugh, and Lizzy never failed to amuse him. She'd been staying at the ranch where he worked for about a month now, and while their interactions were few and far between, they were always entertaining.

She was funny. Unintentionally, of course. She was also annoying, irritating, and snobby. But mostly amusing.

"It's been weeks," Cody pointed out, his clean-cut features still screwed up in confusion. "How long does it take to get over a breakup?"

It was a rhetorical question, of course, but Kit and JJ shared a smirk. He was asking the right guys.

"It can take a while, man," JJ said, his voice a low drawl that gave nothing away. He turned back to his work on the fence, and the Swanson brothers were no closer to knowing the details of their friend's life before he moved to Montana.

"She looks like she's searching for something," Cody said, his expression wary. "Do you think she needs our help?" He winced as he asked the question, and Kit knew what he was thinking.

Cody wasn't exactly fond of females crying. What man in their right mind was? The Swanson brothers didn't have sisters, and he supposed they'd both missed the day at school when men learned exactly how to deal with tears.

The thing with Lizzy was that every time Nash had

seen her in the last month, there'd always been tears. Fountains of them—Nash's precise words.

Who knew what an offer of help could elicit?

Neither brother was keen to find out.

But Kit couldn't stomach the thought of a woman being in need either, so he followed Cody's stare, and sure enough, Lizzy was shielding her eyes and craning her neck like she was searching the grounds.

Kit set his tools aside and brushed off his dirty hands. "I'll go see what she needs."

"Good luck, bro," JJ said.

"Whatever you do," Cody called after him, "don't call her 'ma'am.' Trust me on this one."

Kit shook his head with a laugh. Cody was only two years younger than him, but some days it felt like decades. But then again, he supposed being the single dad of twins tended to age a guy. And right now, he felt world-weary as he walked up the hill for the back porch.

He remembered what it was like to have your world flipped upside down by the person who was supposed to love you. He suspected that was why he let so much slide when it came to the knockout blonde and her spoiled, city-girl ways.

"Morning, sleepyhead," he called out.

Lizzy straightened and turned in his direction. She might as well have been posing for a magazine in that skimpy little sundress of hers. Oh yeah, she was a Gucci girl all right. When her gaze landed on him, she dropped her hand from her eyes with an exasperated sigh.

"Well, it's nice to see you too," he said.

His mama used to say he had a Cheshire cat smile. That smirk typically went over well with the ladies. From old Mama at the diner to the buckle bunnies who came to town along with the rodeo, that smile guaranteed a sweet grin in return. Usually a little flirting too.

But right now his signature charm earned him a scowl.

"Where's my sister?"

"You'll have to be more specific," he said. "Rumor has it you have many sisters."

She rolled her eyes. Apparently she wasn't ready to joke about the fact that she and Emma had recently discovered they were two of seven. Duly noted.

"Kit, do you know where Emma is or not?" she asked, her voice the same exact one he used on Corbin and Chloe when he warned them that this was their last chance to stop the shenanigans before a consequence was served.

"You know I'm not her personal secretary, right?"

Lizzy gave him a baleful look that made his grin widen.

She was just too easy to tease.

"Fine," she said as she started to turn away.

"Now just hold your horses, darlin'."

She turned back with a huff. "Don't call me darlin'."

He ignored that. "I haven't seen Emma this morning, but if I had to guess, she's at the elementary school getting ready for the first day."

Lizzy bit her lip, her brows drawing together to form a cute little crease over her nose. The girl was a beauty, no one could deny that. But right now, without all the makeup and the done-up hair and all the other trappings she normally wore when she ventured out of her room, she looked…sweet. Vulnerable, even.

He felt a tug in his chest that had him talking even though she hadn't said a word.

"You know, my twins are over the moon to be in Emma's kindergarten class this year." Just the thought of his kids had his grin growing. "They've been talking nonstop about it. Chloe's already counting sleeps. She's the only kid I know who can't wait to see the summer vacation end."

This was met by a blank stare, like he'd just spoken in tongues.

He scratched the back of his neck. "My, uh, my kids?"

She blinked, her gaze focusing. "Right." She crossed her arms, her scowl back in place. "So, any idea when she'll be back?"

He let out a huff of amusement. "Are you always such a prickly pear in the morning, or did you just wake up on the wrong side of the bed?"

"It's just…" She gave her head a quick shake as she mumbled, "I'm not having a good day."

She looked away, and he thought he saw…

Oh no.

Oh please no, not tears.

He'd seen Lizzy cry once, the first day she'd arrived, and it had nearly killed him.

"Uh, is there something I can help you with?" He rushed out the words, hoping to distract her before the fountain started to flow.

Her lips moved, her jaw worked…

He winced. She was trying not to cry. He looked around for help with more than a hint of desperation. He saw Cody and JJ watching them in the distance. They were too far away to be of any use. Where the heck was Nash?

"You can't help me." The words seemed to burst out of Lizzy against her will. "No one can."

His brows hitched up at that dramatic comment. "Well, that sounds a little extreme."

Her gaze shot to his, and he clamped his mouth shut.

"Extreme?" she snapped, stomping down the stairs and flicking up dust with her slip-on loafer things that sparkled and were like no sneaker Kit had ever seen before.

Where were the laces? And they seemed kind of high at the back, but he couldn't see the heel part.

Kit stared at the shoes, scratching the back of his head while Lizzy's voice crescendoed.

"Do you happen to know of any high-end boutiques hiring around here?" She threw her arms out wide to take in the acres of sprawling hills around them. "Hmm?"

"Uh…" He looked over his shoulder like some store might magically appear and rescue him from this conversation. "Well, no, but—"

"Do you people even have clothing stores?" Her eyes grew wide with horror. "I mean *real* clothing stores, not that hardware place Emma bought those cowboy boots from. And not some depot that sells whatever it is you're wearing."

She threw a hand in his direction, and he looked down at his T-shirt and faded jeans with a laugh.

"What, you don't like my clothes?" He tried to sound offended, but he couldn't hide his grin.

She rolled her eyes. "Everyone in this town looks like they shop at stores called Mud and Co, or Overalls Are Us, or Barn Wear Extraordinaire." Her words were tumbling out in a rampage that was kinda hilarious.

Barn Wear Extraordinaire?

That was funny.

Or it would have been if she wasn't working herself into such a state. But even so, with her cheeks all flushed and her eyes sparkling with emotion, she wasn't just beautiful—she was breathtaking.

The girl was living fire as she went on and on about some nonsense he couldn't really understand. It had to do with clothes and vogue and some French word he'd never heard of. Couture something?

He tipped his head to the side as he tried to make sense of her tirade. Apparently she had something against plaid.

"Are you saying you don't like the way I look?" he cut in when she finally paused to inhale. "Am I supposed to wear my Sunday best when dealing with horse apples and cow manure? Is that what you're saying?"

She frowned. "What's a horse apple?"

This just made him laugh.

"There's nothing for me to do here!" she huffed.

His mind automatically went to her sister, who'd been stuck with all the responsibilities that came with inheriting this ranch. "There's plenty that needs to be done around here."

"There's nothing I *want* to do," she snapped, her voice accusatory, like he was just trying to rile her.

Maybe he was. It was better than seeing her cry. "Maybe it's not always about what you want."

She growled in her throat. "I hate this place. I'm stuck in the middle of nowhere on a ranch I never even asked for."

This cut his laughter short. *She hates this place?* He found himself looking around at the familiar scenery. Familiar, but still the greatest view on God's green earth.

What could she possibly hate about this haven?

Aspire, Montana, had been his home since before he could remember, and this ranch had been the best work he'd ever had. He didn't like people running it down, even if it was a gorgeous Gucci girl with eyes that sparkled like emeralds.

Unsure whether to laugh again or frown, Kit rubbed a hand over his stubble and said, "If you're so miserable, why don't you head back to Chicago?"

"I can't!" Her voice cracked, and the sound made his heart feel like it was splitting in two.

"Why not?"

She threw her hands up. "Because I'm supposed to be getting married tomorrow." Her breathing grew ragged, and her features screwed up in a way that made his own lungs hitch. "I can't go back and face the humiliation of telling all my friends that my fiancé cheated on me and ruined what was supposed to be the best day of my life."

Kit's chest tightened painfully. He knew what it was like to get punched in the face by life—to suddenly find out that the person you thought you'd die old and happy with actually had other plans. That they didn't love you the way they were supposed to.

He'd do anything to wipe that pained expression off Lizzy's face, to pull her into his arms, cradle her head against his shoulder, and promise her that everything would be okay. But he doubted she'd appreciate that.

She probably needed a decent hug, though, just something to snap her out of this dragon mode she was currently stuck in.

She wrapped her arms around herself again, her expression so injured he'd have done just about anything to take that hurt away.

"What I need is Emma," she muttered, her gaze darting around as if her sister was hiding behind the neighboring barn. "But I can't even go into town to find her because this town's got a population of, like, what? Fifty people? And they're all a bunch of country hillbillies who'd just love another excuse to start gossiping about me again."

She adopted an insultingly twangy accent. "Oh, that's the O'Sullivan girl. Emma's sister, right? I saw her crying in the grocery store that one time she came into town."

Kit moved closer, opening his mouth to protest, but she was on a roll, slinging undeserved insults and mocking the people nearest and dearest to him.

"I heard her fiancé was in love with another woman. Oh really? Well, I heard she had to cancel her entire wedding, which she slaved over for months. Poor girl. How humiliating for her!" Lizzy's voice rose and fell like a storming ocean. "I've seen enough movies and TV shows to know how small towns work. And I'm not putting myself through that."

She was lashing out. He knew that. Her pain was talking, not her. Still, irritation pricked at his skin. "Aspire's filled with good people, Lizzy. If you gave them half a chance—"

"Oh, I'm sure. Grandmas and old men nattering away at tables, cowboys with mud on their boots, and women who wouldn't know good fashion if it slapped them in the face."

"Hey." He frowned. She was taking it too far. He stepped a little closer, ready to bring this rant to a swift end. "That's enough. You don't even know this town."

"I don't need to get to know it. I saw enough driving through it. It's not like it's a complex place." She exhaled loudly as she worked herself up on another wave of irritation. "There's no decent restaurants, no museums, no culture *at all*. This town doesn't even have a gym. I bet you a thousand bucks they couldn't make a decent cup of coffee to save their lives—"

"That's enough, Lizzy."

She continued as if he hadn't spoken. "Even so, that

doesn't stop them from throwing their opinions around, though, right? They'd judge anyone new to town, especially a city girl like me."

A muscle in his jaw ticked. She was talking about his home. His family. And she was talking so fast now he could hardly keep up with her words. The only person he'd ever heard speak like this was the auctioneer at the cattle auctions.

"And why wouldn't they, right?" she continued. "They've got their safe little place in their perfect little world. But there's no room there for me."

He flinched when her voice broke. Blood was rushing to his head, his pulse pounding in his ears. It wasn't just anger at the way she was talking smack about the people he loved. It was her words…

There was something familiar about the way she was talking.

"I don't belong here." His ex-wife's farewell note flashed in his head. *"You'll be better off without me."*

He shook off the memory that he'd thought was dead and buried. It was ancient history. She'd left, and they'd survived.

"…and it's not like I have any other skills, right?" Lizzy was saying.

He frowned. What was she on about now?

"I should just face it. I'm useless!" Her voice broke again. "I have nothing to offer anyone!"

His head was buzzing with anger, and for the life of him, he couldn't say if that emotion was at her or on her behalf. Maybe both. Why was she talking about herself that way?

"I have to get out of this place." She looked up at him with a stubborn glint in her eyes. "I don't belong here."

"I don't belong here. You'll be better off without me."

Lizzy's arms flicked in the air while Kit tried to dodge his ex-wife's words and figure out how to put an end to this rant.

"I don't even know why I'm still here!" Lizzy's voice pitched. "I should just—"

Before he could think better of it, he stepped into her space, lightly pinched her chin, and cut off her tirade with a kiss to the lips. It wasn't a quick peck; it was a firm statement that he poured a fair chunk of his annoyance into, and maybe just a little of the yearning he'd been feeling since the day he met her.

He meant to pull away quickly. This was shock therapy, not a come-on. But her lips were even softer than they looked. And the taste of her was unbearably sweet. Some girly floral scent wrapped around him, delicate and pure, and if he pulled her into his arms, he just knew she'd—

Two firm hands landed on his chest and forced him back.

He released her immediately, raising his hands but looking her straight in the eye.

"You need to stop talking now," he said, as if that kiss hadn't just turned his world upside down.

It had. But even better, it stopped her ranting, and that desperate gleam in her eyes was gone. She still looked mad enough to spit, but at least that anger was better than the downward spiral of insults and self-pity.

"How dare you!" She raised her hand to slap him, but he caught her wrist, lightly holding it and trying not to notice how smooth her skin was.

"It's rude to hit a gentleman."

"You are no gentleman!" She wriggled free of his grasp

and stormed back into the house, slamming the door hard enough to make the house shudder.

He winced as that rush of adrenaline that had prompted him to kiss her faded into a warm, insistent hum of…wonder. He couldn't stop a little grin. His lips were tingling, and even though he probably shouldn't have kissed her like that, it was better than yelling at her to shut up.

Right?

He ducked his head with a chuckle as he headed back toward his friends. Oh yeah, she was likely cursing his name because of that kiss.

But it was worth it.

3

The door slammed shut behind Lizzy, and the room seemed to shake in the aftermath.

But it wasn't the house that was shaking, it was her.

Lizzy stumbled over to a seat at the kitchen table and fell into it just as her knees gave out underneath her.

What. Was. That?

Her fingers came to her lips, which were still warm from Kit's kiss.

Kit's *kiss*. She blinked as she tried to process what on earth had just happened.

Had he really just kissed her?

The tingling in her lips was proof that she hadn't been hallucinating. Her heart was slamming against her rib cage as her lungs labored for air. What was happening to her?

She touched her lips again. They still buzzed, and her skin still felt too sensitive, her senses heightened like that kiss had been a bolt of lightning that singed her all the way through and not just a kiss.

An *unwanted* kiss.

She straightened in the seat, her hand dropping to the

table with a sharp exhale of irritation. At herself, mainly, because while she knew very well that kiss was unwanted, the butterflies in her belly hadn't gotten the memo.

She crossed her arms with another huff.

"Who does he think he is?" she muttered.

"Who does who think he is?" Emma's voice came from the doorway behind her, and Lizzy whirled around with a squeak.

"You're home," she said.

Emma's arms were filled with groceries, and Lizzy leapt up to help her.

"I just ran into town to put some final touches on my new classroom and pick up some groceries for dinner." Emma put one of the bags down on the counter. "I tried to tell you I was heading out, but you were still asleep."

Lizzy set the other bag down before lunging at her sister.

Emma hugged her tight. Her sister always gave the best hugs.

"Hey," Emma crooned in a motherly tone. "You having a rough day?"

Lizzy nodded, not quite trusting herself to talk yet. Her throat was tight with tears. Also, she didn't know where to start.

Kit kissed me! That was what threatened to come out of her mouth if she were to open it right now, but that was stupid. Kit's kiss wasn't why she was on the verge of tears.

He'd been out of line, obviously, and so, of course, she was angry about it, but it didn't mean anything. It wasn't nearly as important as the fact that her wedding day was tomorrow and her life was falling apart at the seams.

And yet, when Emma finally loosened her embrace

and Lizzy pulled away, her mind was still firmly fixed on the cowboy and those amazing lips of his.

His kiss.

No, that *unwanted* kiss.

She gave herself a mental eye roll. Clearly she'd lost her mind if one kiss from a rude, obnoxious, cocky cowboy was messing with her head.

"Did something happen?" Emma asked as she put the groceries away.

"You mean aside from the fact that my fiancé cheated on me?" Lizzy muttered.

Emma glanced over her shoulder with a wry smile. "Aside from that."

Lizzy sighed. "I lost my job."

Silence fell hard and heavy as Lizzy stared at her hands on the tabletop. A slithery, slimy sensation had taken root in her belly, and she couldn't bring herself to look up to see her sister's reaction.

Emma wouldn't be angry or even disappointed in her. She was way too nice for that. But even so, Lizzy's head dipped down farther. Shame. That's what this feeling was. Humiliation.

She'd buried her head in the sand for four weeks and let the last shreds of her life in Chicago fall to pieces.

I'm useless! I have nothing to offer anybody.

Her gut churned as her own voice came back to her. Kit hadn't argued the point.

Not that she'd expected him to.

The rest of the words she'd spewed just a moment ago hit her like a slap in the face and she winced.

She'd been mean. Hurtful. Spouting off about people in his hometown like she knew better.

Emma never would have acted like that no matter how much pain she was in.

And Lizzy couldn't even say why she'd lashed out that way. Kit hadn't done anything wrong—well, not until he'd kissed her.

She shook off thoughts of his manly scent and powerful body—how it ever so lightly pressed against her when he leaned in and stole her words away. He'd been angry. He'd only been trying to shut her up, that was all. And it had worked.

Still, her mind caught on the look in his eyes just before he'd kissed her. She'd been annoying him, sure. That was kinda the point, if she were being honest. His easygoing smile had felt like a physical assault when she was so miserable.

But there was something else in his gaze just before he'd pinched her chin.

There'd been too many emotions to name, but she could have sworn she'd seen hurt. And pain. And maybe even…desire.

Emma's sigh as she sank into the seat beside her jerked Lizzy out of her memories.

"Oh, honey, I'm sorry." She reached out and squeezed Lizzy's hand.

"I loved that job." Lizzy's voice was pathetically small.

"I know you did."

She drew in a deep breath. "But I didn't do anything to keep it."

Emma's wince was sympathetic, but she didn't try to argue.

"This is my own fault. But I don't know what to do about it."

Emma was quiet for a long moment before scooting her

chair back and standing. "Come on. I was going to make some lunch for Nash and the boys. I bet getting some food in your belly will help."

Despite her misery, Lizzy laughed under her breath. "You're going to be one of those moms, aren't you? Forcing your kids to eat whenever they're unhappy. You're already like an old Italian grandma, and you're not even Italian. Or old."

Emma laughed. "You get cranky when you're hungry, and you know it."

"And I get curvy when I'm well fed," Lizzy shot back. "Unlike one lucky lady I know."

Her pointed look made Emma snicker.

"You make it sound like there's something wrong with curves." Her sister rolled her eyes. She hated when Lizzy got hung up on her weight.

"There's nothing wrong with gaining a little weight," Emma said. "You could stand to gain some weight."

"Says the woman who can eat whatever she wants and still wear a size six," Lizzy grumbled.

"Okay, now I *know* you're hungry," Emma teased as she pulled out a casserole dish from the fridge along with some utensils. "But honestly, you haven't been eating enough. And some sunshine wouldn't hurt either. You look like a ghost."

Lizzy opened her mouth to tell her sister she'd just gone outside but thought better of it. They had enough to discuss without wasting words on some meaningless run-in with a cowboy who skipped out on the day they taught manners.

Emma pulled out some fresh baked bread that made Lizzy's mouth water.

"I suppose one of the perks of not getting married

tomorrow is I don't have to worry about fitting into my dress," she grumbled as Emma handed her a slice.

Emma laughed. "See? Now you're looking at the bright side."

Lizzy gave in to an unexpected smile, and Emma stopped what she was doing to stare at her.

"What?" Lizzy wrinkled her nose. "Why are you looking at me like that?"

Emma grinned. "That's just the first real smile I've seen from you since you arrived." She arched her brows. "I know you got bad news about your job, but did something good happen today too?"

Lizzy's mind instantly flashed on Kit's fingers clasping her jaw. The way his lips closed over hers, so firm and hot and—

Ugh. That was so not a good thing.

"No, nothing," she said a little too quickly.

Emma threw the casserole in the oven to heat as Lizzy grabbed them both some iced tea and set the table. She'd eat and be long gone before Nash showed up with the other guys.

She wasn't in a rush to see Kit again, and if he so much as smirked at her after stealing a kiss like that she'd... she'd...

Well, she had no idea what she'd do.

"What's that sigh about?" Emma asked.

Lizzy hadn't realized she'd been so loud, but when Emma joined her at the table and gave her a questioning look, she murmured, "Just trying to figure out what to do with my life now that it's pretty much over, that's all."

Emma rolled her eyes. "Your life is not over."

"Yeah, well." She shrugged. "My life in Chicago is."

"Why?" Emma sounded honestly confused. "You love

Chicago. If that's where you want to be, you should go back. You had more than just Connor there. You have friends, and I'm sure you'll be able to find another job in retail if that's what you want."

Lizzy stirred some sweetener into her iced tea as she nodded. Her sister had a point. She knew that. If she wanted another job even close to the fashion world, she sure as heck couldn't stay here. And Chicago had been her home long before she'd met Connor. But even so…

"I can't go back, Em."

Emma sighed as she reached for her hand. "Why not?"

Lizzy sighed. "It's just too humiliating. I thought I had it all figured out, you know? I thought…" She stopped to swallow a lump. "I thought I had my perfect man and a great job and the wedding of my dreams, and the dress, Emma. The dress."

Emma smiled sadly as Lizzy moaned. "I know, sweetie."

Lizzy threw her hands out wide. "And if I go back to Chicago, I won't have anything."

"That's not true," Emma murmured.

"Isn't it?" Lizzy arched her brows. "You're not going back, and you were my closest friend. And Sarah texted me the other day that if I decide not to return, she's going to move in with her boyfriend to save on rent and blah, blah, blah." Lizzy's hands flew in the air as she worked herself into another state of despair. "All my other friends will be judging me and laughing at me, or at the very least they'll expect an explanation for why the wedding was canceled, and—"

"Lizzy."

Lizzy took a deep breath as she faced her sister's concerned stare. "What?"

"Can I make an observation?" Emma went back into the kitchen, reaching for the bread and starting to carve off more slices for Nash and the others.

Lizzy let out her breath in a long sigh. "Ugh. I hate it when you start a conversation that way."

"Why?"

"It means you're about to criticize my behavior. It's like putting a pretty pink bow on something hurtful so it doesn't appear so bad."

Emma frowned, obviously wounded. "I would never intentionally hurt you. I don't have to say it."

"Great, well, now I'm curious." Lizzy flung out a hand. "So, just…go on. Observe already."

Seeming hesitant, Emma pursed her lips and focused on bread slicing.

Lizzy braced herself, clenching her jaw and telling herself to be a good sister and not bite back after Emma said her piece.

Her sister's voice was light, but the words were heavy and confronting. "Okay, well, over the last month, as you've been processing your pain, I've noticed that the stuff that makes you cry the hardest is your loss of the wedding. You seem more heartbroken over that than what Connor did to you. It's like you're mourning the loss of your big day more than the loss of this man who was going to be your life partner."

Lizzy stilled, unsure how to respond. The observation washed over her like a thick wave of mud she couldn't battle. Drenched and suffocating, she sat at the table struggling to breathe.

That's not true! She wanted to shout it in her sister's face, to prove how wrong Emma was.

I loved Connor! But even as she thought about it, she

wondered…how much?

Because there was no denying that Emma had a point. Lizzy had been grieving the wedding, and the future she'd envisioned for herself, the life she'd had planned out…

But Connor?

Maybe not so much.

Lizzy swallowed hard, but it didn't help to ease this new tightness in her chest.

"I guess I'm just wondering what that means." Emma murmured, focusing back on the bread like she needed to cut it perfectly in order to save the planet.

Was Emma right?

Confusion and fear had Lizzy's belly taking a nosedive. She'd fallen head over heels for Connor on their very first date. She'd known right away he was the perfect guy for her.

But…why?

Because he was the perfect gentleman. How many times had she told Emma that? She'd been swept off her feet by his style and his looks and his manners…

"It's rude to hit a gentleman."

She frowned as Kit's voice filled her head.

A cowboy with dirt on his pants and man-sweat running down his back was no gentleman.

But was a man who had a girlfriend behind his fiancée's back really a gentleman either?

Connor had all the class of a wealthy supermodel—tailored suits, aftershave that must have been made in heaven and sent down via angel post, his hair always styled so perfectly, his face clean-shaven and gorgeous.

Yet he totally betrayed her.

Her chest ached, but her heart…her heart wasn't broken. Not over Connor.

She was hurt though. Her perfect man hadn't cared about her at all. Not the way he was supposed to.

But had she loved him the way she ought to love the man she was going to marry?

The question had her staring at her glass of iced tea long after the ice melted and Emma went out to bring lunch to Nash and the other guys.

She'd known for a month now that she'd been wrong about Connor. But what else had she been wrong about? And for how long?

If he hadn't cheated on her, would she ever have realized that he wasn't the guy for her?

Lizzy crossed her arms on the table and dropped her head on top of them. It was official. She didn't know anything anymore. Heck, she didn't even know who she was without the wedding and the job and her perfect life she'd had so beautifully planned.

If life were a board game, she'd been sent back to square one.

Nope. Nothing demoralizing about that.

One thing was clear—she needed a new game plan. She needed a new *life*. But no matter how hard she tried, she couldn't see how she was supposed to move forward. Her future seemed like a dead end no matter which way she looked at it.

As she puttered back to her room to curl up on her bed, she found her mind returning to her run-in with Kit over and over again.

She'd been too harsh about the town and the people in it. She probably ought to apologize. But everything she'd said about herself being useless and without a hope for the future?

That had never felt more true.

4

Kit had caught a lucky break, and he knew it.

When he returned to Cody and JJ after his run-in with Lizzy, he was sure he'd be hearing all kinds of comments about that kiss.

The kiss.

He dipped his head with a grin every time he remembered that fireworks display. What would have happened if she hadn't pushed him away?

What would it have been like if she'd actually kissed him back?

He was almost afraid to imagine it. The temptation to kiss her again was already brewing; he sure as heck didn't need more.

"Hey, bro," Cody shouted out to him. "You still with us?"

Kit tipped back his cowboy hat with a grin. "What were you saying?"

Cody and JJ exchanged a mocking look at his expense, but Kit didn't care. It had been obvious that Cody and JJ had missed the lip-lock that was seared onto his brain.

Apparently, they'd been having too much fun talking among themselves and placing wagers on when Kit was going to ask the younger O'Sullivan sister out on a date.

Never. The answer was never, which was what he told them.

"We're just about done with the fence. You want to grab a beer with us before you head home?"

Kit shook his head. "No can do. I've gotta take over with the twins before Mom and Dad lose their sanity."

Cody chuckled. "Nah, they love those little munchkins."

It was the truth, obviously. Corbin and Chloe's grandparents adored them, even when they were acting like little tyrants. But all the same, they put in enough hours helping out with day care so Kit could work at the ranch. He tried his best not to take advantage.

"Nash is out too," JJ said. "I just saw him heading to the stables, and he mentioned something about dinner with Emma and her sister."

Kit grinned. "Hope he has better luck with Lizzy than I did."

JJ's smile was slow and taunting. "From what we saw, you managed to make her bad day even worse."

"Yeah, what did you say exactly?" Cody teased, leaning on the newly repaired fence. "One minute she was there talking your ear off, and the next, we turned around to see the door slamming shut."

"Nearly fell off the hinges," JJ added.

"It's not what I said," Kit started as he turned to walk away.

It was what he'd done. But they didn't need to know that. It was sheer good luck that they'd missed the heated, intoxicating—albeit brief—kiss.

But as he caught sight of Nash heading toward the main house, he found himself tensing all over again. His boss had gone back to the house after Emma brought out that amazing lunch for them.

He must have seen Lizzy, or at least talked to Emma.

The closer he got to the house and his truck, the more Kit braced for a blow. Or at least a good talking to. It was likely the least he deserved after kissing a lady out of nowhere like that.

A heartbroken lady, no less.

He winced just as Nash spotted him and waved him over.

"Hey, you want to join us for dinner?" Nash asked.

Kit's shoulders relaxed. "Not tonight. Thanks though."

Nash didn't know about the kiss. If he had, Kit would have heard about it instantly. He might even have a sore jaw over it too. Nash was protective of the women in his life—and right now, Lizzy was firmly in his life.

But for how long?

The question nagged at him, just as her words from earlier had been ringing round his head every time JJ and Cody weren't cracking jokes.

She said she didn't belong here. Did that mean she was leaving?

He rubbed a hand over his chest, wiping dirt off on his already filthy T-shirt.

"You sure?" Nash asked as they both stopped outside the house. "Lizzy will be there."

"All the more reason I shouldn't be, I'd reckon," Kit said with a laugh. "Pretty sure that girl isn't keen on me."

Nash smiled. "That'd be a first."

Kit smirked. He had something of a reputation as a charmer with the ladies in town. Not that it meant anything, really. It was also widely known that after his ex left town, he wasn't in the market for another relationship. At least, not the kind of casual fling that women were looking for when they flirted with him.

He had a certain appeal, all right—that wasn't a secret. But a woman would have to fall in love with him and his kids for him to even consider another relationship.

His kids deserved a mama. One who'd stick around and give them all the love they needed.

"I have it on good authority that Lizzy would love it if you joined us," Nash said. He wore a knowing smirk of his own that had Kit stopping short with a strange pang in his chest.

"Yeah?" he asked, disbelief clear in his tone.

"Absolutely." Nash kept walking. "Emma was saying just this afternoon that Lizzy's having a tough time today, and she doesn't think it helps that she's the third wheel in a new relationship." Nash turned around quickly with his hands raised in defense. "Not that I see her that way. Or Emma, obviously. But being heartbroken is bad enough without having a happy new relationship thrown in your face."

Kit winced. He knew that better than anyone. After Natalie left, it felt like everywhere he'd turned people were pairing off and getting married. He and his friends were that age, he supposed. It was only natural. But it had been hard not to take it as a personal affront every time a buddy or cousin asked him to be best man or join in on his bachelor party, especially in those early days when the twins were still toddlers and his heart felt like a mangled piece of pulp.

"Rain check?" he offered, nodding toward his truck. "I really need to get back to the twins. They'll be waiting."

"Yeah, man, of course." Nash gave him a wave before heading through the back door.

They'd been best friends for as long as Kit could remember, and a part of him sorta wished Nash had heard about the fact that he'd kissed Lizzy. He took off his hat to run a hand through his matted, dirty-blond hair as he climbed into his truck.

Nash had always been the practical sort, and Kit wouldn't mind a heaping dose of reason right now.

He put the truck in gear, already smiling at the thought of the two curtain crawlers who were waiting for him at home.

They might not offer a whole lot of reason, but they were the best distraction anyone could ask for.

His parents' house was a split-level ranch home on the outskirts of town in a nice tree-lined neighborhood where kids were always riding bikes during the summer and sleigh riding during the winter.

He threw open the front door, dropping his voice low to growl, "Fee fi fo fum!"

Out ran two little tow-headed munchkins, giggling and squealing as they threw themselves at him.

"Oh no, they got me," he roared as they climbed his limbs to bring him down to his knees.

When he made a production of toppling over on the ground, Corbin climbed on top of him like he was Mount Everest, and Chloe ran around in circles cheering for their success in taking down the big bad giant.

"All right, all right," his mother, Anna, called as she walked into the room. She was laughing as she took in the sight before her. "That's enough, you two. Go wash your hands. Dinner is almost ready."

"Yes, Grammy," Chloe shouted.

The twins scurried off to do as they were told, and Kit slowly got to his feet, groaning as the workday caught up with him and hit with a wave of exhaustion.

"Thanks, Mom," he said, wrapping an arm around her shoulders and kissing the top of her head as they walked toward the kitchen.

"How was your day, Kit?" his dad called out from where he was standing in front of the fridge.

"Pretty good," he said. "How'd everything go here?"

"Jonathon, grab some juice for the kids while you're in there," his mother called out.

"Oh fine, fine." His dad snagged the juice as requested.

"Kit, go shower up, honey. You stink." His mother gave him a sweet smile, and he chuckled, double-timing it up the stairs, showering and returning within ten minutes to help set the table.

The smell of stew and baking rolls made his stomach growl.

"Did the twins behave?" he asked, flicking wet strands of hair off his forehead.

"Of course!" His mother grinned.

She had never once said anything else when he asked. He was pretty sure Grammy overlooked a good deal of naughty behavior…or maybe she was just way better at getting them to behave than he was.

The kids came back in, and everyone took their seats and bowed their heads as Kit's father said grace.

Kit ladled out the twins' food as Corbin started in on a long story that involved fairy dust and Neverland.

Kit nodded, his expression serious as he listened to the tale.

He was a lucky man, of that there was no doubt.

He wasn't sure what he and the kids would have done

after Natalie left if his parents hadn't offered to take them all in. The twins had been almost one at the time, and while he'd been making enough money for a place of their own, being a single parent to twin toddlers had been more than he could handle.

Even with his semi-retired parents helping out, sometimes it felt like too much. But they made it work. And luckily school would start in a little over a week, so they'd all get a reprieve for most of the day.

"No, that's not what happened next." Chloe's loud interjection in Corbin's story brought Kit back to the present with a jolt. "We went to Narnia next."

He and his parents exchanged knowing smiles as the kids bickered about how exactly their fantastical adventure unfolded.

"And how about you two?" Kit asked. "Ma, how's the florist shop going?"

"Oh, good, thanks." His mother smiled. She worked at the florist part-time, and mostly, Kit suspected, to get out of the house and interact with townsfolk.

She'd always been a sociable type, just as his father had always been highly involved in the community. These days he mainly participated through volunteer work, at the church and in the senior community.

They both told him about their day, but...something was off.

Kit set down his roll as he watched the subtle body language that had him on high alert.

There was a tension here tonight that he couldn't quite explain. A too-tight smile from his dad, a forced laugh from his mom.

Did they have a fight or something?

No. He disregarded that suspicion quickly. They were

sharing looks. Meaningful, knowing looks. The kind that almost always heralded a 'talk' after dinner.

His insides fell flat. Something was up, and he just hoped it wasn't something about the twins.

They were a handful, sure, but they were sweet and loving, and overall good kids.

By the end of the night, he was certain of one thing—something was wrong.

And it had to do with him.

5

Lizzy pushed some food around her plate, her gaze darting back and forth between Emma and Nash as she watched the two of them talk about their day.

"Really?" Nash's handsome face was lit with excitement on Emma's behalf. "So you got the classroom you wanted?"

"Yup. Principal Toulouse said this will be the biggest incoming kindergarten class they've had in a decade, so she was happy to give me the bigger room."

"That's great," Nash said. "Do you need any more help getting the supplies ready?"

"No, but thanks." Emma beamed at him. "I know you've got your hands full this week on the ranch. By the way, how'd it go with the buyer? Did he offer a fair price?"

Lizzy started to tune out again as Nash delved into the specifics of running a cattle operation, but Emma's eyes were wide with interest.

Taking a small bite of the mixed vegetable dish she'd helped Emma make, she watched her sister and Nash go back and forth and decided no one in the history of the world had ever found the topics of ranching and kindergarten so thoroughly fascinating as these two.

They were hanging on each other's words like the world's fate rested on parent-teacher meetings and feeding schedules.

She stabbed at her food as guilt niggled her gut. Her sister deserved to have someone who cared so much about what made her happy. And it was sweet to see Emma take such an interest in Nash's world.

Now her world too, Lizzy supposed.

She reached for her water glass. Maybe she was a little jealous.

Emma and Nash exchanged goofy, lovestruck grins as they laughed over something Nash said.

Okay, maybe she was a lot jealous.

As she watched them, she tried to remember a time when she and Connor had ever looked at each other like that. Or one single occasion when Connor had been this fascinated by her work or her life outside of him and their wedding.

She leaned back in her seat, her appetite totally gone now as she forced herself to admit that she'd never been this interested in Connor's world either.

Heck, she barely even knew what he did for a living. Only that he made a whole lot of money doing it.

She frowned down at the meatloaf on her plate. Did that make her shallow?

Ugh. The fact that she had to ask was probably answer enough.

She slumped down in her seat. As if this day couldn't get any more depressing, now she couldn't even feel sorry for herself.

"That's so interesting," Emma was saying to her boyfriend. She turned to Lizzy. "Don't you think so?"

Lizzy blinked at her sister. Emma was only trying to include her. She and Nash had been going above and beyond to make her feel included, even though she was totally infringing on their honeymoon period, and she knew it.

Lizzy forced a smile. "Yeah. Very interesting," she agreed.

She doubted anyone was fooled, but Emma gave her a grateful smile anyway. For reasons Lizzy couldn't quite understand, Emma truly loved it here on this ranch.

"Did you hear back from any of the others today?" Nash asked.

Lizzy instantly stiffened, dropping her gaze back to her plate.

'The others' were the sisters she and Emma hadn't known about until they'd inherited this ranch.

Emma's sigh sounded weary. "Nothing new. I can't get April to return my calls, and I don't even know if Sierra's gotten any of my messages."

Nash leaned across the table to cover Emma's hand with his own. "You'll get a hold of them eventually."

"Yeah, and then what?" Lizzy muttered. She'd said it so quietly that Emma and Nash didn't hear, moving on to the next topic with ease.

Which was for the best.

Lizzy was enough of a Debbie Downer these days with her constant crying and her mess of a life. She didn't want to add more bad vibes by giving her two cents on the whole new family situation.

As far as she was concerned, the sooner they all agreed to

sell and move on with their lives the better. Or, if Emma and Nash really wanted this place, let 'em have it. That was fine too. But the sooner they could go back to not acknowledging there were other half sisters out there in the world, the better.

They'd gone this long without other siblings, and they'd gotten along just fine. Just like they'd done great with Derek as their stepdad and no Frank O'Sullivan in sight.

If Frank and these half sisters hadn't wanted anything to do with them before, then good riddance, right?

Unfortunately, Emma didn't share her sentiment. She was dead set on tracking them all down—presumably to get an agreement on what to do with the ranch, but Lizzy suspected there was more to it than that.

Her sweet, kind sister wanted to get to know them.

Lizzy sighed, scraping her chair back from the table. "If you guys don't mind, I'm going to excuse myself," she said. "I'll come back out later to clean up, but you two ought to have some alone time."

They both protested, but she ignored them. They were too nice and they'd never ask for privacy, but she was determined to do her best to give them space. It was the least she could do after the way they'd taken care of her for the past four weeks.

She groaned as she reached her bedroom. She still couldn't believe it had been four weeks.

With a wince, she eyed the disaster zone she'd been hunkering down in. Between the empty mugs and discarded Kleenex, the clothes strewn about, and the stale smell of bed linens that hadn't been washed in far too long, she was more than a little disgusted by the sight before her.

The bed was calling, the rumpled covers and sheets

like a handwritten invitation to come back in and sulk the rest of the evening away.

But...four weeks.

The thought of how much time she'd spent wallowing in that bed made her cringe.

Instead of climbing back in, she picked up a crumpled T-shirt and threw it in the laundry hamper.

Oddly enough, that simple act made her feel a little better. She'd never been a slob, and that one act of cleaning up made her feel a little more like herself. Next, she picked up all the tissues and stacked the dirty dishes so she could bring them back to the kitchen when she returned to deal with the dinner cleanup.

Hands on her hips, she regarded the slightly improved room, her head seeming to clear along with each new inch of floor she uncovered.

Reaching for her phone, she turned on her workout playlist. This wasn't exactly the workout she used to do at her gym back in Chicago, but after a month in bed, tidying a messy room seemed daunting.

With the fast-paced beat keeping her moving, she went around the room, sorting clothes and hanging up all the dresses and shirts she hadn't bothered to put away.

She'd gotten to the bottom of a stack of clean laundry when she pulled out the thick, coarse material of...overalls.

Holding them up, she found her lips twitching with the start of a grin.

She remembered these well. Kit had bought them for her on her very first day on the ranch after she'd given him a hard time about the ugly but admittedly useful clothing.

With a huff that was part amusement and part exasperation, she threw them into a pile of their own.

He didn't actually expect her to wear those, right?

She could only imagine the look on his face if she actually walked out of the house wearing the shapeless denim.

He'd laugh, of that she had no doubt.

She clapped a hand over her mouth to stifle a giggle that felt bizarre after four weeks of crying.

Balling up the overalls, she shoved them under the bed, continuing to tidy her room. For reasons she couldn't even explain, she felt better. Actually getting off her butt and doing something was making her feel less useless.

But even with the overalls out of sight, the man who'd gifted them to her lingered in her mind.

Kit.

The scruffy non-gentleman. The man who kissed her.

Would he ask her about her day? Would he care?

He certainly didn't give two figs about appearance.

She caught herself smiling like a fool as she put a pair of pajamas in a drawer.

What are you doing? Stop thinking about him!

She gave her head a shake, turned up the volume of the music, and got back to work, this time determined to not think about the infuriating cowboy and his annoying sense of humor.

By the time she went to help clean up after dinner, her room was nearly tidy. She could hear Emma's and Nash's voices from the back porch as they watched the sun sink over the horizon and continued to talk as if they'd never run out of things to say.

Lizzy smiled at her sister's happy profile visible through the windows and then turned back to tackle the dishes. She might be a little jealous of her sister, but mostly she was happy for her.

And as for herself?

Lizzy scrubbed the pots and pans with renewed vigor. Tomorrow was her wedding day, and in a weird sort of way, she was almost eager to get it out of the way.

Tomorrow might mark the end of an era, but for the first time in a long time, Lizzy felt a flicker of hope at the thought of a new day.

6

"... And they all lived happily ever after." Kit closed the dogeared, beloved storybook and set it down on the end table between Chloe's and Corbin's beds.

"That was the last one," he said as he pulled Chloe's blanket up to her chin and made sure her tattered rabbit, Stuffy, was in its right spot just to the left of her chin.

"But, Dad," Corbin started, his voice high and whiny. Kit knew what he was going to say before he even said it. "Daniel *said* so," Corbin huffed, picking up the conversation where they'd left off twenty minutes ago.

Kit winced and pinched the bridge of his nose. Apparently not even three storybooks could deter his very stubborn son when he had his mind set on something.

"We've been over this, kiddo," Kit said. Several times. Hundreds of times. But who was counting?

He knew very well what Daniel had said.

Daniel was one of their friends from playgroup and the ultimate harbinger of fake news. "Daniel's wrong, bud. Only mommies carry babies in their bellies."

"Yeah, but Daniel says daddies take over being pregnant after the mommies are done," Corbin said, his brow furrowed with the earnest need to understand the birds and the bees right this second. "They take turns, he said. Is that true?"

"Did you carry us in your belly, Daddy?" Chloe asked, her eyes wide and filled with such adoration he was almost tempted to lie.

"No, pumpkin." He ruffled her hair. "You were only ever in your mommy's belly."

Kit held his breath as they both fell silent, their lips puckered in matching frowns as they stewed this over.

Call him a coward, but he hated whenever the talk of mommies came up. Particularly *their* mommy. The older they got, the more challenging their questions became… and the more they understood his answers.

For better or worse.

"But, Daddy—" Corbin started.

"No more buts." Kit shifted to kiss the top of Corbin's head. "Your friend Daniel is mighty smart, but just take my word on this one, okay?"

He saw both their little mouths open, ready to protest.

"Uh-uh," he said. "We've had our bath, said our prayers, had some water, and read three books." He backed away toward the hallway, which glowed bright compared to the night-light-lit bedroom. "Now it's time for sleep."

He shut the bedroom door before they could lodge any more complaints.

With a weary sigh, he headed back toward the living room, where his parents were already settled in for the night to watch the news and their favorite programs.

He stopped short when he reached the cozy, thick-carpeted den with its dark oak paneling and familiar, if slightly worn, old furniture.

His parents were sitting next to each other on the couch, but the TV wasn't on, and by the way they looked at Kit when he walked in, they'd obviously been waiting for him.

Kit scrubbed the back of his neck, fighting another weary sigh. "Okay, you guys, what's wrong? You've been tense all night."

"Tense?" His mother tried to play innocent, but he gave her a baleful look, and she ended up smiling at him. "Oh, okay, fine. But it's actually really good news."

"Good news, huh?" He arched a brow. "So why do you both look so worried, then?"

They shared a glance that made his gut tighten with apprehension.

"Do you remember Gladys and Tom Perkins?" his father asked. "They used to live here when you were just a boy, but then they moved to Astoria, Oregon?"

He shrugged, not really remembering, although he had vague recollections of his parents visiting them a few times.

"Well, we've kept in touch over the years," his mother said, glancing at his father. "And they...well, they've invited us to join them on a cruise."

"Wow. A cruise. That sounds like fun." Kit raised his eyebrows, still trying to figure out what the big problem was.

And then it hit him. And like a sucker punch, it left him winded.

A cruise.

Away from home.

"It'll be for eight weeks," his mother said, her smile

looking more and more like a grimace as she watched his reaction. "We'll be touring around the Mediterranean and parts of Europe."

"Eight weeks," he choked out. "Wow."

A heavy silence fell. Then his father cleared his throat. "We'll actually be gone for about nine weeks altogether, as we'll stay with Gladys and Tom for a couple days before sailing out of Seattle."

His father beamed like he'd won first prize at the state fair, while Kit struggled to form a smile.

Nine weeks. Nine weeks with the kids and no support? How was he supposed to pull that off?

He didn't want to be selfish. His parents deserved this adventure, but he felt like someone had knocked the wind right out of his sails.

"I know this is probably a surprise," his mother said gently. "But the kids are starting school in just over a week, so the timing is actually quite good."

Everything in him tensed at that, like his body was just waiting for another blow. "When do you leave?"

They looked at each other and winced. His father was the one to answer. "The day before school starts."

Kit's head jerked back. "What?"

"Sorry it's so last minute," his mother said on a rush of air. "It's just that Gladys and Tom were supposed to be going with other friends and they had to cancel, so they were looking for people to fill the spot."

"To be honest, son," his father interrupted, "we've been talking about taking a vacation for a while now, so when this opportunity came along—"

"We jumped at the chance," his mother finished.

Kit's head was spinning. Nine weeks. Nine weeks without any childcare help. He swallowed down a wave of panic as he tried to focus on his parents. On the fact that, despite their obvious trepidation at breaking this news, they looked excited. Happier than he could remember seeing them for a really long time.

Guilt nagged at his gut. They'd never complained about how much they'd taken on after Natalie left. But it'd been nearly four years now. Four years of jumping back into parenting two little ones when they ought to have been enjoying retirement.

He ran a hand through his hair and blew out a long exhale. "What about your flower shop?" he asked his mom.

"They're going to cover for me," she said, her smile growing with an excitement she couldn't hide.

Kit nodded. "That's…that's great."

"I've already spoken to Marsha," she added quickly, "and she'll help out with the kids as much as she can. All you have to do is make sure they get to school on time and have someone collect them at the end of each day."

He nodded, his swallow thick.

"If they have to live on grilled cheese sandwiches for a while, that's not the end of the world," his mother said with a little laugh. "Although, I know you're a very capable cook."

He nodded, still struggling for words.

"The thing is, son…" His father cleared his throat. "We feel like this will be a really great test."

Kit blinked. "A test?"

"Yes. A chance for you to prove to yourself how capable you are at doing this on your own." His father's smile was a little too bright.

Kit frowned, trying to figure out what they were saying. His brain felt thick and sludgy.

"We just think..." Anna shared a look with her husband. "Well, we're wondering..."

"Kit, we love you." Jonathan said it firmly. "We love you enough to tell you that you can't keep living with us for the rest of your life. How are you ever going to move on? Heck, how do you expect to find a wife...a mother for these kids...if you continue to live here?"

A mother...

Kit gave his head a shake. He couldn't even think about that right now.

"This time that we'll be away is a great opportunity," his father continued. "You can stay here, obviously, but with the idea that when we return, you and the kids will find a home of your own."

The silence that followed those words nearly crushed Kit where he was standing. He sank down onto the couch opposite his parents, like a dead weight.

They were kicking him out? Him and the kids?

He scrubbed a hand over his eyes, his mind scattering in ten different directions.

"We'll still be here to help with the children after school," Anna said abruptly.

Kit's head came up to face his mother.

"We don't want you to feel like we're kicking you out of our lives or anything like that. We just..." She blinked like she was fighting tears. "We just want to see you happy, and right now, we feel like you're stuck. You've found this rut, and it's about time you step out of it. We're doing you no favors carrying you this way."

His father reached for her hand as his mother's eyes welled with tears. "We're sorry, Kit, really we are, but it's time."

Jonathan nodded beside her, his expression stern—the

look he got when he was trying not to be emotional. It was a look that screamed 'tough love.'

Kit exhaled sharply, dropping his head into his hands. Part of him wanted to be offended. Some childish voice was telling him this wasn't fair, that they couldn't leave him hanging like this.

But the grown man knew that wasn't true.

Deep down he could admit to himself that they were right.

He had been in a rut. This place and this situation were a comfort, but it was never supposed to be the endgame. When he'd first moved in with the twins, it was understood that this was a temporary fix until he got his feet under him.

"We'll leave you to think it over," his father said gruffly, patting his shoulder on his way out of the living room.

"We'll talk in the morning," his mom said, leaning down to kiss the top of his head just like he'd done to Corbin as he'd tucked him in.

His parents loved him. He knew that. But he wasn't a child anymore, and they couldn't keep taking care of him.

He understood. And he wished he could tell them that, but he was too overwhelmed to even speak.

He'd tell them in the morning.

He heard the familiar, comforting sounds of his parents getting ready for bed, the kids quiet and no doubt deeply asleep in their room.

For Kit, sleep would be a long time coming.

He tried to calm himself, but as he sat there in silence in the darkened living room, all he could see before him was stress and chaos.

Nash would be lenient with his hours, and his parents

were right—with school starting, a good chunk of the twins' weekdays would be covered. But there was still a whole lot of time unaccounted for that he'd need to fill. Just the thought of dinner and bedtime routine without his parents to give him a hand felt like too much.

Yeah, maybe that made him pathetic, but right now, that was exactly how he felt.

He fell back against the couch with a groan. He was a grown man with a decent job and kids of his own.

But right now, he felt green behind the ears, like he was about to leave home for the very first time.

He tilted his head back to stare at the ceiling.

Pathetic?

That was an understatement.

7

The next morning, Lizzy found herself in a showdown with the wall calendar hanging in the bathroom.

Clearly she'd been in the wild west for too long, because the theme song to *The Good, the Bad and the Ugly* played in her mind as she brushed her teeth and faced down the calendar that taunted her with today's date.

Her wedding day.

She spit.

"It's you or me," she grumbled to the seemingly benign country landscape print.

It didn't answer. Because it was a calendar.

"Fine. You asked for it." She snatched the bottom edge and ripped it off the wall, tossing it into the trash with a satisfied sigh.

Clapping her hands together, she finished up her morning routine. She blow-dried her hair out straight the way she liked it, and for the first time in a month, she even pulled out her makeup bag and put on a little blush and lipgloss.

When she was done, she found herself facing her reflection with a little smile. She might have no idea what she was doing with her life, but for the first time in a long time, she recognized herself when she looked in the mirror.

That was something.

Padding through her newly cleaned room, she headed into the common area. She hadn't slept the whole morning away today, but the house was still eerily silent.

She had a feeling she'd have to get up a whole lot earlier than nine o'clock to catch the early birds who lived in this house.

"Emma?" she called.

No response. She hadn't really expected one.

Grabbing her phone, she texted her sister.

Lizzy: *Are you around?*

Emma: *At school working in my classroom. Do you need something?*

Lizzy: *No, that's cool. Just wondering where you were.*

Emma: *Help yourself to anything in the fridge or pantry. Let me know if you want me to pick anything up on my way back from town.*

. . .

Lizzy sent her a thumbs-up, then wrapped her arms around herself.

Now what? Normally she'd make herself some coffee and then head straight back to her room. But today?

Today she wanted to *do* something. She'd spent so much time hiding in her room, it was a wonder she didn't have bedsores and stiff joints. There was a restlessness inside her that she couldn't shake.

Coffee in hand, she found herself pacing the length of the first floor of this sprawling ranch home.

Emma had given her a quick tour her first week here, but Lizzy had barely registered anything outside of her own misery. Now she felt like she was seeing it all for the first time.

Heading down one hallway, she stumbled upon what was clearly Nash's room and quickly backtracked. This was ridiculous. Sipping her coffee, she had to remind herself that she wasn't a snoop.

Even so, she felt like some nosy neighbor as she made her way through the ground floor, poking her head into a small office and a den with a large flat-screen TV on the wall. From there she wound her way to the other side of the ground floor, where Emma had made a little area for herself.

Her sister had clearly made this house her home.

A stab of envy nearly stole Lizzy's breath, and she took a big gulp of her coffee. She wasn't jealous that Emma had a home here, obviously. Aspire, Montana, definitely wasn't where she *aspired* to end up.

She smirked at her own joke as she left Emma's wing and headed toward the staircase leading to the second floor.

That feeling of being an intruder grew as she padded

along the thick carpet on the upper landing, a long row of windows at the top giving a breathtaking view of the land that sprawled out as far as the eye could see. She might not have been all into nature like Emma, but even she could admit it was pretty here in a peaceful, picturesque kind of way. It was actually rather breathtaking…if you liked that kind of thing.

Lizzy found herself standing there for far too long just taking in the sight of all those rolling hills and the way the world seemed to go on forever. She couldn't decide if the landscape was beautiful or terrifying. Or maybe it was a little of both. Like staring up at the stars at night, the sight of all that space sprawled out before her made her feel…small.

Lonely.

And like she had no idea where she belonged in the world.

A shiver raced through her, and she clutched her warm mug tighter in her hands as she turned away from the view and continued her exploration.

She came to Frank's room next, and the door creaked open when she touched it.

She'd been in here before with Emma, but there was something almost sacred or eerie about the space, and the sisters didn't linger. Now, she paused in the middle of the room, still and quiet as if maybe she could feel some sort of connection if she tried hard enough.

She shook her head with a huff of amusement at her own silliness. Of course she couldn't feel a connection. It wasn't like Frank was a real father to her, and she hadn't even known he'd had a wife when he'd died. Even if she believed in ghosts, she wouldn't have found one here. If he hadn't taken an interest in Lizzy when he was alive, why on earth would Frank O'Sullivan want to get to know her now?

The thought left a bitter taste in her mouth that the coffee couldn't quite dispel. Shoving all thoughts of Frank and his wife firmly out of her head, she moved on to the next room.

April's room. Lizzy frowned at the bedroom which had so obviously been decorated with a young girl in mind. The bunk beds. The purple walls.

Lizzy would have loved this room when she was young. Why had her father never invited them to the ranch?

Hurts she didn't even know she harbored stirred in her chest, and she quickly turned away, racing out and back to the stairs. This house was too big and too creepy to be wandering around on her own like this. It was haunted, all right. Just not with ghosts. It was filled with memories of people she didn't know, no matter how much blood they might share.

It was filled with the lives of a man who hadn't wanted to know her when he was alive and a sister who clearly didn't want to know her now.

She made a beeline for the stairs and ran down as if those bare, empty bedrooms were coming after her.

What was she even doing here? How could Emma stand living in this place when it was one big reminder of the man who'd given them up without a second thought?

By the time she reached the main floor again, that wave of unease had passed. Her pulse slowed to normal, and that rush of panic was replaced with embarrassment for acting like such a ninny.

Emma would be home soon. Nash too. And then this

place wouldn't feel so empty. She just had to find a way to keep herself occupied in the meantime, that was all.

She reached the kitchen and looked around her.

Now what? What was she supposed to do with her day?

Her mind instantly rushed to fill her in on what she would be doing right now if things were different. If Connor hadn't cheated on her—or even if she hadn't found out.

Her stomach fell as she leaned against the counter. Would that have been better? To not know? Would she be happier living in ignorance and having the day of her dreams?

She pushed away from the counter with a sound of disgust, because she wasn't sure. Logically she knew she shouldn't want to be marrying a man who was sleeping around behind her back. But there was a part of her—a big part that she didn't even want to admit to—that wished she'd never found out the truth. That wished she could still have had her day and avoided all the humiliation and—

Ugh.

She set her coffee cup down by the sink and headed toward the back porch. The fresh air was a welcome distraction, and she watched some horses graze in the distance. Oddly enough, the sight calmed her a little, but it didn't stop the questions from plaguing her.

Had Emma been right? Had it really just been about the wedding?

Was she that shallow? That self-absorbed?

"Maybe it's not always about what you want."

Kit's voice rose up in her memory, unwanted but unavoidable. She couldn't seem to shake him.

Or that kiss.

She sank onto the porch swing.

The kiss she needed to forget about.

But he'd had a point when he'd said there was plenty to be done around here. Maybe her sister could make her a list of the chores she could help out with when Emma started teaching next week.

It wasn't exactly a new career or a life plan, but at least it would get her out of the house, right?

From where she sat, she could see the sun hit the top of the red barn in the distance, and a family of birds rose from the roofline. In the distance she could hear men's voices calling to one another. The ranch hands, no doubt. As the voices drew closer, she recognized one low growl in particular.

Kit?

Her belly did a flip and she straightened, her heart picking up its pace as her mind scrambled to think of what she ought to say to him about that kiss.

She should chew him out, obviously. Put him in his place and tell him never to do something like that again.

But the owners of the voices never came into view. They stayed just out of sight even as their conversation continued.

"Why not?" Kit snapped.

Yeah, that was definitely his voice. She wondered why he sounded so annoyed.

"Because it's a bad idea, brother."

Lizzy craned her neck and had an obstructed view of Kit and his younger brother, Cody, arguing near the pigpen.

"It'd only be for a couple months." Kit sounded kind of...desperate.

Lizzy drew back onto the porch swing. She should go inside. This was a personal conversation.

Instead she found herself sitting still, curiosity winning out over manners.

Cody scoffed. "I'm not moving in with you while Mom and Dad are away. That will defeat the whole purpose of their plan."

"It's a stupid plan," Kit growled.

"No it's not. You're just scared you can't manage."

Lizzy heard Kit scuff the ground with his boot. She leaned forward again, oddly desperate for a glimpse of him. She'd never heard him sound so upset before. He was almost always easygoing…even when he was being a brute and kissing a lady out of the blue.

But all Lizzy could see was the edge of his cowboy hat.

"Look, I'm not trying to be mean, okay?" Cody said. "I'll pick up extra hours on the ranch to help you out. Nash has already agreed to let you start late in the mornings so you can take the kids to school, and if Marsha can collect them at the end of the day, then you can at least bug out early in time to make dinner. It'll all work out."

Kit shook his head. "Easy for you to say."

"Come on, man. You can do this."

"They want me to find a place of my own." Kit's voice was taut with emotion, and Lizzy felt an answering pang in her chest.

"For me and the kids," he continued. "Did you know about that?"

Lizzy winced. The laid-back, devil-may-care cowboy she'd come to know was nowhere to be found. For some reason, that made her anxious.

"Yeah, I know." Cody's soft voice was kind and understanding. "Don't take it personally, man. They're doing this for your own good."

"Yeah, I suppose. I just… It feels like it's out of the blue is all."

Lizzy leaned forward and saw Kit take off his hat with a sigh, running his hand through his hair.

"I guess I've been blind and selfish, just assuming they were going to help me out forever."

"They will help you out forever," Cody offered. "Just not so hands-on."

Kit nodded.

"I'm serious, brother. You *can* do this. You're a wonderful father. Your kids adore you. You know how to feed 'em, bathe 'em, and get 'em into bed at night. It's gonna be okay."

Kit cleared his throat and nodded again. "I know. You're right. I'm feeling pretty pathetic right now, that's all. I shouldn't have let it get to this point. I should have had it all figured out by now."

Lizzy's eyes stung with an unexpected surge of sympathy.

No, it wasn't just that. It was understanding. She'd never thought she could relate to a cowboy before, but right about now…

She got it.

She felt pretty pathetic too. And hearing him admit it made her want to give him a hug.

Instead she leaned back in her seat. It wasn't her place to make him feel better. His brother was there for that, just like Emma had been there for her.

"You're not pathetic," Cody was saying. "You're just processing the news. Don't worry about it."

Their voices started to fade again. They were heading

back toward the stables, and Lizzy could see the slump of Kit's shoulders as he walked away.

She should go inside. Maybe clean the kitchen and get some lunch going to give Emma a break from all the cooking she'd been doing.

But first…

Lizzy lifted her gaze to the big, cloudless blue sky and offered up a prayer. For Kit. For her. For both of them to find their way forward.

8

T*his is it.*

Go time.

Kit checked his watch and winced.

Scratch that. It'd been 'go time' ten minutes ago. Now they were officially running late. Not that the cute little munchkin currently glaring up at him seemed to care.

"Chloe, I'm sorry, sweetheart, but I don't know how to do a French braid."

He didn't even know what that meant, to be honest. But she looked so horrified that he vowed to find out the next time he was online.

Or maybe he could ask Brooke from the hair salon. She'd know.

"But, Daddy, it's my first day," she said, her tone so high and plaintive, it made his headache intensify ten times over.

"It's just school, pumpkin," he said. "You don't need to have a French braid."

Her scowl said she believed otherwise.

"Look, when Grammy gets back—"

"I miss Grammy!" Her sudden tears tore his heart out, but when he reached for her, she ran away. "I'll do it myself!"

"Chloe, we don't have—"

Slam.

His words were cut off as the bathroom door banged shut.

"Time," he muttered to himself.

Running a hand through his hair, he turned to find Corbin. "Buddy, you ready?" he called as he headed into the den.

"Almost," Corbin mumbled.

Almost, apparently, meant not at all to Kit's son. "Corbin, you don't have pants on."

Corbin's lower lip came out as he continued to play dinosaurs in his Spider-Man underwear. "I don't think I want to go."

Kit rested his hands on his hips and could barely suppress his sigh. "Corbin, we've been over this."

About two hundred times, but who was counting?

"I don't feel good." Corbin's forehead puckered.

Kit huffed, crossing his arms and narrowing his eyes. "Is that true?"

"No," Corbin mumbled.

"What did we say about fibbing, buddy?"

Corbin didn't answer. Kit scrubbed a hand over his face. Two days. It had been two days since his parents had left, but it already felt like his world was falling apart.

Jabbing a finger at his son, he used his best no-nonsense tone. "Pants on. Now."

He waited until he saw Corbin slowly crawling to his feet. He was moving like molasses, but at least he was moving.

Kit ran into the kitchen to grab their lunch boxes along with the paperwork to finalize their enrollment. He'd meant to drop it off earlier in the week, but Lucy, at the school office, had been very kind and assured him today would be fine too.

He looked at the stack now, praying he hadn't forgotten anything important.

A checklist on the fridge told him he'd forgotten at least one thing.

"The pictures!" he groaned. He was supposed to have printed out a picture for each of them to hang on their cubbies or their bins or lockers—whatever it was Emma had called it.

He pinched the bridge of his nose and took a deep, fortifying breath. He could bring that tomorrow. They could surely last one day without personalizing their storage bin.

"I'm ready," Chloe said in a singsong voice that told him she was already over her crying fit from a minute ago.

"Oh thank heavens, you—" He stopped talking abruptly as he caught sight of her.

Her smile was precious. Her braids?

Not so much.

Lumps of hair stuck out at odd angles, the braids wilting to a messy finish. The hair ties she'd twisted were barely hanging on, and she'd missed a few big locks of hair that haphazardly sat on her shoulders.

"Uh, sweetheart?" he started.

"What happened to your head?" Corbin said as he came up behind Chloe in the hallway.

"Does it look bad?" Chloe's bottom lip trembled, and Kit wished his mother was there. She always knew how to smooth things over with Chloe, but he was often at a loss for this girl who was so much like her mother it killed him.

"Um…I just think you might be more comfortable with your hair down?" Kit tried to gently persuade her.

"Why?" Her eyes glassed over with tears.

Corbin snorted. "Because it looks weird."

Whipping around to face her laughing brother, she pointed at him. "Corbin, shut up!"

"Hey, don't talk to your brother like that."

She sniffled. "He's laughing at me!"

Kit glowered at his son. "Stop laughing."

"I'm trying, but her hair looks…" He got the giggles and couldn't even finish his sentence.

Chloe stomped her foot. "I! Need! Grammy!" she started wailing. "I don't want to go to school! I'm staying home." Plunking herself down on the ground, she crossed her arms and pouted her lip. Tears trailed, unchecked, down her rounded cheeks.

Kit was about ready to tear his hair out and start crying himself.

"If Chloe's staying home, I'm staying home too." Corbin crossed his arms, his chin set in defiance.

Kit's heart started to pound. He would not panic, dang it. Taking a deep breath, he let it out slowly.

Right.

I can do this.

One twin at a time, that was all.

He turned to Corbin first. He was just being opportunistic right now, and it didn't take a child psychologist to figure out why. "Look, buddy, I know you're nervous about school."

"I just don't think I'll like it," Corbin said. His glower was replaced with a wide-eyed look of terror that had

Kit crouching down so he could meet his son at eye level.

"Trust me, I get it."

"You do?"

Kit nodded. If Chloe was just like her mama, then Corbin was his mini-me. If it were up to Corbin, he'd be outside from sunrise to sunset, riding horses and feeding the livestock.

"But you know who needs schooling?" he asked.

"Who?"

"Cowboys," he said. "You can't run a ranch like Uncle Nash without having a good head for numbers. And you definitely couldn't be a veterinarian like Dr. Peterson if you don't learn about science." He arched his brows. "Should I keep going?"

Corbin still pouted, but he shook his head.

"Besides, you know Miss Emma is all about fun and play. Remember the rocket and how she said her class went to space?"

"That was just pretend."

"You love playing pretend." Kit grinned. "Come on, cowboy. What do you say?"

Corbin shrugged.

Not exactly the response Kit was hoping for, but it was a step in the right direction.

Taking a deep breath, he turned back to Chloe. She was outright weeping now, her head buried in her hands. "I want Grammy!"

"I want Grammy too. And Grandpa. Where are they?" Corbin asked.

"Where are your pants?" Kit shot back.

Corbin knew very well where his grandparents were. A still-pantsless Corbin spun around with a roll of his eyes.

"Here's what we'll do, pumpkin," Kit said as he crouched beside Chloe. "Let's take these braids out for now, and tonight after dinner I'll learn how to do the French braids you want, all right?"

"No!" she wailed. "I want them now."

"This way it'll be a sorta before-and-after event," Kit continued. Was the desperation in his voice obvious?

It felt obvious.

He was trying too hard, but one glance at his watch and he knew he'd do just about anything to get these two out the door. They'd already be late even if he didn't hit a single red light.

"What does that mean?" Chloe asked with a sniffle.

She was still moping, but at least she was distracted. Kit scooped her up in his arms, snagging the lunch boxes and shouting for Corbin to hurry.

"Before and after shots," he said. "It's a thing they do in fashion magazines and whatnot."

"They do?"

Kit kept talking, only half aware of the nonsense coming out of his mouth—like he read fashion magazines! But he'd seen the odd one lying around. Enough to sell the idea to his daughter. He got Chloe and the lunch boxes in the back of his truck and strapped her in.

The screen door slammed shut behind Corbin. "Ready!"

Kit held his breath, praying that this time Corbin had pants on.

Ugly braids were one thing, but he was pretty sure Aspire Elementary School had rules about wearing pants.

He sighed with relief at the sight of Corbin, fully dressed and launching himself up into the back seat beside his sister.

Kit was bone weary by the time he got into the driver's seat and set off toward school.

And this was only the first day.

His head fell back against the headrest as he internally groaned.

This was going to be a very *long* school year.

9

Lizzy was back on the porch swing when Nash came out to find her.

"You sure you're okay being here alone all day?" he asked.

His brow was furrowed with genuine concern, which made Lizzy smile. Her sister sure had found herself a good one. And no one deserved a good guy like Nash more than Emma.

"I'll be fine." She nodded. She'd been painting her toenails a pastel shade of blue, and she held up the nail polish and brush with a grin. "See? Lots to keep me busy."

Nash chuckled.

"Besides, I told Emma I'd take over the great sister hunt now that she's teaching all day, so I've got some homework on my plate."

Nash shifted, fidgeting with the cowboy hat in hand. "I'm real glad you're helping Emma out with that. I know it means a lot to her that you've been so understanding about her wanting to stay."

Lizzy's smile widened, and she set the nail polish to

the side. Funny, she'd been here for about five weeks now, and this might have been the first real one-on-one conversation she'd had with Nash.

Not for any lack of trying on his part. She'd just been too caught up in wallowing to make much of an attempt.

"You know I'm happy for her, don't you?" she asked. "I'm glad she found someone who appreciates her for the amazing woman she is. And I'm so happy that she found a place where she feels she belongs. She deserves that."

Nash nodded, his chin tucking down and a smile tugging at his lips in a way that made Lizzy's heart clench with joy on her sister's behalf.

Get thee a man who looks like that *at the mere mention of your name.* She nearly laughed aloud at the thought. But there was some truth to it. Nash couldn't so much as talk about his girlfriend without getting a goofy grin on his face.

Sappy and corny, perhaps. But so very sweet.

"We're lucky to have her," Nash murmured.

And by that, Lizzy knew he meant *he* was lucky to have Emma.

Lizzy certainly wasn't going to argue.

"Anyway," he said, backing up a step, "I just wanted to say thanks for the way you've been chipping in around the house while Emma starts her new job. And the whole inheritance thing…" He trailed off, no doubt unsure how to continue.

Even when Emma was with them, they rarely talked about the as-of-yet unmet sisters. Emma had spoken to a few of them on the phone, but Lizzy had made it clear she had no interest in getting to know them.

But no matter what Lizzy felt, that didn't change the fact that all of the sisters had to be contacted and come to some sort of agreement over what to do with the property. Frank made it very clear in his will that the decision was to be unanimous.

"None of us can really move on until this is dealt with," she said, gesturing broadly to indicate the ranch and the house. "I'm not exactly in love with the idea of talking to these women, but I know how much it means to Emma that they see the property before making any decisions."

He nodded. "Well, I appreciate it, and I know Emma does too. It's been a lot for her."

Lizzy nodded, her throat tightening with guilt. "And I haven't made it any easier."

Nash was quick to disagree, but she ignored his protests.

She hadn't been helpful—not since she'd arrived and made it her mission to wallow. But not before then either. She'd been so caught up in her wedding plans, she hadn't done anything at all to help ease the burden that came with this inheritance.

Guilt had her ducking her head, turning her attention back to her toenails. "Anyway, I've got plenty to keep me busy," she said.

"All right, then, I'd best get back to work," he said.

She nodded. "I'll be heading in soon too."

She took her time with her nails, letting them dry before adding a second coat. It felt absurdly good to be doing normal things again. Every day this week she'd tried to tackle one task in her life. Sometimes that was something as simple as giving herself a pedicure. Other days it had been something more difficult, like getting on the phone with Sarah to sort out how they were going to end their rental agreement and when they could get her belongings moved into storage for the time being.

She'd been putting off even looking at the file Emma had about their half sisters. But with Emma gone all day and Nash busy with ranch business, there were no more excuses.

"No use putting off the inevitable," she mumbled to herself before finally pushing off the porch swing to head back inside.

Emma had left all sorts of things for her on the kitchen counter. There was a stack of papers related to the sisters—the contact information she had for the three she'd talked to, as well as all the information she'd gathered on the two who seemed just as content to ignore this whole newfound family situation as she'd been.

She pursed her lips as she read over April's page.

She couldn't exactly blame the girl. How would it feel to know that two women you'd never met—who you might not even have known existed—were currently living in your childhood home and debating what to do with your land?

Lizzy set it down with a sigh.

Nope. She couldn't even imagine what April was thinking. As for Sierra, the mystery sister who couldn't be found?

Lizzy frowned at her name. She wasn't sure what she could do that Emma hadn't already. It wasn't like Lizzy was Nancy Drew. What did she know about tracking down a missing sister?

She slid into a seat at the kitchen table with a sigh. The sisters could wait. She'd start first with the will and the documents that detailed what they'd inherited.

The dry reading was interrupted by a call from her mom.

"Is there anything we can do for you, sweetie?" Her mother's voice held a forced brightness. She felt Lizzy's heartbreak as if it were her own, but she was doing her best to be chipper.

"No, thanks," Lizzy said. "You've already done so much."

Her mom and Derek had done a lion's share of the work when it came to unplanning the wedding. They'd made all the calls and answered all the questions.

Through it all, Lizzy had tried to keep some distance from her mom.

Not because she didn't love her and miss her—she did. It was just that sometimes Lizzy was so like her mom that being around her was tough.

Lizzy could admit that she was a bit...dramatic. Or she could be, at least. Two drama queens in one room wasn't always easy. When there was a celebration to be thrown, Lizzy and their mom were all over it. But when there was a crisis, Emma was the one everyone looked to.

"Oh, honey..." Her mother's voice wobbled, the brightness disintegrating as she obviously fought tears.

Lizzy grimaced. This right here was what she'd been trying to avoid. It was why she'd fled to Montana rather than take a much easier and quicker trip out to the suburbs surrounding Chicago to stay with her parents.

"I'm fine, Mom," she said quickly.

Please don't make me cry again. Please don't make me cry.

"You're not fine, sweetheart." Her mom sniffled.

Thanks. That's very encouraging.

"And now you're so far from home," her mother continued. "I'm glad you and Emma have each other."

Lizzy nodded, her gaze fixed on the open file before her. "And five other sisters," she said with a sigh. "If we can track them down."

Her mother went quiet for a beat, and Lizzy tried to figure out what that silence meant.

But after a little sniff, her mother's voice picked up again. "Well, anyway, I'm glad you're not having too hard of a time today."

Lizzy gave a huff of rueful amusement at the way her mother managed to gloss right over any mention of these newfound sisters. She'd been doing that a lot lately.

Her mother had been everything to her and Emma growing up. She and Derek, who'd filled the role of father so thoroughly they rarely even knew what they were missing.

But throughout the years, her mother had done a phenomenal job of not really talking about Frank O'Sullivan. She'd never truly explained why he'd never wanted to be a part of their lives, or the fact that he'd had other daughters and had remarried. Twice.

Granted, her mom hadn't known the extent of it, but she'd known about Sierra, the eldest. Lizzy rubbed a hand over her eyes as her mother's voice filled the line with small talk about the trip she and Derek were planning to take for their anniversary.

Lizzy tried to give her the appropriate responses, but oddly enough, all she could really hear was Kit's voice in her head. Again.

"Maybe it's not always about what you want."

She frowned at the folder before her. Why was she thinking about that now?

And why wouldn't that irritating cowboy get out of her head already?

"...and you know we wish you were here with us," her mother was saying.

Lizzy smiled. "I know, Mom. And thanks for everything."

She meant it. Her mom and Derek had been such a help, it was churlish to stay hung up on the fact that her mother hadn't told them about their sisters.

Wouldn't you have done the same?

Lizzy frowned as her mother said her farewells and hung up. She lowered the phone and stared at it.

Would she have done the same?

The question nagged at her, making her pace the length of the kitchen as she tried to put herself in her mother's shoes.

Heck, she didn't even have to go that far. She could just think back to how she'd responded to the news that she and Emma were two of seven O'Sullivan sisters.

What had she done?

Nothing. She'd let Emma handle the responsibility of dealing with the will, the attorney, the estranged sisters. She'd had her hands full with a wedding, yes, but she'd shoved all thoughts of these sisters out of her skull, glossing over the topic just like her mother had done their entire life. Whenever they'd asked questions about Frank O'Sullivan, she'd redirected and dodged until they pretty much gave up asking.

Maybe she was more like her mother than she thought.

Guilt weighed on her shoulders as she sank back into the seat, forcing herself to read the rest of the will and other legal documents that detailed all that made up this property.

It was a lot. More than Lizzy had realized. She'd

known they stood to earn a nice amount of cash if they sold, but she hadn't actually understood why until now.

Pushing out of her seat, she strode over to the back door. It was one thing to read about this property and its buildings, cattle operation, and house, but it was another thing entirely to see it with her own eyes.

She gave her legs a much-needed stretch by roaming around the grounds, taking in the view with new eyes.

This was hers. Well, hers and her sisters'.

She bit her lip and rested her hands on her hips as she surveyed the view with this new understanding.

What had Frank been thinking when he'd left them this land?

She sighed, dropping her arms and continuing her walk. She couldn't even begin to guess, not when she'd never even known the man outside the occasional card for the holidays.

She'd never known him…and now she never would.

Truthfully, she wasn't sure how that made her feel. It wasn't exactly sadness that had her slowly ambling the grounds between the stables and the house. It certainly wasn't grief. But it was…something.

Like being homesick for something she'd never even known.

She shook her head to rid herself of the maudlin thought. There was no going back, Derek used to always say. Only forward.

Stopping near the pigsty, she wrinkled her nose as she took in the pigs Emma insisted were cute. Even with the same parents and raised under the same roof, she and Emma were just about as different in personality as two women could get. She couldn't even imagine what these half sisters would be like.

But maybe it was time to find out.

She'd likely have to get to know them since Emma was dead set on getting them all here to see the place before a decision was made. It was no secret that Emma wanted to keep the property. Lizzy didn't, of course—what use did she have for acres of land in the middle of nowhere?

But she refused to fret about the fact that she and her sister had differing opinions. It hardly mattered now, not when there were seven opinions to take into consideration.

She supposed Emma thought that if she could bring all the sisters here, they'd fall in love with this place just like she had.

Lizzy snorted. "Good luck with that."

The biggest pig blinked ridiculously long lashes at her, her gaze fixed on Lizzy as if she'd spoken to the pig and not herself. Lizzy wondered which was crazier, talking aloud to herself or addressing a giant pig with eyelashes that Miss Piggy would kill for.

"How did you get such pretty eyelashes?" she murmured.

The pig snorted.

Lizzy let out a giggle before clapping a hand over her mouth. Goodness. To think, she was supposed to be leaving for her honeymoon right now, flitting off to a tropical island in the Caribbean. Instead she was here.

Talking to an ugly, smelly pig.

"No offense," she said, as if the pig could hear her thoughts.

Lizzy folded her arms on the top of the fence, then set her chin on her forearms. "What's that? You think Connor is a pig too?"

She sighed dramatically, her grin widening. "I suppose you have a point."

The pig moved even closer, and the two smaller ones followed.

“I suppose I just swapped out one pig for another, huh?”

The pig snorted, and Lizzy laughed. “I’ll take that as a yes.”

10

This was a nightmare.

Kit took off his hat to rake a hand through his hair as he stared down the mutinous little sweethearts glaring at him from the back seat.

"Come on, you two," he said. "We're already late."

"I'm not going," Corbin said. He wore an angry pout, but telltale tears welled in his eyes.

He was scared. Understandably. Heck, Kit's gut hadn't stopped churning with anxious dread all morning. The thought of his babies alone in a whole new world tore his heart out.

Well, alone with Emma. And around fifteen other kids their age. But still.

"I'm not going either." Chloe folded her arms over her chest for emphasis.

She'd finally stopped crying, but only a few seconds ago. Her red, splotchy cheeks were still tearstained, and her nose was running something awful.

Kit looked around for a tissue and came up empty.

Grabbing the bottom hem of his T-shirt, he leaned forward and swiped it over her face.

He could only imagine how disgusted Lizzy would be if she saw him do something so gross. But little kids *were* gross. It was in their nature.

"Daddy," Chloe whined, pushing him away and wiping her nose on her new, clean shirt instead.

He sighed. Now they were both gross.

Wonderful.

"I don't have time to argue with you." He huffed, his gaze darting from his daughter to his son and back again. "You're going to kindergarten, you're going to have fun, and that's final."

His voice rose with aggravation and…

And now they were both crying again.

Kit put his hands on his hips and looked down at his boots as he took a deep breath and counted to ten. "I'm not angry," he said in the calmest voice he could muster. "I understand your trepidation—"

"Our trepi-what?" Chloe asked.

"I'm not trepidated." Corbin's chin rose with stubborn defiance.

"No, of course you're not," Kit muttered under his breath. "Look, we're already late. Let's just get in there and see Miss Emma. You guys love Miss Emma, right?"

Chloe and Corbin exchanged looks. It was moments like this that Kit fully believed the twins shared some sort of psychic link. He found himself holding his breath until they turned back to him with earnest nods, their little fingers already fumbling for the latches on their seat belts.

Kit actually let himself breathe with relief as they entered the elementary school. The halls were empty, which confirmed the fact that they were very late. Everyone else was already in their classrooms.

"Come on," Kit said as he all but dragged Corbin by the hand while holding Chloe in his arms.

She'd taken her hair out of the wackadoo braids, but now it was an unruly blonde mess with curls sticking out in every different direction.

He found their classroom and threw the door open, only to freeze when the entire room turned to look at them. Emma was in the front of the classroom wearing a beaming smile while a whole lot of little ones sat in a circle at her feet. In the back of the classroom, a solid handful of parents were staring at him with curious expressions, like they just couldn't imagine why he was running late on such an important morning. It was the first day of school!

He forced a smile for the room at large. He was just being paranoid, that was all. No one was actually judging him.

Right?

"We have two new people joining us." Emma walked to the back of the room to greet them. "How wonderful. Chloe and Corbin, why don't you come in and join our circle?"

Corbin dumped his bag on the floor, his angry glower back in full force. The poor kid looked wary as all get-out, but when Emma smiled and pointed out where the book-bags were supposed to be stored, he dutifully took his bag and Chloe's over to the hooks on the far side of the room.

Chloe, meanwhile, clung to Kit like a limpet, squeezing her legs around his waist and gripping his neck with an iron hold.

She wouldn't let Kit put her down.

"Come on, peanut," he said softly. "Time to join the circle."

"I don't want to." She buried her face in his neck.

"You can sit with Corbin," he tried.

She shook her head against his neck. Some of the other parents were giving him sympathetic smiles as he found a spot on the mat between a redheaded boy with glasses and a little girl who was staring up at him like he was an evil ogre from a fairy tale.

Sitting there among the kindergarteners, with Chloe tucked in his lap, he felt like a giant.

Emma launched into a welcome speech, addressing the kids with gentleness and understanding but without any baby talk or coddling. She treated them with respect and made it clear she expected the same in return.

Kit was impressed. He could learn a thing or two about how to talk to his own kids.

After a couple minutes, though, he could hardly even pay attention to what she was saying. His gaze kept traveling to the clock on the wall. He was late.

So late.

His insides churned uneasily. He hated being late. Even more, he hated letting people down.

Oh sure, Nash, JJ, and Cody would all understand. But he didn't want to be that guy who got a free pass. The guy who everyone else had to pick up the slack for because he couldn't manage his own life.

He broke out in a sweat as Emma—Miss Emma, as the kids called her—continued with her greeting and then went into instructions for their first activity. He was fairly itching to run out of there. As soon as Chloe was set up with her task, he'd go.

But once all the kids ran to the table to get started, Chloe's grip on his hand increased.

"I have to go, pumpkin," he whispered, giving her one last hug. This was now his fifth 'one last hug.'

"Nooo." Chloe burst into tears. Corbin watched from where he sat at the table, his own eyes widening with fear at the sight of his sister's distress.

All the other parents had filed out with no scenes. No fuss.

What am I doing wrong?

Emma came over to assist just as Kit was starting to think he might have to take Chloe with him.

"She'll be okay." Emma grinned, hauling Chloe out of his arms with a firm but gentle grip. "First-day jitters. Leave it with me. I've got this."

Chloe didn't fight Emma, but she turned back to him with impossibly wide eyes. "No, Daddy, you have to stay."

"I've got to get to work, but I'll be back to pick you up at the end of the day, okay?"

"No. Stay. Please, stay." Her voice was high and tight and filled with so much despair, he couldn't take it. Her big eyes, that little pout, the tears. It was doing his heart in.

"Chloe, Daddy has to go sweetie," Emma said softly. "You're going to be just fine. Here, let's start coloring in our picture together."

"No!" Chloe was outright bawling now, and Kit's own eyes stung as he backed away.

Emma looked at him and nodded. "Just go. She's gonna be fine."

It broke his heart, but he walked out of the classroom, Chloe's wails for "Daddy!" echoing down the hallway.

11

Emma had been trying to sell Lizzy on the myriad benefits of pros and cons lists for as long as Lizzy could remember.

Lizzy scowled at the open notebook in her lap as she shielded her eyes from the morning sun.

How exactly was this supposed to be helpful?

She tapped the end of the pen against her own handwriting as she considered what she'd already written.

After reading through all the documents Emma had left behind, making no progress tracking down Sierra—again, she was no Nancy Drew—and leaving another voice mail for April to add to Emma's eight hundred that she'd already left, she'd decided to tackle her own life.

Starting with trying to find a new job.

Her feet were pulled up on the porch's swing bench, which had become her favorite place to sit and think. She wouldn't say she was fond of the sprawling landscape view, but it was growing on her.

Besides, it was sort of peaceful out here, and Nash kept assuring her that she ought to take advantage of the nice weather now because snow would be here before she knew it.

She wiggled her freshly painted toenails. She supposed that meant she should show off her prettiest nail polish colors now too, before they were hidden in snow boots.

The thought had her head jerking up and her breath coming in a gasp.

What the…?

What was she thinking?

She wasn't going to be here long enough to need snow boots. Of course she wasn't.

With renewed energy, she turned her attention back to the list. She'd decided to take Emma's suggestion to heart and started by making a pros and cons list about her old job—what she loved, what she'd been particularly good at, and what she'd rather do without.

Her list wasn't exactly a long one, and it wasn't exactly sparking a flurry of ideas about what she ought to do next with her life.

She was just about to give up when a truck barreled up to the side of the house, kicking up a cloud of dust as it came to an abrupt halt.

Kit climbed out, and his every movement was…wrong.

She frowned as she watched him get out and gather some tools from the back seat. She hadn't seen Kit since she'd overheard that emotional conversation between him and his brother, but just like then, he seemed to have misplaced the easygoing, fun-loving cowboy she thought she knew.

That cocky smirk had been replaced with a furrowed brow and a hint of a frown.

The man was brooding.

Her lips parted when he turned in her direction.

Goodness. Brooding looked good on him.

His smile was even better though. Seeing him without it put her on edge for reasons she couldn't begin to explain.

She was up and out of her seat before she knew what she was doing. Tossing her notebook and pen on the bench, she wiggled into her sandals and headed in his direction. He was so lost in his own thoughts that he didn't even notice her until she was almost on top of him.

He turned and gave a start at the sight of her before leaning back against his truck with a sigh.

"Sorry." Her lips were twitching with amusement despite herself. "Didn't mean to scare you."

"You didn't scare me," he said quickly.

Maybe just a little *too* quickly.

She pressed her lips together to squelch a giggle. But the urge to laugh faded fast as she caught a better look at him.

Her chest tightened and her belly sank as she took in the tightness in his jaw, around his eyes.

He wasn't just brooding, he was upset.

"Kit, are you...um, are you okay?"

He looked away from her. "Just having a tough morning."

"I can see that." She bit her lip as she watched him turn away from her to gather the rest of his things.

"I should get to work," he said. "I'm already late as it is."

Lizzy nodded, backing up a step. She shouldn't have come over here in the first place. She wasn't sure why she had. This was the guy who'd kissed her without warning —when she'd been in the middle of a tirade, no less. She was supposed to be angry with him.

But as much as she told herself that, she couldn't summon up any negative emotion. Not when he was like this.

"Want to talk about it?" She fell into step beside him as he headed toward the barn.

"What?" He glanced over at her with a furrowed brow like she was some curious new creature he'd never encountered before. "Uh, no. Thanks."

He added the 'thanks' belatedly and maybe a little grudgingly.

She should leave him alone. He clearly didn't want her help. She had her own worries to think about. Her pros and cons list wasn't going to finish itself, right?

They reached the corner of the house. Her notebook was in view where it sat on the porch swing, and any second now he'd peel away and make a beeline for the barn.

So good. Great. She wasn't about to stop him. It wasn't like she wanted to hear about his problems or anything.

He started to turn away.

"Is this about your parents leaving town?" she blurted.

He froze with his back to her. When he swiveled back, his brows arched in clear disbelief, she took a step back. What was she doing? Just because he was upset didn't suddenly make them friends.

She had a sudden flash of those dang ugly overalls he'd gotten for her on her first day at the ranch. That had been the first and last time she'd laughed—albeit grudgingly—for a full month.

The memory had her feet stopping before she could backpedal any further. "Well?" she said.

"I... How...?" He stopped, took off his cowboy hat,

and raked a hand through his hair in a gesture she was starting to recognize. "What do you know about that?"

Heat crept up her neck and into her cheeks. "Oh, well, um..." She shrugged, giving him an apologetic wince. "I sort of overheard you and your brother talking about it."

"You—" He cut himself off, his eyes wide with shock. Then his head fell back with a groan. "Great," he said as he turned away. "Just great."

He started to walk away from her again, but she hurried to catch up to him. His legs were longer, and, unlike her, he wasn't wearing delicate heels, so she had to do a little jogging to keep up.

"I'm sorry," she said quickly. "I wasn't trying to eavesdrop." *Much.* "But if something's the matter—"

"Nothing's the matter," he said, his tone harsher than she'd ever heard it.

"Oh." She came to a halt, her stomach falling. She swallowed down a wave of hurt...which was ridiculous. She wasn't his friend, and he wasn't hers. What did she care if he confided in her?

She didn't.

She gave a short nod and was just about to turn on her heel to head back to the porch when he let out a sharp exhale and beat her to it.

Spinning around to face her, he threw his hands up. "My parents couldn't have timed this any worse, you know?" He didn't wait for a response.

She suspected he wasn't expecting one, but she nodded all the same.

"I know I'm probably being selfish right now," he continued, his gaze roaming over the landscape but clearly not seeing it. "I could have used some warning."

She opened her mouth to sympathize, but his eyes

widened and he hurried on like a man possessed. "Who knew girls' hair could be so dang hard to braid? I mean, double French braids? I can't even tie a ponytail!"

Lizzy narrowed her eyes, her lips still parted. "Um…what?"

He sighed and shook his head, scrubbing a hand over his face as his eyes lost that desperate glint. "It's Chloe's first day of school, and she wanted to look pretty."

"Ah," she said, his braid tirade suddenly making sense. "Yeah, I get that."

His gaze narrowed on her with suspicion, like he thought she was mocking him.

She wasn't. Lizzy nodded her understanding. "She wanted to look nice for her first day of school, and you couldn't help with her hair."

His shoulders fell. "I tried. I really tried, but then we were late, and when we got to school she wouldn't let me go, and then she lost it when I had to leave."

He looked away, his jaw working to the side.

Lizzy's insides did something odd. They seemed to tighten and swell at once. The sight of this big, burly, smug cowboy getting all worked up over his daughter's bad hair day was just…

"She'll be okay," Lizzy said.

She winced when he gave her a baleful look that said he didn't believe her.

And why should he? She didn't know the first thing about kids. But she knew Emma, and Emma would make sure his little girl was okay.

"She was calling my name, Lizzy. Wailing it as I walked away from her."

Her lungs hitched at the gruffness in his voice.

He drew in a deep breath and let it out with a long

sigh. "But Emma told me it was normal and that once I left she'd be fine."

"I'm sure she's right," Lizzy offered.

"But it's killing me." When his gaze met hers, it was filled with all the pain he was feeling.

Lizzy wasn't sure she'd ever felt more helpless than she did right now, because she had no idea how to make him feel better.

Now times that by a million and you might have an idea how he's feeling.

She pressed her lips to keep from offering meaningless platitudes. She suspected that was the last thing he'd want or need right now.

His head dropped back so he was staring up at the sky. "My little girl, who was so excited for kindy to start, was a wreck, and I feel like the world's worst father."

"You're not," Lizzy said quickly. "You're just doing the best you can."

"Yeah, well..." He ran a hand through his hair, messing it up and sighing. "It sure doesn't feel like it."

Lizzy felt another tug in her chest. For just a second, she wished they really were friends so it wouldn't be weird for her to go up and wrap her arms around him.

He looked like a man who could use a good hug.

But they weren't friends, and despite his predicament, he was still Kit-the-Irritatingly-Cocky-Cowboy, so she took a step forward but didn't hug him. She settled for patting his upper arm, telling herself sternly as she did so that she was most definitely not feeling him up.

Even though his biceps were freakin' fantastic. Raw, hard muscle that told of manual labor and all things cowboy. A hot flush raced through her, and she quickly lowered her hand.

"I'm sorry she was having such a rough time," she said. "But I'd be willing to bet that right about now, Chloe is happily playing with her new friends, and her crying from before is a distant memory."

His brows drew together as he gave her another incredulous stare. That look said he knew very well she had no idea what she was talking about.

She brought her chin up in defiance. He was right, she didn't know the first thing about kids. But Emma did. "Emma tells me all the time about how her students can lose it when their parents first leave, but she manages to distract them with fun, and it's like the tears never happened in the first place." Lizzy gave a short nod. "It affects the parents way more than the kids. That's what she says. And you know as well as I do that Emma's a pro when it comes to this sort of thing."

Kit regarded her in silence for a long moment, and Lizzy felt another inexplicable surge of heat in her neck and cheeks. She looked away quickly, not sure what to make of his scrutiny.

When she glanced back, she saw the ghost of a smile tugging at his lips. It was a half-hearted gesture, and nothing like his normal easygoing grin, but she supposed it was better than nothing.

"Yeah," he said, already turning away toward the barn. "Emma's probably right. Thanks."

She watched him walk away, his shoulders still slumped and his gait heavy.

She stood there long after he disappeared inside the red wooden structure.

He was still upset. And that was not okay.

She wasn't sure why her own insides were twisted into

knots over his bad mood, but she did know there was one thing she could do about it.

Her phone was sitting next to the pros and cons list.

For a second, she hesitated.

She could just go back to her list. Mind her own business and focus on salvaging her mess of a life.

She could do that.

Maybe she *should* do that.

But…

Maybe it's not always about you.

She sighed as she reached for her phone and started to type.

Hey, Emma. I know you've got a busy morning, but if you have a sec, I need a favor…

12

Mucking out stalls wasn't exactly Kit's favorite part of the day, so the fact that this chore was currently the highlight of his morning was really saying something.

He reached over to the beat-up old stereo JJ had set up in the back of the stables and turned up the country song that was playing on the radio.

JJ and Cody were already out on the range, and Nash was in the office working. He'd been hoping to have a little company when he arrived to help distract him from Chloe's parting wails.

But instead he got this.

He dug his pitchfork into the hay as he hummed along to the familiar tune.

A grudging smile tugged at his lips as he thought of Lizzy and the way she'd actually tried to comfort him.

He supposed she'd been a bit of a distraction. And she'd tried to help, which was really sweet of her.

He tossed the manure and then straightened with a jolt at the sound of a squeal behind him.

He spun to find Lizzy standing there, a look of horror on her face as she stared at the pile of manure that had just narrowly avoided hitting her.

"You okay?" he asked. His gaze raked over her from the top of her pretty blonde waves to her shiny white sneakers.

No sign of manure on her, thank goodness, but she pinched her nose shut with a pout that brought Chloe to mind all over again, and he found his gaze caught at the ground by her feet as a wave of heartbreak hit him.

Maybe I should go back to the school and check in on her. Or maybe I could call just to see—

"Why are you staring at my shoes?" Lizzy asked.

He blinked, his gaze focusing. Oh brother. He was still staring at her bright white, totally impractical shoes. But at least she'd changed out of those crazy heels she'd been wearing a little while ago. They might have made her legs look amazing, but she could roll an ankle wearing heels out on the dirt like that.

"What are you doing here?" He dragged his gaze back up to find her frowning at him, her nose still pinched.

"I need to talk to you." Her voice was nasally, and he had to hide his grin. She was cute…at times. When she wasn't acting like a spoiled brat. She nodded toward the open door. "Outside?"

He chuckled and gestured for her to lead the way.

The breeze and sunshine were a welcome relief after the dark and stale air of the stables. He led her over to a nearby fence and leaned against it as he brushed his hands off on his jeans. "What's up?"

He braced himself.

This was it. He'd known it was just a matter of time before Lizzy confronted him about that kiss.

Heck, he knew very well he should have apologized by now. He'd been out of line. And even if the kiss had been sweeter than sweet, it'd been wrong.

He didn't regret it. Not for one second.

But that didn't mean he didn't owe her an apology.

She had her head tipped down and she was on her phone, a little frown of concentration on her lips.

"Look, Lizzy, if this is about—"

"Here." She lifted her head and thrust the phone into his hands.

He blinked down at her screen, straightening away from the fence with a sharp inhale of surprise at the familiar faces he saw there.

"I texted Emma, and she sent me these." She moved to stand closer to him and reached over his arm to scroll through a few pictures. "They're all photos of Chloe laughing with two other girls and then one of her reading to a doll."

He gaped at the screen, his heart aching and twisting and then finally expanding with a surge of relief as he took in her sweet little smile and the happiness that lit her eyes.

"See?" Lizzy said, her head right next to his shoulder as she looked at the pictures alongside him. "Chloe is happy and content at school."

Kit's throat grew so choked he could barely speak. "Thank you." It came out all gravelly and harsh, but she smiled at him in return.

"Thought that might make you feel better." Her smile was smug, and the cutest little dimples winked up at him.

This close, it was impossible not to be struck by her beauty. She was gorgeous, he'd always known that. But the way her eyes danced with laughter, the way her smile lit her features and gave her this radiant glow…

Lizzy would always be a knockout, even when she was crying and scowling and moping and ranting. But this…

Whoa.

Nothing could have prepared him for this.

He tore his gaze away, drawing a breath into his paralyzed lungs. He found himself staring at her phone again, and his heart kicked against his rib cage like a stubborn mule.

He blinked at the smiling image of Chloe. Lizzy had done this. For him. "Thank you," he said again. He turned to meet her gaze. "Seriously, thank you."

She nodded, her smile deepening, which only made her dimples appear and her cheeks pinken. "No problem. Hope your day gets better from here."

She took her phone back and started to walk away.

"Lizzy, wait."

She paused, turning around with arched brows.

His mouth went dry. *Aw heck.* He'd never been nervous around a girl a day in his life. Not even around Natalie. He'd always had confidence when it came to flirting with the ladies.

But right here and now?

He felt like he'd suddenly hit puberty all over again.

She cocked her head to the side, a question in her green eyes.

He wanted to kiss her again.

Heaven help him, he had to fight the impulse to move to her and draw her into his arms and—

"Kit?" Her brows were furrowed now, the question in her eyes morphing to concern. "You okay?"

"Yeah, I just…" *Want to kiss you.* He shook off the thought. Kissing Lizzy had been a mistake the first time around. Hadn't he just been thinking that? He cleared his throat. "I just wanted to say I'm sorry."

Her brows hitched up.

"For kissing you," he added.

Her lips parted with surprise, and he could have sworn he caught a hint of a smile. "You're sorry, huh?"

The ire in her tone was belied by a tinge of amusement. His shoulder muscles relaxed a little. She couldn't be that angry with him if she was at least a little amused. He shrugged, flashing her that Cheshire cat grin that never failed to get him out of trouble.

"What can I say?" he teased. "I needed to get you to stop talking."

She planted her hands on her hips and narrowed her eyes. "And kissing me was all you could come up with?"

He shrugged again and she looked away, but not before he caught another twitch of her lips. "What else could I expect, I guess," she said in a too-mild tone, "when dealing with someone so uncivilized."

A laugh burst out of him, surprising them both if her smothered smile was anything to go by. He took his hat off and held it in his hands, deepening his natural twang to exaggerated effect. "Yes, ma'am. I suppose you're right, ma'am."

She rubbed a hand over her mouth, but not before he caught her grin. Her eyes narrowed in suspicion. "Did Cody tell you how much I hate being called 'ma'am'?"

He widened his eyes in feigned innocence. "No, ma'am."

She laughed for real this time, and the sound was like sunlight after a long, cold winter.

He dropped his gaze, alarm shooting through him at

that errant thought. Sunlight after a long, cold winter? What was he thinking?

"Well, anyway," she said, starting to back away again. "You shouldn't just go around kissing ladies. It isn't right."

His gaze came up and clashed with hers. He felt a spark of…something. A fire of some sort, like she was issuing a challenge or daring him to try it again.

The urge to tease her was too much. It was too tempting to make those cheeks turn pink and her eyes glimmer with life and laughter. "I already told you, darlin'. I didn't know how else to shut you up. You were speaking a load of nonsense and—"

"A load of nonsense?" She arched a brow. "You know this apology is starting to turn into an insult, right?"

He chuckled, leaning in closer and lowering his voice. "What would you have done, then, if the shoe were on the other foot?"

"If I wanted you to quit talking already?" she shot back, her tone saying this was exactly what she wanted —right now.

"That's right," he said. "How would you shut me up?"

She blinked, and then her gaze dropped to his mouth. Her lips parted, and he…

He forgot how to breathe.

Was she thinking about kissing him?

With an audible inhale, she snapped her gaze back up to meet his. "That's not the point. The point is, you don't just shut a woman up," she continued. "You let her speak."

"You were talking nonstop," he pointed out. "And did I mention it was nonsense?"

She pursed her lips. "Well, maybe some women have a

lot to say, and if you don't like that, maybe you shouldn't hang out with some women."

She gave her head a haughty toss that made her blonde locks fly.

"Who should I be hanging out with, then?" he asked.

Her eyes narrowed with a dangerous spark. "I assure you, I don't care. Just so long as it's not me."

"Such a little spitfire," he teased.

He laughed a little louder as she huffed like that was an insult. It wasn't. Not to him, at least. He knew far too many women who never called him out on any of his crap. Sparring with Lizzy was like a breath of fresh air.

"Lizzy O'Sullivan, you are one entertaining lady."

She rolled her eyes. "I'm so glad I can make you laugh."

With another flip of her hair, she turned and walked away, her hips sashaying with each step.

He couldn't drag his gaze away if he'd tried.

She turned to spot him staring, but rather than looking away, he met her gaze with a bold smile.

He could have sworn he heard her huff of exasperation even from so far away. It wasn't until she turned away the second time that he realized how unsettled he was, because…

Well, dang it, was he getting himself a crush on some spoiled city girl?

He rubbed at his chest, where his heart was pounding far too hard considering he was standing still.

He wished he could blame this uncomfortable tension inside him on the morning he'd had or the thought of the nine weeks to come. But as he watched her pale sundress disappear into the ranch house in the distance, he knew that wasn't true.

She'd gotten to him, and each new run-in made him like her more and more.

Which was bad.

Really, really bad.

He had enough on his plate being a single dad to the twins. He didn't have time to date. And even if he did, he owed it to the twins to date someone who might want a serious relationship.

Someone who wanted to be a mother, and who wanted to stick around.

Definitely not some gorgeous, fly-by-night visitor who'd be out of this town and out of their lives just as soon as she got back on her feet.

He shook his head and went back to work, throwing his all into tasks around the ranch until he was a sweating, aching mess. But not even sore muscles were enough to rid his mind of Lizzy's dimpled smile when she'd given him the most thoughtful gift he could imagine.

By the time he went home to take care of his kids, he couldn't deny that this was, in fact, a crush.

And the only thing he could do about it was to steer clear of Lizzy O'Sullivan.

13

Lizzy stared at the mess before her. "This was such a bad idea."

"I'm sure it's not as bad as you think." Her mom's voice came from her phone, which was leaning against a stack of cookbooks on the counter.

Lizzy arched a dubious brow as she reached out to jab a fork at the doughy glob in the middle of what was meant to be a chicken pot pie. "You're right. It's worse."

Her mother's laughter filled the air. "It's the thought that counts. Emma knows that."

"Uh-huh." Lizzy pursed her lips in irritation. "Is that your way of saying this pie is unsalvageable?"

"Well…" Her mother's voice was hesitant. "You said the edges are burnt to a crisp?"

"Yes," Lizzy sighed.

"And the inside is uncooked?"

"Looks that way." Lizzy blew out an exhale that sent a lock of hair flying off her face.

"Then I think you might want to order a pizza," her mother finished.

"I don't think any place delivers out here." Lizzy sighed again, fighting the urge to snap at her mom. Her mother was only trying to help. After not speaking much at all for the past month, her mom had been more than a little surprised to get a second phone call in one day.

But really, when it came to trying to save dinner, Lizzy hadn't known who else to call.

Besides Emma, obviously. But the whole point of her cooking dinner was to surprise Emma with a hot meal when she got home from her first day of teaching.

Instead, she'd be surprising her sister with a charred, inedible dish and a kitchen that looked like it had been hit by a tornado.

"Sorry I can't be more help," her mom said.

"It's okay." Lizzy forced a lighter tone for her mother's sake. "I'll manage something."

She was already rifling through the pantry as she spoke. Emma had to have stocked some noodles and tomato sauce. Even Lizzy could handle boiling water.

Right?

Her hand paused while skimming over a spice rack.

Man, how pathetic was she that she couldn't even make one lousy dinner on her own?

"Well, I'll admit, I'm glad you called," her mom was saying. "Derek came home after I spoke with you this morning, and he thinks you ought to know..."

Lizzy stilled as her mother's voice faded. "I ought to know what?"

"Oh, it's nothing." Her mother's voice had an artificial ring to it that Lizzy knew well.

"Mom, just tell me."

"Well...Connor's been trying to insist that we pay for the deposit money that was lost—"

"What?" Lizzy whirled around, her voice sharp with anger.

"It's fine, dear," her mother continued quickly. "Derek will handle everything. He just wanted you to know in case Connor reaches out—"

"I don't plan on speaking to Connor," she said stiffly, the mere thought making her blood run cold. "Ever."

"That's what I told Derek," her mother hurried to say. "Of course you don't want to talk to him. And you shouldn't have to. That's why Derek will handle everything. He's dealt with some pretty wayward characters in his time as a school principal. I'm positive he can handle one arrogant, overinflated, slimy weasel."

Lizzy nearly laughed at her mother's string of insults, but the sound evaporated before it could form. Instead, she swallowed, torn down the middle between gratitude and humiliation. She loved that her parents were always there for her. Emma too. But at the same time...

She was thirty years old. She'd been this close to marrying and starting to run a house of her own. Shouldn't she be handling the gory details of her breakup and canceled wedding herself?

For as long as she could remember, her parents had been helping her—from choosing a college to moving in with Emma. She'd always had either her stepdad or her sister handling things for her.

Her mom kept talking, but Lizzy was frozen solid in the pantry. She put a hand to her belly as it churned with a new, unpleasant realization.

Her family had always taken care of her...and Connor had done the same. He'd always taken charge of everything, from choosing where they ate to figuring out their vacation plans. In hindsight, she could see that he'd treated her more like a child than a partner. Sure, he'd given her free rein with most of the wedding plans, but now she realized it was just a chance for him to spend more time with his other woman.

Ugh!

Why had she ever fallen for him?

Was it because he'd been yet another person who would handle life for her?

The thought was too depressing to consider.

"And Trina was asking about you the other day when I went to the salon. I didn't give her the details, of course, but I'm sure you'll be seeing her soon enough when you get back to Chicago."

Lizzy winced. When she got back to Chicago? More like *if* she went back.

Her silence went too long, and she squeezed her eyes shut as she waited for the inevitable questions. It was a miracle she'd avoided them on their call this morning. There was no way her mom would let this opening pass.

"When will you be coming back, dear?"

Lizzy squeezed her eyes shut. "Um…"

"I know they love you at your job, but they won't hold that position for you forever."

"No, they…they won't."

She left the pantry to pace the kitchen, her heart racing.

"But I'm sure they'll be happy to have you as soon as you return."

I should tell her. I should just tell her the truth.

Snatching the phone, she wandered to the back door and went out onto the patio as her mom kept talking.

I don't have a job to go back to. Why was that so hard to say?

Because it felt impossible. Because admitting it meant she'd get *that* tone from her mother.

It would be sympathetic, maybe even pitying…but not surprised.

Because wasn't she the irresponsible flake of the family? Her biggest accomplishment to date had been finding a rich, handsome man to marry, and she'd managed to screw that up royally.

Okay fine, *he'd* messed that up.

But she still felt like an idiot for not having seen the truth in front of her face. She was the world's stupidest screwup for having fallen for a liar like Connor in the first place.

In the end, she blurted out the embarrassing fact while her mother was in the middle of talking. "I lost my job!"

The silence that followed was deafening. And then came the tsking sound she'd been dreading. "Oh, honey."

Lizzy took a deep breath. "Yeah. So…" She swallowed hard. "I don't know when I'll be back exactly."

"Okay, sweetie." Her mother's voice was too nice now. Almost patronizing. "There's no rush. I'm sure Emma is happy to have the company, and you know there's always a place for you here when you're ready."

"I know, and I appreciate that," she said.

Her throat felt tight. Would she really end up moving back in with her parents in the suburbs? She scrubbed a hand over her eyes. Would she go back to her childhood bedroom and let her mom do her laundry and cook her dinners?

She winced.

No. She might be pathetic, but she wasn't ready to take two steps backward.

So where will you go?

She shoved the question aside. She'd figure it out. Eventually.

A wave of panic crashed over her.

Right?

"Mom, I'd better go. I have to clean up this mess I made."

"Okay, honey. You take care of yourself. And call more often!"

She let out a huff of rueful amusement as she hung up.

I have to clean up this mess I made?

Honestly, she wasn't even sure if she was talking about the kitchen or her life. It was applicable to both.

She was about to go back inside when she caught sight of JJ and Cody heading out of the stables. Even from here she could tell they were covered in dust and sweat.

Her lungs hitched, and she found herself holding her breath as she waited for Kit to follow in their wake. But there was no sign of him.

She exhaled with a heavy sigh.

Something inside her deflated, which was just plain bizarre. It wasn't like she'd been hoping to see Kit again today. One run-in with that boorish, arrogant macho man was more than enough.

Although…

"Lizzy O'Sullivan, you are one entertaining lady."

A smile tugged at her lips before she could stop it. She'd seen the way he'd been looking at her when she'd walked away, and the memory of the heat in his eyes was enough to make her flushed all over again.

Lizzy was used to being admired by men. She'd always been pretty, and she'd taken pride in that. She loved playing up her best features and feeling confident in what she wore and how she wore it.

But it wasn't just his look of appreciation that had her humming as she'd set about cooking this afternoon. It was his laughter, his smile, and his parting words that had her smiling like a fool before she told herself she was behaving like a silly girl.

But honestly, he didn't just make her feel appreciated for her looks. He made her feel like maybe he enjoyed talking to her. Maybe he found their teasing and their spats as electrifying as she did.

She frowned. She had no business getting all hot and bothered over some guy she barely knew and wasn't even certain she liked. Oh sure, he could be nice enough, she supposed. And his adoration for his kids was awfully sweet.

But that didn't change the fact that he was a cowboy, which meant they had nothing in common.

You had everything in common with Connor, and look where that got you.

She ignored that little voice and waved as JJ and Cody grew closer.

"Hey there, Lizzy," JJ said in that deep drawl of his.

"Howdy, ma'am," Cody said.

Lizzy planted her hands on her hips and arched a brow. Cody's wince had her stifling a laugh.

"I meant, howdy, Lizzy," Cody amended.

She hadn't realized her gaze had gone back to searching for Kit until JJ asked, "Did you need something?"

"Oh, no," she said quickly, tearing her gaze from the stables to face them. "Just…um…" *Where's Kit?*

No. She couldn't ask that. Why would she be asking about Kit?

"Um…"

They continued to stare at her expectantly.

"Is there a pizza place that delivers out here?" she asked abruptly.

They exchanged a look and some snickers. "No, ma—" Cody started but caught himself quickly. "No, Miss Lizzy."

She and JJ both burst out laughing at his attempt to cover up the 'ma'am.' "Miss Lizzy, huh?"

Cody grinned and ducked his head. He was adorable. Handsome like his older brother but without all that infuriating swagger.

"Makes me sound like a kindergarten teacher. Like Miss Emma," she teased.

JJ chuckled. "No offense, but I can't picture you as a kindergarten teacher."

"No offense," she shot back, "but I wouldn't be caught dead taking care of a bunch of little tykes." She gave a fake shudder that made both men laugh.

Lizzy saw her opening and took it. "Speaking of kindergarten..." She looked past them to the stables, but there was still no sign of Kit. She turned back to Cody. "How'd your niece and nephew do?"

Cody beamed. "They did great. Kit cut out a little while ago to pick them up, and he texted us to say that Chloe and Corbin made it through their first day with flying colors."

Lizzy grinned. "That's great news."

But despite her genuine happiness over Chloe and Corbin's success, she felt another stab of disappointment.

JJ glanced back at the stables and then to her, his expression just a little too knowing. "Kit will be back tomorrow," he said mildly. "I bet he'll be itching to tell you all about it."

She smiled and looked away, her cheeks warming with embarrassment. Did JJ think she had a crush on Kit?

He couldn't be more wrong.

She was just bored here at the ranch, that was all. She was bored, and Kit was a distraction.

Yeah, that was all this was.

Straightening her shoulders, she pasted on a big smile. "If you'll excuse me, I've got to get back to making dinner."

They said their goodbyes as she walked inside to clean up the epic mess she'd made.

14

Chloe's nose was wrinkled up in disgust. "Daddy, is it supposed to smell like that?"

Kit whipped around from where he'd been cutting carrots into slices to see smoke rising from the oven. With a muttered oath, he reached for pot holders and pulled out the tray of slightly charred chicken strips. "It's fine," he said, prodding one lava-hot strip to make sure that was an accurate assessment. "It's just a little overcooked."

Corbin's frown was filled with doubt, and Chloe's nose was still crinkled.

Corbin pointed to the freezer. "Grandma said she left frozen dinners for us to heat up."

Kit sighed as he dished out his best attempt at a home-cooked meal. "Yeah, buddy, I know. But I'm saving those for nights when I can't take off early," he explained.

He felt bad enough for leaving early today, but considering it was their first day, he'd made the exception.

Tomorrow, he wouldn't be able to leave. Some cattle buyer was set to visit, and Nash would need all his men out there on the range to help.

On cue, he saw Nash's text come through. He was asking after the kids, but at the end of the text, there was a reminder about the important buyers arriving the next afternoon.

Nash: *You sure you can make it? I can bring in some outside help if you need to take off early.*

Kit went to type back a reassurance right away but thought better of it. After serving up dinner, Kit called Marsha, a woman who lived two doors down and helped babysit on occasion.

Once he confirmed that Marsha was able to pick them up from school, he shot Nash a response.

Kit: *I'll be there.*

He set his phone aside as he joined his kids at the dinner table and started the meal with a quick prayer of thanks.

"So," he said, leaning back in his seat as he munched on a chicken strip of his own. The bitter charcoal clung to his tongue, but he powered through, grabbing the ketchup bottle and squirting a large blob onto his plate. "Tell me everything."

He chuckled as Corbin and Chloe launched into animated stories simultaneously. He tried to nod and respond to both, which was tough since they were telling wildly different stories.

"And then Bobby pretended to be Superman, and I was Captain America!" Corbin's voice rose with excitement.

"But she said she plays with her mom's old Barbie collection. She has twenty-five dolls! Plus the car and the house and the horse. She also has a bunch of outfits that her mom made. So, can I go play one day?" Chloe gave him her 'I'm cute and persuasive' smile, and all he could do was grin at her.

"I'll see what we can work out." He cleared his throat, wondering how the heck he was supposed to get this little girl's mother's phone number and then arrange some kind of playdate. Even that small task seemed too big.

He shifted in his seat, grabbing another charcoal strip and dunking it in ketchup. "So, what did you learn today?"

The kids both looked at each other, then shrugged.

Kit chuckled. "Come on. Just one thing." He held up his pointer finger.

"Um…well, I liked music time. We had to copy Miss Emma's claps. It was fun." Corbin speared a tater-tot and popped it in his mouth, then proceeded to clap a rhythm, which Chloe copied.

And the next five minutes disappeared as all three of them took turns making up claps, just like Miss Emma did.

Kit laughed and reveled in their joyful excitement.

"So I think it's safe to say you both had a good day."

His comment set off another round of stories, and for a little while, Kit leaned back and let himself soak in the win. It was only one day. And he had no idea how he was going to make it through tomorrow. But at least today was a success all around.

When dinner was done, he got the kids situated in

front of a Pixar movie that they could already repeat verbatim as he went about cleaning up the kitchen.

The sweet satisfaction of having survived today was starting to wane as it sank in that he was going to have to do it all again tomorrow, and the day after that, and the day after that.

He sighed as he scrubbed the charred pan. He could do this. It was like today was a test run, that was all. Now he knew he needed a whole lot more time in the morning for Chloe's hair, plus some buffer time for Corbin if he decided to protest by not wearing pants again.

For a moment he stopped his scrubbing and rested his elbows on the counter's edge as he dropped his head with weary exhaustion. Tomorrow would be easier.

It had to be. Because nice boss or not, Kit couldn't show up late every day. And he sure as heck couldn't cut out early.

But this was fine. He was fine. He'd just have to make sure they all stayed on schedule.

Dishes done, he went back to the living room to spend some more quality time with the twins…only to find them fast asleep on the couch.

He glanced at the clock. It was a little earlier than they normally went to bed, but they must have been tuckered out by their big day.

Slowly and quietly, he got them upstairs and tucked in for the night. For a long moment he sat on the edge of Corbin's bed and watched them sleep.

Was this how it was always going to be? Feeling like he was torn in twenty different directions at once just to survive?

All he wanted was to give them a good life and be the sort of parent they could rely on.

He wanted them to have the same stability he'd grown up with.

He wanted to do an honest day's work and still have time to be everything his kids needed.

Leaning forward on his elbows, he sighed. Why was that so hard?

A prayer came to mind, and he murmured a quick plea for strength and endurance, then took the time to bless his children.

"Amen." Pushing to his feet, he turned off the bedroom light and went back to the living room. He snagged his old laptop, which he barely ever used, and booted it up in his lap as he kicked his feet up on the coffee table.

The Pixar movie was still playing in the background—oddly comforting since he'd seen it so many times alongside the twins. Aside from the movie, the house was silent. So very quiet.

Was this what it would be like when he and the kids moved into their own space?

He already knew the answer, and the heavy sensation in his stomach made him wonder if the charcoal chicken they ate for dinner had actually been rocks.

With slightly shaky fingers, he typed in the website for a local real estate agency, turning up the movie's volume to make up for the silence that made him lonelier than he'd felt in a long time.

He'd been content to just have his family around, grab the occasional drink with his coworkers and buddies, and flirt with the ladies who sidled up to him at the pool table when they went out.

That and his kids…it had always been enough.

But now, alone and wondering how he was going to do

it all again the next day, his parents' words came back to him.

"You've found this rut, and it's about time you step out of it. We're doing you no favors carrying you this way."

Now that his pride wasn't stinging and the shock was over, he could see the truth in their reasoning.

Maybe it was time for him to move on. It was time for him to make a new life for himself. For his kids. It was time they were their own family.

With a weary sigh, he started to scroll through the options. He'd been setting money aside over the years. He had a nest egg he could dip into for exactly this moment.

He wasn't sure what he was looking for though. Something affordable. Maybe with a little land. Something that felt like a home. A place where he could imagine raising the twins into full-fledged adults.

He chuckled softly at the image of them going off to college and starting lives of their own.

It seemed like a lifetime from now, but he suspected he'd blink and that day would be upon them.

Still, right now?

He dropped his head back against the couch as the rest of the school year spread out before him.

One day down.

He took a sip of his drink.

And twelve years to go.

15

Lizzy tilted her head to the side, soaking in the late afternoon sun as she watched the paint on her nails dry.

It wasn't that she was bored, necessarily. She pursed her lips as she held her fingers up for closer inspection. She just wasn't sure she was fond of that pale turquoise she'd applied yesterday, that was all.

Her phone dinged beside her, and, careful not to smudge the polish, she hit the button to answer.

"Hey, Emma," she said. "You heading out soon?"

She gave a little wince. Had that sounded desperate? It was just that this place got kinda lonely without Emma and Nash around.

"No, I have to stay late." Emma sounded uncharacteristically frazzled. "Actually, that's why I'm calling. I need your help."

Lizzy straightened, her gaze locked on the phone. "What's up?"

"Marsha was supposed to be picking up Chloe and Corbin after school, but she's had a family emergency with her own grandchildren, and she's had to leave town." Emma's words ran together, and Lizzy blinked in surprise.

Who was Marsha? And what did this have to do with her?

"Okay," she said slowly.

Emma let out a loud exhale. "I can't reach Kit. Which isn't surprising. I know he's with Nash and they're on the range today with this buyer."

Lizzy frowned. "They don't have cell reception out there?"

A brief silence followed that. Had that been a stupid question? Maybe. But Lizzy had thought that in this day and age, cell reception was everywhere.

"No," Emma said simply. "They don't. Which means I can't get ahold of Kit—"

"So you need me to track him down?" Lizzy was already looking around, as if she might be able to spot Kit riding on his horse in the distance. She couldn't. No surprise there. But it did get her thinking—just how big was this land they owned, anyway? "I'll keep an eye out," she said feebly.

What else was she supposed to do? Hop on horseback and ride aimlessly around until she spotted them?

No thanks.

"Lizzy, listen to me," Emma said. "I need you to come and collect the twins. Take them back to Kit's place and look after them until he gets home."

Lizzy balked. "What? Me? Why?" Panic laced her words, but honestly… "I don't know what to do with children."

This was not an exaggeration.

"Kids freak me out. You know that, Emma."

"It's not that hard," Emma said.

"Says you! You know how to keep those feral little creatures tame. You have a gift, Em. A gift I do not share."

"Lizzy, they're not feral, just energetic."

Lizzy scoffed.

"They're harmless, I swear," Emma added.

Lizzy was fairly certain she could see Emma's smile, as well as her eye roll. She thought Lizzy was being a drama queen. And maybe she was. But right now, the dramatics felt warranted.

"You just have to drive them home, give them a snack, and look after them until Kit shows up." Emma was using her teacher voice now. The one that was all calm and gentle—and didn't fool Lizzy in the slightest.

"Oh, that's all, huh?" Sarcasm laced her tone. "Just feed two little devils until Kit deigns to return home?"

"Lizzy," Emma said.

"Why can't you do it?" Guilt speared through her at Emma's tired sigh.

"I have an important staff meeting that I have to go to," Emma said. "Look, I wouldn't be calling you if I wasn't desperate. Please, Lizzy, you're the only person I know right now who is free and available. I need your help."

"Free and available"?

Lizzy looked around her at the discarded folder of sister names and the remnants of her lunch. Yeah, she was definitely free and available.

She really hated the fact that she was so free and available. She wished she was busy working at a job she loved. Dang it.

"Lizzy, please."

She tipped her head back with a sigh. "All right, fine. Now tell me again what you need me to do."

A little while later, Lizzy found herself staring down

the largest truck she'd ever seen. It was Nash's, and it was huge.

"You're a beast," she whispered.

She toyed with Nash's keychain until it unlocked, and then she hauled herself inside.

Or rather she *tried* to haul herself inside.

Her first attempt ended with her sliding back down, her heels landing with a squish in the mud.

She really should have changed her shoes. But she'd been in such a frenzy, finding Nash's keys and gathering up her belongings, it hadn't occurred to her that this scenario might require a wardrobe change.

She moaned at the sight of her dirty shoes before latching on to the seat belt and the driver's seat, wedging one foot on the runner as she threw herself up again, this time landing on her belly in the driver's seat.

Graceful it was not, but at least she was in.

"Right. Step one complete," she mumbled as she stuck the keys in the ignition.

It came to life with a roar that terrified her. She settled her hands on the wheel tentatively.

Was anything about this truck *not* overly large?

She replayed her conversation with Emma.

"I don't know how to drive a stick."

"Yes, you do," Emma had shot back. *"Derek made us both learn, remember?"*

"I remember, I remember," Lizzy muttered now as she put the truck in gear. "I also remember that I haven't had to actually use this knowledge for, oh...six years or so?"

She was talking to herself now. A tendency that was becoming way too frequent. She'd have to quit this new habit when she returned to civilization or she'd be that crazy cat lady, talking to herself as she raided the freezer section of the grocery store for pints of ice cream.

After a couple jerky starts, she got the truck in motion and headed for the dirt path leading to the main road. "We've got this, Beast," she said, patting the dashboard for good measure. "Yup. We have totally got this."

Her voice sounded shaky and her knuckles were white, but by the time she reached the gates that opened onto the main road, she was feeling a little more comfortable driving this hulking vehicle.

"Just like riding a bike," she whispered. "A loud, giant, powerful bike."

It wasn't until she was on the main road and seeing signs for Aspire's downtown when she realized this was another reason her belly was twisted into knots.

She hadn't left the ranch since she'd first arrived. This was her first time going out into the world on her own, and her pulse raced with nerves that she couldn't quite explain.

"It's fine," she told herself. "I'm just going to the school. Emma will be there. She's got the car seats and she'll know how to install them and get the kids fastened in..." She winced as she turned onto Main Street.

She hadn't taken much notice of her surroundings on her one outing into Aspire with Emma. She'd been too caught up in her own overwhelming grief. And then there was the fact that everyone and their mother had recognized Emma and wanted to stop for a chat.

Lizzy had hated it. The attention, the curious stares, the whispers. It had felt like nails raking over her raw skin. Her humiliation had been painful enough without a bunch of nosy neighbors clambering for a better look at her tearstained face.

Or those ladies who'd been all too eager for a glimpse of Kit. She frowned as she remembered a pretty brunette who'd all but drooled over Kit when he'd dropped them off in town.

No wonder his ego was so out of control.

This time as she drove down Main Street, she could admit it had a certain charm. If you liked that whole Hallmark, Norman Rockwell vibe. Two-story brick buildings lined the few blocks that made up the so-called downtown, and the stretches of buildings were dotted with parks and flowers and streetlights that gave the area pops of color and life amid the old-fashioned signage and architecture.

With mountains as a backdrop and that famed big blue sky...

Yeah, she could see how this place might appeal to Emma. It was pretty. One might even say quaint.

She sniffed as she followed Emma's directions and turned down the side street leading to the school. She might be able to appreciate the homey atmosphere and the small-town charm, but that didn't mean it appealed to her.

No, sir. She'd be bored to tears in a place like this.

Her eye was caught by a cute little boutique that was nestled along the side street. She felt a familiar yearning.

It had definitely been way too long since she'd been shopping. Not that Aspire would have the sort of clothes she liked. But even so, she made a mental note to check out that shop when she had some free time.

Which was basically all the time. Except for right now.

She flinched as the redbrick, white-pillared elementary school came into view. Even if the sign didn't announce it as a school, the yellow buses and playground equipment out front gave it away.

She pulled up to an empty space along the curb and gripped the giant wheel with a sigh.

Taming this terrifying beast of a truck seemed like child's play compared to…

Well, child's play.

The thought made her laugh under her breath.

She reached for the door handle with a long suffering sigh. "All right, you little monsters. Let's get this over with."

16

Life was good as Kit rode his stallion over the east ridge. The O'Sullivan homestead and surrounding buildings spread out in the valley below looked as pretty as a picture.

"I think that went as well as could be expected," Nash was saying as he brought his horse into stride alongside Kit's.

Kit nodded. "By the sounds of it, you'll be earning the new owners a good payday this year."

JJ and Cody sidled up alongside them. JJ was chewing on a piece of straw, looking thoughtful as he said, "I'm curious, Nash. Are you going above and beyond because you're dead set on being the world's best foreman—" He gave Nash the side eye. "—or are you just trying to impress the new owners?"

Kit dipped his head with a chuckle as Nash gave an exasperated sigh.

Kit envied the heck out of Nash with his new relationship, but he didn't envy his friend all the teasing he'd been withstanding ever since he'd fallen for an O'Sullivan.

"The fact that I'm dating Emma doesn't change anything," he said stiffly, which made Cody and JJ laugh all over again. "I've always done what's best for this ranch."

Kit looked over at his friend. "Everyone knows that, Nash. They just like to tease you."

Nash huffed, but his irritation was tempered with a rueful smile. "They can have their fun," he said, loudly enough for the other two to hear. "Because at the end of the day, I'm going home to Emma."

His smug smile put Kit's Cheshire grin to shame.

Not one of the men could argue that. Cody had never had a serious girlfriend. JJ could have a slew of girlfriends all over the state for all they knew because the private mountain man never talked about his love life—or lack thereof. And as for Kit…

Well, everyone knew he'd been flying solo since Natalie left.

"You're all just jealous," Nash added with that smug smirk.

Not one of the other men argued.

The conversation had Kit's head spinning with what-ifs. They were crazy thoughts…thoughts he'd been trying to dispel for nigh on twenty-four hours now. Heck, maybe even longer.

But try as he might, every time he wasn't paying attention, his mind kept drifting to thoughts of a certain blonde bombshell and the way it had felt when his lips touched hers.

He nudged his horse faster, as if he might be able to outrace his insubordinate brain.

He blamed it on his parents' departure. Having so

much alone time at the house put a spotlight on the fact that he was lonely.

He took off his cowboy hat, the bright sun glaring down on his face as he scraped a hand through his messy hair.

He couldn't deny it any longer—he *was* lonely.

Oh, his kids kept him busy, and his friends were great for a laugh, but at the end of the day, he wished there was someone at his side. A partner. A friend. Someone who wanted to tell him everything that happened in her day and who took an interest in his day too.

The desire for companionship had become more apparent now that he was alone with the kids, but it was thoughts of Lizzy and that kiss that made what used to be a nagging sense of lacking feel like a giant void in his chest.

He shook his head with a rueful huff of amusement.

That little drama queen must've been rubbing off on him. A giant void? Yeesh. He needed to get a grip.

"You all right, Kit?" Nash asked.

The other two had fallen into conversation among themselves, and Nash was watching him with a curious gaze.

"Yeah. Of course."

Nash nodded, tugging on the reins as he slowed his steed and cast another sidelong look in Kit's direction. "It's just that I know this has been hard on you. Going from having your parents' support to doing it all on your own…"

Kit sighed. "It's not easy, but luckily for me, my boss is also my friend." He shot Nash a grin that made him laugh. "And besides," he continued, his spine straightening with pride, "I made it through day two with flying colors."

Apparently Cody overheard him, because he laughingly called out, "The day's not over yet, big brother!"

JJ chuckled behind him.

Kit laughed it off. No, the day wasn't over, but compared to yesterday, this day was already a win. He'd gotten the kids to school on time and without any meltdowns. That right there was huge. Add in the fact that both kids had eaten a semi-nutritious breakfast and he'd managed a decent ponytail to satisfy Chloe, and he was feeling like the king of the world.

His gaze latched on to the ranch house below them as they crested the hill toward the stables.

Was Lizzy home?

Of course she was. She never left this ranch. Which was a shame, really. How was she ever going to get a better opinion of Aspire if she never gave the town a chance?

He suspected she might actually like some aspects of town if she kept an open mind. And if she had the right tour guide…

A smile tugged at his lips as he imagined taking her out on the town. Introducing her to some of the town's quirkier residents and showing off the local sights.

They might not have spas and gyms and whatever else it was she'd been going on about, but as a town that catered to tourists, they had their fair share of nice things.

Not even a snobby city girl like Lizzy could complain about the steak dinner at The Roadhouse or the pie at Mama's Kitchen—

A ding from his phone cut through his daydream just in time. Why on earth couldn't he get that woman off his mind?

He fished out his phone as Nash's phone dinged and then Cody's.

"Guess we're back in cell range," JJ drawled. He was the only one not scrambling to turn on his phone.

"Uh-oh," Cody muttered.

"Emma texted," Nash started slowly.

But Kit already knew what he was going to say, because he'd gotten multiple texts from Emma too—plus a handful of missed calls from the school, which made his heart pound with worry.

His eyes flickered over her texts, relief flooding him when he realized they weren't hurt, and then—

"What the...?"

"No way." Cody chuckled.

Nash made a hissing sound as he winced. "Lizzy's watching your kids?"

Kit brought the horse to a halt beneath him so he could focus on Emma's last text.

Emma: *Sorry for all the messages! Nothing to worry about. Lizzy's taking the twins home and will watch them until you get done. Take your time, she's got it covered.*

"She's got it covered?" He clutched the phone tighter, an uneasy sensation tightening his chest.

Dang it, just when he'd thought this day was going to go smoothly.

Kit rounded on Nash. "Does Lizzy know anything about taking care of kids?"

"Er..." Nash winced. "I don't know."

"Does she have any experience whatsoever with children?" he continued, hoping for a little reassurance.

He caught the exchange going on behind him and turned his horse to face his brother and JJ.

"What is it?" His brow puckered, the tightening in his chest increasing to uncomfortable.

They shared a wary look. "Nothing, just…" Cody cleared his throat. "She made it pretty clear the other day that she's not a fan of kids."

"Actively dislikes them, actually," JJ added, his lips twitching with amusement.

Kit's eyes widened. "What?"

He felt like he'd just taken a kick to the chest. His rib cage ached, and it knocked the wind out of him.

His kids were with a woman who didn't even like children?

And also…

Lizzy hated kids?

Ouch. That blow was brutal.

He scrubbed a hand over his eyes. It didn't matter.

Except…

How on earth did she not like kids? Didn't all women like cute little ones?

A stabbing disappointment had him rounding on Nash again. "Is this true?"

Nash shrugged, his gaze fixed on his phone and his own brow furrowed. "How should I know? It's not like I've ever had a heart-to-heart with her about this topic."

Kit growled low under his breath. Everyone else here was way too amused while his children's safety was on the line.

Cody shifted closer. "I think our boy Nash here is more worried about Lizzy driving his truck at the moment."

Nash's head snapped up. "That's not true." He turned to face Kit. "Look, whether she likes kids or not, Emma wouldn't leave her in charge if Lizzy couldn't handle it. She'd never put your kids at risk, and you know it."

Kit sank back in his saddle as some of his tension eased. Nash had a point. Emma wouldn't have let Lizzy watch them if she didn't think she were up to the task.

Suddenly Kit had a vision of what Lizzy had in store for her. He could just see the twins running her in circles with tantrums and tears and demands. He swallowed a snicker at the thought of them all muddy and grimy after playing outside. One of them would surely find a way to muss up Lizzy and her precious clothes.

"You're right," Kit said with a nod. "She's probably the one I should be worried about. I'm sure she can take care of two kids for a couple hours."

"Yeah, but can she handle Nash's truck?" JJ asked. His low voice held a world of mischief, and Kit's gaze darted back to his best friend.

"She took your truck?" Cody's comment from moments ago was only now registering. Kit hadn't even thought about how Lizzy would have gotten to the school.

Cody looked like he was trying not to laugh. "She took his truck."

JJ let out a low whistle. "That's an awfully big truck for such a little lady. Think she'll be able to handle it?"

Nash looked a little pale.

"Sure hope she knows how to drive a stick shift," Cody added.

If Kit could have reached his brother, he would have punched him in the arm. They were torturing poor Nash. "Emma wouldn't trust her with Nash's ride if she thought she couldn't handle that either." He arched a brow at Nash. "Would she?"

"No." Nash breathed out wearily. "No, she wouldn't

put her sister at risk if she thought she couldn't drive it safely."

All four of them fell into silence. Nash was no doubt thinking about his precious truck while Kit was trying not to imagine everything that could possibly go wrong with an inexperienced babysitter at the wheel.

"She doesn't like kids," he muttered, trying to reconcile that with the foolish daydreams he'd been harboring like some lovesick teenager.

"That's what she said," JJ said.

Kit glared at him, and Cody held his hands up in defense. "She was probably just kidding around. Exaggerating or whatever."

Kit turned to Nash. "What do you think?"

Why did it matter? She didn't have to like kids to keep them safe for a couple hours. And yet...

"Nash?" he prompted.

"I told you, I don't know," Nash huffed. But his gaze darted away guiltily. "Emma kind of indicated to me that Lizzy didn't want to have kids. That's totally different."

The words were a second blow that made Kit's swallow thick and painful.

He shouldn't care that Lizzy didn't want kids. He *didn't* care. In fact, he was grateful. This was exactly what he needed to know to get over his stupid crush.

They slowly rode closer to the stables, and Kit quickly dialed Emma, but it went straight to voice mail. He left a frustrated message before hanging up. He turned to Nash. "Do you have Lizzy's number?"

Nash winced and apologized. "Sorry, man. She's always at the house, so I've never needed it."

"This is just great," he muttered. Even if he hurried

back to the stables and finished his chores for the day, she'd still have been alone with them for way too long.

"I'm sure it'll be fine," Nash said. "Emma would have given her clear instructions for what to do."

Kit took a deep breath as he imagined the worst. "And she won't crash your big truck with my kids in it?"

Cody chuckled. "Of course she won't. She's not going on any major highways, and the speed limit in town is so low that she can't get into too much trouble, even if she is driving a beast of a truck. Besides, she's not totally incapable." He shot a mischievous look in Nash's direction. "Clipping a wing mirror or two is not crashing a truck."

"She's not going to clip any wing mirrors," Nash barked.

JJ shrugged, his gaze thoughtful. "She kind of is incapable, though, don't you think?"

"She's been trying," Nash said, his tone defensive. "She's come out of her room, and she's been real great about trying to help out around the house."

Kit arched a brow in disbelief and saw that JJ and Cody were fixing Nash with the same shocked stares.

"What?" he said, still defensive on his girlfriend's sister's behalf. "She's been up and about the last few days. Seems to have found herself some energy and spirit. I say she's gonna be fine." Nash nodded. "Now, get back to work."

Kit frowned, going back to his duties and trying not to worry.

It wasn't like Chloe and Corbin were babies anymore. Lizzy could cope with two five-year-olds, right?

He winced as he remembered the nightmare they'd put him through the morning before...and he'd had experience with them since birth!

"Just hang tight, kids," he murmured as he kicked his horse into motion. "And try not to drive Lizzy completely insane."

17

Lizzy's smile felt awkward and forced under the scrutinizing stares of her two new charges.

"Hi, I'm Lizzy." She waved.

The boy frowned. The girl's nose wrinkled up like she smelled something rotten.

"They hate me," Lizzy whispered.

Emma straightened from where she'd been adjusting the straps on the second car seat. "Don't be ridiculous. They're going to love you." She patted Lizzy's arm. "Just be yourself."

"Be myself?" she whispered as she headed back toward the driver's seat. Somehow she didn't think two five-year-olds wanted to hear what *Vogue* had to say about the latest fashion trends.

For a long moment, she stared up at the high seat as she imagined the ungraceful scramble that was in store just to get into the beast.

It seemed like an oddly fitting metaphor for what she was about to do.

She was so very out of her element.

Emma came over and wrapped her arms around Lizzy's waist from the side. "Thank you so much, sis. You're the best."

Her chest tightened at her sister's gratitude. It wasn't every day that Lizzy got to be the hero in their relationship. Squaring her shoulders, she promised herself she wouldn't let Emma down.

Or Kit.

She heaved herself up and into the bucket seat with only one embarrassing grunt. When she was sitting upright, she turned to face her passengers.

They stared right back.

She smiled.

They didn't.

Lizzy's heart jumped into her throat. Corbin looked straight at her, his gaze assessing, and all she could see was a mini Kit. Her smile grew, and he dipped his head.

"Hi." With another awkward wave, she greeted the kids again. "I'm Lizzy."

"We know." Chloe's brows drew together.

"You said that already," Corbin pointed out.

"You're Miss Emma's sister," Chloe continued. "And you're going to drive us home and feed us a snack and let us watch cartoons all afternoon."

"Chloe Swanson, I did not say that," Emma reprimanded from the back door, then leaned in to talk to the twins. "Now, remember what I said. Lizzy's in charge, and you need to do what she says. She's going to take you home and feed you, but she's the boss this afternoon, just like Aunt Marsha is when she's looking after you, okay?"

Chloe pouted. "But Aunt Marsha lets us watch TV or play on the iPad all afternoon."

"Well, Lizzy might do the same, but that's up to her."

Emma tucked a wild lock of hair behind Chloe's ear, and Lizzy could immediately see how desperately it needed a decent brush and style. Poor kid.

Emma smiled at the kids. "When you come back to school tomorrow, I want a glowing report on how amazing you were for my sister, okay?"

The twins shared a dubious frown before looking back at Lizzy, who had to hide her fear with a great big smile. It was too big. Too cheesy and they no doubt saw right through it, because their frowns deepened.

Clearing her throat, Lizzy threw her shoulders back. She wouldn't let two five-year-olds get the better of her. "Let's go have some fun!"

Yikes. She faced forward with a wince. That had been way too loud and frighteningly enthusiastic.

Emma moved so she was standing next to Lizzy, her hand on the driver's side door. "You're seriously the best. I'm so grateful."

Lizzy smiled. "Anytime."

Emma slammed the door shut, and Lizzy was alone in a silence that made her skin crawl.

They were probably planning her demise.

Not that she was paranoid or anything.

Lizzy put the truck in gear.

"Do you know where you're taking us?" Corbin asked.

"To your home," she said.

"Do you know the way?" Chloe added.

"No." She gave them a smile in the rearview mirror. "Do you?"

For a second they looked horrified, but then Corbin cracked a smile. "You're teasing."

She held up her phone. "I have the power of the interwebs at my fingertips. All hail Google Maps."

"You're weird," Chloe said, but she was giggling, so Lizzy called that a win.

With their address in her phone, she gritted her teeth and started the short but stressful drive to Kit's house.

Kit's house. I'm going to Kit's house.

Lizzy shifted in her seat as a girly giggle bubbled up in her. She had the sort of fluttery butterflies in her belly she hadn't known since high school.

She gave a snort of exasperation. Her body had a mind of its own.

And it was all well and good for her body to have a crush, because she most definitely did not. She glanced in the mirror. No, sir. Even if he wasn't an arrogant, testosterone-laden Neanderthal, Kit lived *here,* and he'd always live here. Plus, he had kids.

Lizzy didn't even want kids of her own let alone someone else's.

She straightened and focused her gaze on the road, ignoring the butterflies with a new determination because it was decided. She did *not* have a crush.

Eventually—finally—they turned onto Kit's street, and Lizzy let out a sigh of relief. Not even a tiny ding in this big old beast. She brought the truck to a stop at the curb in front of an older white split-level home that was tucked back into the tree line at the end of a long driveway.

"Why are you parking here?" Corbin asked. "Why not pull into the driveway?"

"Aunt Marsha always parks up by the house," Chloe said.

"Marsha, Marsha, Marsha," Lizzy said under her breath in her best Jan voice.

"What?" Corbin asked.

"Nothing. I just, uh, I wanted to leave room for your

dad when he gets home." There was no way she would admit to these two that she didn't trust herself not to take out Kit's mailbox.

Lizzy climbed down from the driver's seat and then opened the door to the back seat.

She was on Chloe's side and helped the girl get out of her straps. She reached for her to help her down, but Chloe shook her head. "I can do it by myself."

Lizzy arched a brow in disbelief. It was a long way to the ground.

Chloe arched one back. "I do it all the time."

Lizzy shrugged and took a step back, and the young girl openly assessed her from head to toe.

"I like your shoes," Chloe finally said. "They're tall."

Lizzy laughed. "Yeah, well, I can be a little short sometimes."

Chloe grinned. "Can I try them on when we get inside?"

Lizzy blinked, surprised by the question. "Of course."

She was usually a little precious about her shoes and jewelry—all her possessions, really—but she just got a smile out of a five-year-old. Of course the little girl could try on her shoes.

Lizzy went around to Corbin next, and he actually let her help him down, although he somehow managed to get a smear of mud on her pants in the process. She bit back a whimper as she looked down at it. She loved these pants.

Chloe jumped out her side, and the painful sound of fabric ripping rent the air. Lizzy gasped as she raced around to Chloe's side of the truck.

"Oh no!" Chloe wailed. "My dress!"

The amount of tears that suddenly sprang from Chloe's eyes rendered Lizzy temporarily frozen.

"Haha! I can see your underwear!" Corbin pointed at his sister and laughed, which only made Chloe cry harder.

"Hey, it's okay. It's okay. Uh…" Patting the girl's shoulder, Lizzy held the dress together at the side and led the kids around to the backyard, dodging sports equipment and a plethora of toys that had been scattered as if a toy box had exploded.

"Got the key!" Corbin pulled it out from under the potted plant and helped open the door. Chloe continued to wail while Corbin shoved open the door, dropping his backpack on the floor and announcing, "I'm starving!"

"Uh…" Grabbing the bag, Lizzy placed it on the table and looked around the house. The furniture was worn and the carpet had seen better days, but the sunken living room had a cozy air about it. The sofa was outdated, but it practically begged to be snuggled up on for a rainy afternoon filled with movies and popcorn.

There were framed photos covering every inch of the walls and a bookcase that was filled with kids' books and board games.

"I need food!" Corbin shouted above Chloe's tears.

"Yeah, uh…sure. Let me just…" She walked into the kitchen. Everything about it cried *home,* from the worn linoleum tiles to the lingering smell of spices. There were cute little signs all over the walls with sayings like 'God Bless This House' and 'A Messy House Is a Happy House.'

"You have to wash your hands first, Corbin!" Chloe shouted. "Grammy says that's the first thing we have to do." She sniffed and slashed a hand under her nose, then dumped her backpack on the kitchen floor while Corbin raced to the bathroom.

Lizzy started going through cupboards and fridge, and she managed to unearth a few snacks. Popping them on plates, she arranged them to look nice, then walked to the table.

"Can we eat in front of TV?" Corbin asked, his puppy-dog eyes doing a number on Lizzy's heart.

She blinked, surprised by the tug in her chest. "Uh... are you allowed to?"

"Uh-huh." Corbin bobbed his head, all innocence and sweetness.

Lizzy had no idea if he was telling the truth but figured this afternoon was all about survival.

"Well, okay, but not on the couch. Just kneel in front of the coffee table." She remembered the rules from her mother and hoped that was okay.

Placing the food down, she turned to Chloe, who was still sniffling and not moving into the living room. "You coming to eat, sweetie?"

"I'm not hungry." She pouted, fingering the torn fabric of her dress.

"I don't like banana!" Corbin held up the yellow fruit.

Lizzy glanced over her shoulder. "Okay, well, just eat everything else, then."

"Can I have an apple?" he asked.

"I'll get you some in a minute. I'm just going to help Chloe first."

Corbin huffed and turned back to the TV, reaching for the remote and starting to flick through channels. He settled on a cartoon, and Chloe shouted, "You're not allowed to watch that one!"

"Yes I am!"

"No, Grammy says there's too much fighting in it."

Corbin let out a disgusted scoff but didn't change the channel.

Crossing her arms, Lizzy sighed and walked back into

the living room. "Corbin, are you allowed to watch this show?"

"Sometimes." His voice was so small, it nearly made Lizzy laugh.

She pressed her lips together to stay serious, then managed, "Sometimes, as in when no one knows you're watching it?"

He nodded, fingering the little fish crackers on his plate.

"Okay, well, I'll tell you what. I'm gonna give you a chance to change the show to something you know you're allowed to watch, or you can just let me choose for you. I'm sure there's some Barbie movie or something we could all enjoy."

"Eww!" He scoffed and quickly grabbed the remote. A moment later, *Paw Patrol* was playing, and Lizzy felt kind of triumphant as she wandered back over to Chloe.

Crouching down, she lightly touched the girl's arm. "Do you want to go change?"

"I love this dress." Her chin bunched. "It's my favorite."

"It's so pretty." Lizzy fingered the fabric. "I love this peachy-pink color so much. It really looks good on you."

"But it's ruined." Tears lined her lashes again.

"Here, let me take a look." Spinning Chloe to the side, Lizzy inspected the dress and concluded that Chloe was right. This kind of fabric couldn't easily be stitched back together, especially where the tear was. With a sad sigh, Lizzy quietly told the girl, "You're right. This can't be fixed."

Chloe's chest heaved, and a fresh wave of tears started to trickle down her cheeks.

Lizzy winced, and her heart went out to the girl. This

she could totally understand. She'd be bummed too if her favorite dress were ruined. Heck, she might even cry. She nibbled on her lip before blurting, "But the good news is I can make you a new dress, just like this."

Chloe blinked, her lips parting. "You can?"

"Yeah. That's what I do. I'm into fashion, and I studied design at college. I can make a killer dress, and you could help me design it. So it can be everything you want it to be."

Chloe let out a squeak, staring at Lizzy like she'd just offered her the moon.

Lizzy grinned, a strange pang in her chest at the girl's wide-eyed stare. This little one was adorable. Glancing down at her watch, she did a quick calculation, then spontaneously said, "Hey, is there a fabric store in town?"

Chloe nodded. "I think so. There's a place that sells wool and stuff. Grammy takes me there sometimes because she knits booties for the babies in church."

"Perfect." Lizzy grinned. "Do you think you can show me where it is?"

"Main Street," she said promptly.

Lizzy chuckled. "Of course it is."

"Why don't we go there right now, before it closes, and you can pick something pretty?"

"Really?" Chloe jumped up on her toes and started clapping her hands.

Lizzy straightened, feeling slightly in control of the situation for once. Snacks and sibling bickering? Not so much. But a new dress and a trip to the fabric store? This was totally her jam. "You go get changed, and I'll get your brother ready."

"Okay!" Chloe raced up the stairs while Lizzy wandered into the living room.

"Let's go, Corbin. We're going to make a quick trip into town."

Corbin groaned. "I don't want to. We only just got home, and my show just started."

Some of Lizzy's confidence faded in the face of his stubborn pout. "Come on, help your sister out."

"I don't wanna." He didn't tear his gaze away from the TV.

Holding her sigh in check, Lizzy walked back into the living room and crouched down beside him. "You know, I've heard that brothers who do gallant things like making their sisters feel better when they're sad get rewarded with ice cream."

He perked up, his back going straight as his eyes darted to her face.

Lizzy played it cool, checking her nails and shrugging. "It's just something I heard. But that's cool. If you don't want ice cream, we can stay here."

"I want it! I want it!" Clicking off the TV, he jumped to his feet, and Lizzy couldn't help a laugh.

These kids were hilarious, and she felt like she was winning some kind of epic battle every time she got them to do what they were supposed to.

She crossed her arms as she watched Corbin hurriedly stick his feet in his shoes.

Maybe she could survive this afternoon after all.

18

"They're fine, they're fine, they're totally fine." Kit tapped the steering wheel as he repeated the mantra.

It didn't help.

The closer he'd gotten to the end of the workday, the more worried he'd become of what he was going to find when he walked through his front door.

His parents' front door.

He winced as he passed the familiar landmarks on his route home.

Lizzy O'Sullivan was currently in his parents' house.

He blew out a long exhale. Nope, this wasn't humiliating at all. He'd never minded much that he was that guy —the one who had to move back in with his parents. Everyone in Aspire had known all about his situation, and of course they'd been sympathetic, so he'd never actually had to explain to anyone why he was a grown man living with his mom and dad.

Now, though...

He shook off the thought. It didn't matter what some

stylish Gucci girl thought of his situation. And besides, he was in the process of finding his own place.

He nodded. He'd already known his parents had been right to push him out of the nest, but right now he was more grateful than ever for their nudge.

Although clearly, when he moved out on his own, he'd have to find more reliable babysitter backup than just Marsha. He'd need to have a network in place for occasions like this one.

He ran a hand over his hair but gave another nod. This was fine. He could do this. It would just take time to adjust and get all the moving pieces into place, that was all.

And honestly, all that mattered right now was making sure his kids were healthy and happy—and that they hadn't done anything horribly bad to Lizzy.

He had an image in his head of Lizzy weeping in the corner as his kids went into full just-ate-an-entire-Easter-basket-full-of-chocolate mode.

Nope. She wouldn't survive that level of sugar high. And no one should have to.

But she wouldn't let them eat whatever they wanted, right?

Man, he hoped she had more sense than that.

He pulled into his driveway and leapt out, racing up to the front door, bracing himself for whatever scene he might find.

He threw open the door, ready for tears or screams or—

Nothing.

"Hello?"

Still nothing.

"Chloe? Corbin? I'm home!"

The house remained still. Noiseless. And it set his already frayed nerves on edge.

His hand fell and his brows drew together in confusion as he turned in circles, like his kids might be hiding behind the bookcase. He didn't have to go far into his house to know they weren't there.

Even so, he called out Lizzy's name a couple times, knowing he'd get met with silence once more.

He spun in circles again, his mind spinning.

Where could they be? What had Lizzy done with them?

He crossed over to the front door again. No truck.

He should have noticed that right away. Nash's truck wasn't exactly easy to miss.

Oh crap. He scrubbed a hand over his jaw as he tried to calm his racing heart and think clearly.

Lizzy was alone with his kids...and she was in Nash's truck.

Do not panic, he ordered himself.

He pulled out his phone and dialed Emma again, but she didn't pick up. He glanced at the time on his phone. No doubt she was either still in that after-school meeting or driving back to the ranch.

He started to pace. "Who else could track her down?"

The sheriff.

He stopped short. How long did one have to wait before filing a missing person's report?

He stood there for way too long with his phone in hand, weighing his options.

Nash's truck was noticeable. If she were anywhere within Aspire's town limits, someone would spot that truck.

He started with Mama's Kitchen, but the busboy who

answered hadn't seen anything. He tried the flower shop next—the owner loved him. She'd closed early, so she was no help.

He was just starting to seriously consider putting out an APB when the front door opened and his family came bounding inside.

"Daddy!" Chloe squealed. She ran into his arms, clutching a shopping bag to her chest.

"Hi, Daddy," Corbin said. He was grinning from ear to ear, and the reason why was melted all over his face. Kit choked on a laugh at the sight of chocolate painting his lips, chin, and a spot by his ear.

"Ice cream, huh?" His gaze lifted to meet Lizzy's.

She shrugged with a cute little grimace. "Is that bad? I didn't know what the rules were on sweets, but it was the only way I could lure him away from the TV."

He stared at her as Corbin wiggled his way into the family hug, smearing that melted chocolate ice cream all over Kit's shirt, though Kit couldn't bring himself to care.

He inhaled deeply and let it out slowly, his heart aching with relief at having them in his arms again. They were safe. They were cared for. They were…

They were *happy.*

And that happiness burst out of them in a torrent of words.

"Daddy, guess what Lizzy can do?"

"Daddy, she let me pick two flavors of ice cream!"

"…and Miss Emma liked my picture."

"…but I told Jack I wasn't allowed to do that so…"

Their little voices filled the air, tumbling over one another and making Kit's head spin as he looked back and forth to nod and respond.

It was the sound of chaos. And he loved every second of it.

He glanced up to see Lizzy watching on with an affectionate smile that made his heart slam against his rib cage.

"Guys, I can't wait to hear all about your day, but I've got to get dinner started, and I see two faces that need a good scrub." He pointed to the bathroom. "Let's see who can wash up the fastest."

They were off like lightning, their bickering already starting up about who was going to win.

Lizzy's gaze turned to follow them, and she still wore that smile.

That smile.

He hadn't thought he could love her face any more than he had the day before. But that smile had been one of gleeful smugness and laughter. This one made his heart feel like warm goo. Because this one spoke of tenderness and warmth, and it…it…

Aw heck, it slayed him.

"Thank you, Lizzy," he said when their voices were muted by the sound of running water.

She turned to face him, her hands clasping and unclasping in front of her. Almost like she was nervous.

But that couldn't be the case. This was not a girl who got nervous around a guy—definitely not him.

"It was nothing," she said, shifting toward the door.

"Funny," he murmured, moving toward her slowly as he shoved his hands in his pockets. "I never took you for a liar."

Her brows arched in surprise, and her lips parted. "What? Why would you—"

"Lizzy," he cut her off, grinning as he came to stop

right in front of her. "Taking care of my kids is a lot of things…but it's not nothing."

To his shock, her cheeks grew a little pink, and she looked away. "They were cute. Funny." She shrugged, looking up at him through thick lashes. "You've got pretty cool kids, you know."

His chest swelled as he nodded. "Yeah, I know."

They both glanced over at the hallway, where the twins' voices were getting louder.

"You seem to have made a big impression," he said, not trying to hide his admiration. "They like you."

Her blush deepened. "Yeah, well, turns out kids aren't so bad. They're just little people, right?"

He chuckled. "Right."

She grinned at him for a moment, then jerked a thumb toward the door. "Well, anyway, I should–"

"Wait," he blurted. When she stopped and gave him a questioning look, his heart started to race. "Uh, it's just…" He reached for his wallet. "I need to give you—"

"Oh no, no, no," she said quickly, waving her hands in a quick motion. "No way. This was just a favor for Emma."

"But–"

"No," she said sternly. "Honestly, I know I'm kinda pathetic and unemployed right now…" Her cheeks pinkened even more. "But I can still do a favor for a friend."

He blinked. A friend. Was that what they were?

Her brows drew together slightly, and he suspected she was wondering the same thing.

"Besides…" She shrugged, flashing him a hesitant little smile that made his lungs hitch. "It was kind of fun."

"All right. Well, if you're sure—"

"Daddy! Can Lizzy stay?" Chloe's voice interrupted

their awkward goodbye, and in a second his twins were flanking him.

"Daddy, tell her to stay for dinner," Corbin said. "I want to show her my Teenage Mutant Ninja Turtles."

"Oh, that's—" Lizzy was wincing as she edged away. "I don't want to intrude."

"I owe you dinner at the very least." Kit shamelessly latched on to his kids' excuse so he didn't have to say good night.

"Um..." Lizzy bit her lip, her gaze filled with uncertainty.

"She has to stay, Daddy," Chloe said, her gaze so earnest it was hard to keep a straight face. She held up the shopping bag she was still clutching. "Lizzy's gonna make me a new dress."

Kit's brows shot up, and his gaze darted up to meet Gucci girl's. "She is?"

Lizzy shrugged, her grin sheepish but her eyes dancing with laughter. "If her daddy doesn't mind."

He felt a laugh bubbling up, that warmth in his chest spreading and growing. "I don't mind at all. But if you're making my daughter a dress"—he arched one brow—"I'm going to have to insist that you stay for dinner."

"Please, Lizzy," Corbin said, his tone wheedling.

"Yay, she's staying!" Chloe cheered. Apparently she thought it was a done deal.

They all looked to Lizzy, whose smile grew until it lit up the whole house. "Yeah, okay. But only if you let me help."

19

"Why do I feel like this is a case of the blind leading the blind?" Kit asked.

Lizzy giggled. "Shh. I'm trying to concentrate."

"You're reading the back of a box, Lizzy," Kit drawled, coming to stand just behind her. "It can't be that complicated."

"Well, then, you can handle the pasta," she shot back.

"No, thank you." Kit chuckled, stepping away with his hands up. "I've got my hands full with the vegetables.

Lizzy emptied the boxed linguini into the boiling water and set a timer on her phone. She found herself biting her lip to hold back a silly smile.

She'd been acting like a giddy teenager from the moment she'd walked in and found Kit waiting for them. She wasn't sure what it was, but being here at his house, with his kids...

It felt so different from every other run-in she'd had with him. He didn't have that cocky swagger when he was dropping to his knees and hugging his children. And the way he'd looked at her had been anything but taunting.

She'd gone from feeling jubilant about her success handling the twins to nervous as a schoolgirl in the face of her crush.

So stupid, she told herself. But as she watched Kit slice bell peppers beside her with a frown of concentration so intense it looked like he was performing surgery, she couldn't stop her heart from doing a backflip in her chest.

"You know," he said after a beat, "when you offered to help cook, I sort of thought maybe you knew what you were doing."

She watched his lips twitch as he fought a smile.

Resting a hip against the counter, she crossed her arms. "That's funny, because when you said you wanted to repay me with dinner, I sort of thought maybe you knew what *you* were doing."

He shot her a sidelong glance and a small smile that made the butterflies in her belly go wild. "Fair point."

She laughed, loving this new side of him. He still teased and he still had confidence to spare, but it was tempered by something warmer and softer. No doubt that had more to do with his kids' bickering presence at the kitchen table behind them than her, but it was still nice to see. It made him more human somehow. More relatable. He was more than just some macho cowboy. He was...

A friend?

She stared at his profile as she nibbled on her lower lip. That's what she'd said earlier. She'd called him a friend. Was that all he was?

She turned away with a huff.

Of course that's all he is. That's all he can be!

"Chloe," Kit said, "it's your turn to set the table."

"What can I do?" Lizzy asked. "I mean, aside from

watch the water boil, which I am doing a supremely good job of, I might add."

"I am very impressed," he said evenly. "Julia Child's got nothin' on you, darlin'."

The term of endearment made her toes curl as warmth spread through her. He was just teasing. She knew that. But it still sounded affectionate.

In fact…

She turned to watch Chloe reaching up on tiptoes for the plates as Corbin played in the corner with his turtles.

There was so much warmth in this house. So much love, even when they were all just going about their chores.

"Corbin," Kit said, "time to put the toys away and help your sister."

"Aw, but, Daddy," Corbin whined, "I didn't get to show Lizzy."

Lizzy grinned, her heart melting at that. "Personally, I don't want to have to rush through my introduction to these turtles. If you put them away now, we'll have plenty of time to play together after dinner."

Corbin's eyes widened with excitement, and he hurriedly scooped up his toys.

Lizzy turned to see Kit watching her with a small grin that made his eyes crinkle at the corners. There was amusement there that had her a touch defensive.

"What?" she asked.

"Nothing." He shook his head like he was clearing it. "Just… You're good with them, that's all."

She shrugged. "They're good kids."

"Yeah, but…" He cleared his throat, turning back to his task. "Never mind."

"No, go on. Say it."

He turned to her with arched brows. "Some of the guys were saying you don't like kids. Or..." He scratched the back of his head as he ducked it sheepishly. "I don't know, that maybe you don't want kids?"

"I don't," she said quickly. And then, as soon as it was out of her mouth, she found herself wondering if that were true. She frowned, her gaze fixed on the food they were preparing as if the answers might be found on a cutting board.

"Oh. Right." Kit nodded, a muscle in his jaw clenching for just a moment. "I was just surprised that you're such a natural, that's all. I didn't mean to offend you—"

"No, it's okay." She cut his apology off before it could get awkward. "I was just thinking..."

"About?"

"I guess I never really gave kids much thought when I was younger." She reached over and stole a slice of pepper, popping it in her mouth. "I wasn't like Emma, who always dreamed of a husband and kids and a white picket fence."

He nodded. "That's not a surprise. You and Emma don't seem all that similar, aside from your crazy good looks."

She gave a huff of amusement and turned her head before he could see her blush. "Yeah, well, I'd never really thought about it until Connor came along. And then he made it clear that he didn't want kids, and so I sort of decided I didn't either, and now..."

She was frowning again, the slice of pepper forgotten in her hand.

Kit snatched it from her and ate the rest of it. "You'll figure it out."

He sounded so certain, and so...nonjudgmental. She

wasn't sure where to look or how to respond. "I sure hope so."

He turned back to the vegetables, using his hands to scoop them into the salad bowl. "After my wife left…" He cleared his throat.

Lizzy held her breath when he didn't immediately continue. She was afraid if she spoke he'd remember who she was and stop talking.

He took a deep breath and gave her a rueful smile. "It can take a while to figure out who you are when you're no longer part of a couple." His expression grew rueful. "I guess maybe I'm still figuring it out and it's been, what? Four years?"

His self-deprecating wince made her laugh. She patted his shoulder. "You'll figure it out too."

He chuckled, and for a moment they both fell into their own thoughts.

"Go have a seat." Kit nodded toward the table with a smile. "I think I got it from here."

"You sure?" she teased as she backed toward the table where the kids were taking their seats. "Because boiling water can get a little complicated, so—"

"I know where to find you if I need your assistance." He grinned and winked, sending a fresh wave of butterflies bursting through her system.

Honestly, Lizzy. Pull it together!

A little while later, Kit joined them at the table.

"Chloe, your turn to say grace," he said.

Everyone bowed their heads and clasped their hands.

Chloe's brow furrowed with earnest concentration. "Thank you, God, for Daddy and Corbin and for the pretty lady who is gonna make me a new dress so I will look so pretty and everyone will talk about how pretty I am."

Kit cleared his throat while Lizzy clamped her lips together, trying not to crack up laughing.

"Oh!" Chloe's eyes popped open, then squeezed shut again. "And thank you for the food! Love you! Amen."

Kit glanced across the table and gave Lizzy a wincing smile, but she just grinned at him and picked up her fork. She was smiling as she dug into her food. It felt like her first real smile in a long time.

It was hard to wallow on her troubles with Chloe chattering away a mile a minute and Corbin interjecting occasionally, seemingly just to rile his sister.

"All right, you two. I'm remembering. It's time for—" Kit started.

"Oh!" Corbin's hand shot into the air. "I want to go first."

Lizzy paused with the fork halfway to her mouth. "Time for what?"

"Rose and Thorn," Chloe answered as though she and her brother were telepathic or something. Her grin was wide and even cuter with the addition of a milk mustache. "We play it every night, except we forgotted last night because we were so busy telling Daddy about our first day of school. But Daddy promised that we wouldn't forget tonight."

Lizzy arched a brow in Kit's direction, and he wiped his hands on a napkin as he sat back in his chair.

"It's simple," he said. "We go around the table, and everyone tells us one good thing that happened to them today and one challenge they faced. If you really had a big day, you can share a bud too."

Lizzy couldn't help a smile as her chest swelled with emotion. "What's a bud?"

"Oh, that's if you did something nice for someone," Chloe said.

"Or your bud can be if you're excited about something coming up tomorrow," Corbin added.

Lizzy nodded, careful to keep her expression thoughtful to match their seriousness. "Got it."

"Don't worry." Kit grinned. "We don't keep score or anything." He gave her a little wink that the kids missed. "These two just like to have rules to play by."

"I see." And she did. Having been around them for the better part of the afternoon, it was clear these two were big on keeping each other in check.

And she'd thought she and Emma were competitive.

She stuck a bite of carrot in her mouth to smother a laugh.

The game was fun and lighthearted, which was why Lizzy refused to cry. Even if both of the kids named her as their rose for the day.

Nope. She was definitely not choked up over that.

She took a big gulp of water.

"Your turn, Daddy." Chloe pointed at him.

"Let's see," he said, leaning back and crossing his arms. "I'd say my thorn was worrying about you two." He gave the twins a mock glare that sent them into a fit of giggles. "And my rose..." His gaze lifted to meet Lizzy's.

She found herself holding her breath.

"Well, my rose was finding out that Lizzy had taken such good care of my little lovebugs."

She felt a flush of warmth all the way from her head to her toes at the kindness in his eyes when he looked at her.

She dipped her head and speared her food with her fork.

"Mine's easy," she said nonchalantly. "My thorn was

finding out I am woefully behind on my American Girl knowledge." She shot Chloe a look that made the little girl giggle. She turned to Corbin. "And my rose was having an excuse to eat ice cream in the middle of the afternoon."

He met her grin with a beam of his own.

Kit cleared his throat. "Yeah, speaking of that, Corbin, you need to eat those carrots, buddy. You and your sister are running on pure sugar at this point. You need some vegetables to counter the attack."

Corbin's mouth instantly set in a stubborn pout. "I don't like 'em."

Kit rolled his eyes, and Lizzy could practically feel his exasperation. She'd bet this was a conversation they had most nights.

Lizzy remembered the battles her mom went through to get her to eat broccoli, and she stepped in to help before she could even think about it. "How can you not like carrots? They're orange, one of the happiest colors in the world. Why wouldn't you want to eat happiness?"

Corbin blinked, like he was trying to figure out what she was saying, then shook his head. "They taste yuck."

"Joy tastes yuck?" Lizzy pulled a face. "Wow. Okay."

Chloe giggled. "Does eating carrots really make you happy?"

Lizzy had to force a straight face, especially after noticing Kit's expression. He was trying so hard not to crack up laughing.

Popping a piece of carrot in her mouth, she munched it, then gave the twins a silly smile.

They started giggling, and she wiped her mouth like a lady before telling them, "It's clinically proven."

She had no idea how this was all blooming in her head, but she was running with it.

"Oh really?" Kit's voice was filled with laughter as he pointed at her with his fork. "And which study did you get this information from?"

She leaned back with a haughty toss of her hair. "Well, if you went to the same medical school I did, you would know this."

His lips twitched, his chest shaking as he contained his laughter. "And which school is that?"

"The, uh…the Institute of Commonus Knowledgeus, of course. And believe me, it takes a lot of experience to graduate from that place, so you should really listen to me."

She had to look away because Kit was dying across the table, trying to play it cool while holding back his laughter.

The kids glanced between them, then settled on their dad for confirmation.

"Is that true, Daddy?" Corbin asked.

He swallowed and nodded solemnly. "You should listen to her. Dr. Lizzy says carrots make you happy, so eat up."

Corbin frowned, gazing down at his four little sticks of carrot, then plunging his fork into the first one. Taking a big bite, he scrunched his nose up, but he kept chewing.

Lizzy leaned forward and lowered her voice. "Enjoy the happiness, my little friend."

Kit chuckled, and she glanced across the table at him, throwing him a little wink and surprising them both.

What? She was the winking one now?

She seriously did not know what was coming over her.

But man, was she having fun.

20

Carrots make you happy.

Kit couldn't believe it. He ducked his head and tucked back into his meal. This woman was surprising him at every turn. Funny, smart, quick-witted. He couldn't remember the last time he'd enjoyed a meal this much. And he couldn't believe he'd doubted Lizzy's ability to look after his kids. She'd done a stellar job.

All he could think was *Stay, stay, stay!*

Which was ridiculous. Just because she'd helped him out and they'd enjoyed one nice meal together did not mean she'd want to stay. Or even that she should.

Clenching his jaw against those inappropriate thoughts, he took a bite of his meal, trying and failing not to keep glancing across the table at this beautiful woman.

She was just neatly placing her knife and fork in the middle of the plate, proving what a lady she was, when Corbin let out a loud and proud burp.

Lizzy's eyes widened. Corbin beamed while Kit smothered his chuckle with a hand over his mouth. "No burping at the table, Corb. You know that."

His son's expression was comically innocent. "The bubbles just came up. I couldn't stop them."

Kit just barely held back a sigh. "Well, what do you say after it happens?"

"Excuse me." Corbin rolled his eyes and pushed the last of his salad around the plate with his fork.

Then out popped a little fart from Chloe's rear end.

"Really?" Kit glanced across the table at her, mortified by his children's behavior, although, truth be told, he was swallowing down a surge of laughter as well.

Chloe covered her mouth, then started giggling.

Lizzy ducked her head. He couldn't see her expression, but clearly she was horrified by their manners.

Kit winced, scratching his head with embarrassment. Lizzy would never want to eat at their table again.

But then it happened. A giggle escaped before Lizzy could cover her mouth. Even with her mouth covered, her giggles got the better of her and she started laughing. Then…out came a loud snort.

His kids cracked up instantly as she gasped and ducked her head.

For a long moment, Kit could only gape at the woman across from him.

She was obviously mortified, and it was the cutest thing he'd ever seen. He couldn't contain his roar of laughter, and soon all four of them were laughing so hard they were clutching their bellies. Chloe even had tears popping out the corners of her eyes.

And all the while, the only words buzzing in Kit's brain were *Stay, stay, stay.*

He tried to shake it. He really did. But when the laughter subsided and Lizzy helped Corbin clear the table while he and Chloe put away the food, the urge kept growing.

He didn't want to see her leave. He sure as heck didn't want to say good night not knowing when he'd see her again.

He rubbed at his chest as he snuck a glance of her and Corbin, giggling among themselves as they got Corbin's stool in place so he could help with the dishes.

Kit really ought to be putting an end to this. Nothing good could come of his children getting attached to this woman he was growing fonder of by the second.

But as much as his brain knew that to be true, his body and his heart seemed to be of a different mind altogether.

After they were done cleaning up, Corbin held Lizzy to her word and dragged her off to their room so she could ooh and ahh over his Ninja Turtle collection.

He and Chloe watched from the doorway, and his little girl slid her hand into his, tugging him down so she could whisper in his ear.

"I like her, Daddy."

His heart gave a jerk at those sweet, simple words. So easy for her to say. She'd been too young to understand when her mama left.

She didn't know what it was like to have her heart broken. She and Corbin didn't have any defenses built up to protect themselves against it.

Which was why he needed to protect all their hearts for them.

By the time the turtle presentation was over, Chloe pointed out that it was nearly bedtime and begged shamelessly to have Lizzy read their nightly stories.

"You don't have to," Kit started.

"That's okay." Lizzy grinned. "I don't mind."

He got them into their pajamas and brushed their teeth—the whole process easier with Lizzy goading them along. And when they were all tucked in, Chloe handed Lizzy one of their favorites.

Kit leaned against the doorframe, just as transfixed as his children as Lizzy dove into the story with the air of a real actress. She even used all the voices, something he was terrible at.

Corbin and Chloe were wide-eyed with awe by the time he came over to kiss their heads and turn off the light.

Lizzy followed him out into the living room.

"It's getting late," she said, stifling a yawn with her hand.

He should let her go. Heck, he should escort her to the door.

Instead, he heard himself say, "Stay for coffee?"

She blinked up at him in surprise. "Isn't it a little late for that?"

He lifted a shoulder in a half-hearted shrug. Yeah, it was. He normally never had coffee this late, since he rose so early. But though he knew it was wrong, he didn't want this night to end.

"I don't want you sleepy when you drive back," he said.

This was true, and after a second, she nodded. "You're probably right. Driving that beast is intimidating enough without worrying about falling asleep at the wheel."

A little while later, they were settled on the couch with their coffee, Lizzy's feet tucked up beneath her, and the whole situation so dang cozy and sweet, it seemed like the most natural thing in the world.

Which was crazy. He never had women over.

Ever.

And they'd certainly never taken part in family time or snuggled up on his parents' worn, faded couch.

That thought made him flinch. "I'm moving out, you know."

She blinked. "You are?"

He took a deep breath as he filled her in. It was more than a little embarrassing to admit that his own parents were nudging him out of the nest, but he suspected she knew as much anyway.

"That'll be nice," she said when he told her about one of the rentals he was looking at. "For you and the kids."

"It will," he agreed. "I wish it hadn't taken this long for me to feel like I'm capable of standing on my own two feet, but..." He shrugged. "I'm grateful that I have the kind of family who I know will always be there for me."

Lizzy looked thoughtful as she nodded. "I'm grateful for my family too. I wouldn't have gotten through this whole ordeal without Emma and my parents."

He stayed quiet because he got the sense she still had more to say.

"I just wish sometimes it was me being there for them, though...you know?" She looked up, and her gaze was heartachingly vulnerable.

He nodded, his throat choked with emotion. "Yeah. I do know."

They sipped their coffee in silence for a little while.

"Emma's always had her life under control. She's always been so reliable, and now she has Nash, who's such a great partner." Lizzy took a deep breath and shot him an impish grin. "Maybe one of these new sisters I've inherited will be in need of a fashion-savvy flake of a sister."

"You're not a flake," he said quickly.

She shrugged. "I don't want to be. I want to be someone people can rely on." She leaned forward slightly and gave him a cute little smile as she nudged his arm. "Like you. You're a good dad, and your kids obviously know they can count on you."

His heart warmed at the praise. "I think having kids forced me to be that kind of person. I'm not sure who I would be or how I'd be acting if I didn't have them in my life."

She nodded. "They're lucky to have you."

He looked away, a little embarrassed by the attention. "Well, someone had to step up when Natalie left."

Lizzy frowned. "You mentioned earlier that she left, but…" She bit her lip. "Is it rude if I ask how and why?"

He gave a huff of amusement. "Lizzy, you got my son to eat carrots and charmed my daughter into thinking you're a real-life fairy godmother. You're officially allowed to ask anything you want."

She chuckled. "All right, then. What happened?"

She sipped her coffee while he gathered his thoughts.

"We met one summer," he started. "I was visiting some old family friends in Santa Rosa and I saw her on the beach. I asked her out within ten minutes of talking to her, and we spent the summer stuck together like glue. We were stupid. Thought we knew everything. Fell instantly in love. By the end of the summer, I proposed and convinced her to move to Aspire." With a sharp huff, he shook his head.

She gave him a sympathetic smile.

"My parents tried to persuade me to slow things down, but they liked Natalie and accepted the fact that we wanted to tie the knot. I thought I knew what it meant to be married." He scratched the tip of his nose as he winced.

"I thought I knew what it meant to be in love." He shot her a sidelong look. "Have I mentioned that I was young and stupid?"

She laughed, but it was a sad, husky sound.

He took a deep breath. "We didn't actually intend to have kids so soon. We'd only been married a year. It was a happy surprise...for me." He winced again.

Lizzy's eyes were filled with so much sympathy he had to look away. "Not for Natalie?"

He shook his head. "She'd already been trying to convince me to move away. She wanted to travel, see the world, explore. I kept saying we needed more time to save. She'd argue that we could just wing it." He tutted and scratched his whiskers. "She felt trapped here, and then she got pregnant. The sensible move was to stay put, be around family support, you know? We'd have to spend every spare dime on the kids. She wasn't happy about it from the start, but I thought...well, I think we all thought that once she held those babies in her arms, she'd have a change of heart."

"But she didn't," Lizzy said.

"I think she really tried, but... When I look back, she was restless from the day I put that ring on her finger. We were both just so keen to make it work. To prove any doubters wrong. We didn't stop to think about the fact that if it was difficult before the start, it wouldn't necessarily get easier." He cleared his throat as if that could get rid of this knot of shame he felt whenever he was forced to think about this time in his life. "I wanted what my parents had, but I couldn't make it happen. I did everything. I...I tried so hard." His voice wobbled for just a second, but he cleared his throat again and powered through the rest. "But I guess I didn't really see her...hear her. I didn't understand what she was trying to tell me, because I didn't want to admit defeat. So she left. I got home from work, and the twins were crying in their crib, and…there was a note."

Lizzy gasped. "Oh my gosh. That must have been so awful."

He nodded. "It was a shock."

She leaned forward again, this time resting a warm hand on his shoulder. "You're a good father."

He shook his head, his chest tightening. Did she have any idea how much he needed to hear those words? "I just do the best I can."

"You're doing great."

He turned to face her. "You did great today too."

She laughed, her hand dropping, and he felt the loss of its heat instantly.

"I surprised myself, actually," she said. "It was fun."

He winced. "Enough that maybe you feel like doing it again?"

He hated to even mention it, but with Marsha still out of town, he had no idea who else to ask.

She smiled, pausing to think about it before eventually nodding. "I can help you out until Marsha gets back."

"Thank you." He had this urge to reach out to her, to brush his knuckles over that dimple in her cheek, to wrap an arm around her shoulders and tug her close against his side.

He wanted to run his fingers through her hair, pull her close, and kiss those lush lips again.

But she stood from the couch before he could act on any of his desires.

"I should really get going," she said.

"Yeah, of course. Let me walk you out." He tried to

imagine her driving the big truck home on the dark country roads, and his chest tightened with worry. "You sure you'll be okay?"

She nodded. "I'm getting the hang of driving that thing. Just like riding a bike." He arched a brow in doubt, and she snickered. "I'll take it slow."

He nodded. "I wish I could drive you back myself, but—"

"The kids," she filled in quickly. "I know. I get it. You stay here and take care of those two. I've got this."

He walked her out to the truck, and they both paused by the driver's side door. They lingered there for so long that he wondered if she felt it too, this pull. This desire to stay together. Like there was still so much unsaid between them.

"Thank you for everything you did today. You saved my bacon." He skimmed his hand down her arm, unable to stop himself from touching her.

"That's okay." She smiled. "I'm glad I could help. Your kids are great, Kit. You should be really proud."

"I am."

They smiled at each other, and something sparked between them—an invisible magnetism that seemed to unnerve them both.

"Well, I should..." She nodded to the truck.

Was it his imagination, or was her voice slightly breathless?

She wet her lips and he nearly groaned, his gaze catching on her mouth, his mind filling with memories of what it had felt like to kiss her. What it would feel like to kiss her again.

"I'm not sure I want you to see this," she said softly.

He blinked, jarred out of his thoughts by that comment. "Excuse me?"

She winced and glanced behind her. "Um, it's a really big truck," she said. "And getting into it…" She wrinkled her nose. "It's not exactly pretty. So, if you don't mind…"

She nodded for him to return to the house, and he couldn't stop a low laugh as he reached for her.

"Or," he said as he settled his hands at her waist, "I could give you a hand."

"Oh." Yep. Her voice was definitely breathless before. Just like it was now. "Or…or that."

He paused. She froze. He wasn't sure how long they stood there like that, so close he could feel her breath in the cool air. His hands on her waist but not moving because…

Aw heck, because he didn't want to let her go.

But he couldn't draw her close, either.

He wanted to. He ached with that desire.

But common sense told him this was trouble.

Her eyelids fluttered, and her lips parted.

Was she remembering their kiss too?

He was certain he saw the moment she came to her senses, just as he'd done. With a crooked smile, she batted her lashes. "If you don't mind, I'd happily take you up on that lift."

He chuckled before tugging open the driver's side door and returning his hands to her waist. This time he lifted, setting her away from him, even though every muscle in his body was begging to pull her close.

And when he shut the door behind her and watched her buckle her seat belt, his mind was only capable of saying one word.

Stay.

21

Lizzy turned to face Emma as her sister brought her SUV to a stop by the curb. "Thanks again for the ride, sis."

Emma grinned. "I can't think of a better way to spend my lunch break."

Lizzy rolled her eyes, but she was still smiling. "Yeah, yeah. I know I've been something of a recluse since I got here, but you don't have to make such a big deal out of it."

Emma leaned forward to draw her into a crushing hug. "I'm just so proud of you, that's all. It takes guts to move forward after you've been hurt."

Lizzy patted her sister's back. Moving forward. Was that what she was doing? She still hadn't come up with any real plan for her future. All the pros and cons lists she'd been making hadn't helped as far as her career goals were concerned. Heck, she still didn't even know where she'd be living next.

But she supposed there was some truth to what her sister said. She was voluntarily leaving the ranch, after all. That was something.

She eased back, trying to pry herself out of her sister's arms. "Well, thanks again."

"You sure you're good from here?" Emma asked.

Lizzy nodded. "Nothing in Aspire is too far away. And I could use the exercise after a month of lying in bed."

Emma's eyes held a hint of motherly concern. "If you're sure…" She arched her brows. "Do you need a lift after you watch the twins?"

Lizzy smiled as she reached for the door handle. "Kit's already arranged for Cody to pick me up later."

Lizzy's heart gave a weird little flutter at the mention of Kit. She bit her lip to squelch a goofy smile as she slid out of the SUV and shut the door behind her. She really had to nip this burgeoning crush in the bud. Sure, he was hot. And yeah, dinner the night before had been the most fun she'd had in a long time. But that didn't change the fact that she had no idea what she wanted from her life.

She had no plan for her future, but it most likely did not involve sticking around in Aspire. If she'd learned anything from this breakup, it was that she needed to have her own plans, not base her life on someone else's.

Even as she reminded herself of all this, she was still smiling as she headed toward the fabric store entrance. Kit's mother had a sewing machine, but it was outdated, and she wanted to be sure she had all the right equipment to get started on Chloe's dress today.

The owner of the fabric store greeted her with a wide smile. "You're back!" She glanced around. "Now where are those adorable Swanson twins?"

Lizzy laughed. "Still at school. I had a hunch that I might be able to shop a little easier without them in tow."

The owner laughed. "What can I help you find?"

Lizzy rattled off her list and followed the shopkeeper

throughout the store, the kind older woman keeping up a steady stream of small talk all the while.

The day before, when she'd brought Chloe and Corbin, she'd been a little afraid she'd have a repeat of her first experience in Aspire, when she'd come into town with Emma and had been the object of a whole lot of stares and even more whispers.

But the older woman who owned this place had been nothing but gracious and welcoming. She'd asked after Emma, so obviously she'd recognized her name, but that was where the questions had ended.

Once she had all her supplies in hand, she paid for her items. She glanced at the time on her phone. She still had an hour before she walked over to fetch the twins, and she hadn't yet explored Main Street, so this would be the perfect opportunity to check it out.

"You know," the store owner said as she was piling Lizzy's purchases into a bag, "you really should go visit my daughter at her boutique around the corner."

Lizzy arched her brows in surprise, and the older woman's cheeks pinkened sweetly. "I'm not fond of gossip, but it's rather hard to avoid in small towns," she said. "I've heard you work in fashion."

There was a question in her voice, and Lizzy nodded. "That's right."

"Well, my daughter shares that passion, and I just know she'd adore meeting you." She leaned over as if letting Lizzy in on a secret. "It's not easy for her to find like-minded ladies in town, if you know what I mean."

Lizzy laughed. "I can imagine. And I was just wondering how I was going to kill time. I'd love to go check out her store."

"Wonderful! You just ask for Trina, and you tell her that her mama sent you."

A little while later, she followed the shopkeeper's instructions and found herself standing in front of the cute little boutique she'd spotted the other day.

A woman in a perfectly tailored black dress and a chic black bob stood behind the counter.

The door creaked a little when Emma opened it, and the woman looked up, her eyes sparkling with curiosity.

"Hi," Lizzy said, walking toward her while eyeing the racks of clothing on either side of the store. They were grouped by color, and Lizzy instantly loved the layout. The owner had used the space intelligently. It was both aesthetically pleasing and practical. Yep, this was her kind of store. Stopping at the counter with an impressed smile, she asked, "Are you Trina?"

The woman's face lit with a grin as she stuck out her hand to shake. "I am. Trina Belle Clemmons, at your service."

Lizzy opened her mouth to respond, but as she slipped her hand in Trina's, the other woman continued, her speech fast and clipped.

"And you must be Lizzy, Emma's sister, am I right? Of course I'm right." She grinned. "You're the spitting image. Now tell me." She leaned forward over the counter, resting on her elbows. "Is it true that you work at Nordstrom?"

Lizzy hesitated for a moment, waiting to see if the other woman was going to continue. When she didn't, she answered for herself. "That's right." She winced slightly as she corrected herself. "Or…I did. Before I came here."

Lizzy shifted awkwardly, waiting for questions, dreading the moment she'd have to explain that she'd been fired after ending her engagement and—

"Well, their loss is my gain," Trina said with another bright smile.

Lizzy's brows arched. *It is?*

Before she could ask why that might be, Trina was sliding an iPad across the counter. "I'd love to hear your thoughts on the new winter lineup I'm putting together."

Lizzy blinked in surprise, but a jolt of excitement raced through her as she eyed the wholesale clothing site.

Trina seemed to misunderstand her hesitation for unwillingness. She winced. "I'm sorry. That was rude of me. You probably have other things to do and–"

"Oh no," Lizzy said quickly. "It'd be my pleasure."

"Wonderful." Trina clapped her hands together with unbridled excitement. "I'd just love to hear your thoughts."

Trina was in luck, Lizzy decided, because she definitely had thoughts. She had so many thoughts.

The hour flew by as she and Trina talked over each other, their hands flying around as they chatted excitedly about the latest trends and designers. Lizzy was outright breathless with excitement by the time she spotted the clock on the wall. She flinched. "Oh dear. I'd better get going soon. I don't want to be late picking up the twins."

"Is it that time already?" Trina's face fell with clear disappointment. "I sure do hope I get a chance to talk to you again soon." Her brows arched. "Any idea how long you're sticking around in Aspire?"

"Uh…" Lizzy started. There was no hint of prying for information or trying to gather fuel for the local gossip mill, but her mouth opened and shut pathetically as she struggled for a response.

Trina leaned forward and patted her hand. "Doesn't matter. I'd just love to grab coffee with you before you go."

Lizzy exhaled sharply with relief. "Oh yeah. That I can definitely do."

Trina brightened. "Great! How does tomorrow work for you?"

"Tomorrow's great."

They made their arrangements, and Lizzy was gathering up her purse and fabric store shopping bag when Trina came around the counter and surprised her with a tight hug. "We sure are blessed to have you here in Aspire. You and your sister. I know my daughter, Maddie, adores Miss Emma."

"Is she in her class?"

"Yes. She had the best first day. Couldn't stop talking about it last night." Trina laughed.

Lizzy grinned in understanding but didn't want to admit that she'd shared dinner with Kit and the twins last night.

"Are you going to the school now too? We could walk together," she said.

Trina raised her hands and shook her head. "Oh no. My father has insisted on doing school pickup duty. He wouldn't even let me collect her after her first day yesterday." She laughed. "Those two have some special kind of bond, and I wouldn't dare get in the way of that."

"Aw. That's really sweet." Lizzy grinned, and Trina bobbed her head in agreement before giving her a heartfelt smile.

"You know, your sister has been such a blessing to this town, and she sure does love having you here. She told me just last week."

Lizzy's eyes widened in surprise. "She did?"

"Yes. I'm heading up the PTA, and I always try to connect with each teacher before the school year starts. I popped in to introduce myself, ask her what things she might need funding for, and we got chatting. She sure is a sweetheart."

Lizzy smiled. "Yes she is."

Trina's eyes glimmered. "I know you might not be here long, but while you are, I sure could use a sister who rocks the fashion world." She leaned in as if letting Lizzy in on a secret. "I've been trying to liberate these Aspire folks from plaid since I moved here ten years ago."

Trina winked at her, and Lizzy knew she was talking to a kindred spirit.

Lizzy feigned seriousness. "I'd be honored to help you with this critical mission."

Tina laughed and was still laughing as Lizzy headed out the door, a new bounce in her step.

A little while later, she'd picked up the twins and walked them home. It was a bit of a trek, but watching them run ahead of her, chatting and laughing and spontaneously stopping to twirl or throw rocks, Lizzy was convinced that letting them work off some of their energy was for the best.

"What did they feed you for snack time?" she teased. "Pixy Stix?"

Chloe turned to her with wide eyes. "Oooh, what are Pixy Stix?"

Lizzy opened her mouth to describe the sugar-filled straws she'd loved in her youth but thought better of it. The less they knew about sugary temptations, the better.

"Never mind." She held up the bag of sewing supplies with a grin. "Who wants to help me make a dress today?"

Chloe jumped up and down. "Ooh, me! Me!"

Corbin wrinkled his nose. "Not me."

She laughed as she tousled his hair. "That's fine. You

can watch some more *Paw Patrol* while your sister and I work. How does that sound?"

He lit up. "Great!"

Once they reached the house, Corbin and Chloe ate a snack, and then Corbin situated himself in front of the TV.

Chloe followed Lizzy into the small room where Kit's mom kept her crafting supplies and helped clear the way so Lizzy could pull out the old machine. She eyed it critically.

"Not the best," she mumbled. "But it'll do the trick."

They set up shop in the living room to keep Corbin company, although he was far more interested in the television than in their dressmaking plans.

Once everything was ready, Lizzy turned to Chloe with a pen and notebook. "All right, missy, what exactly do you envision for this dress?"

Chloe blinked, and then her eyes widened to the size of saucers. "You mean…I get to choose?"

Lizzy fought a smile. "You already picked out the fabric, didn't you? Now comes the really fun part." She leaned in close. "Designing the dress."

Chloe's lips parted, and her gaze filled with awe. "I've never designed my own dress before."

Lizzy nodded, trying her best to remain serious in the face of Chloe's adorableness. "Most people haven't. Which is a shame, really. Nothing tells the world who you are—who you want to be—more than the clothes you choose to wear. It's an outward expression of your personality, right?"

Chloe nodded eagerly. "Right."

Lizzy choked on a laugh. "Okay, then. What is your dress going to say?"

Chloe took a deep breath, her eyes sparkling with excitement. "Fairy princess," she breathed.

Lizzy nodded, her face aching with the urge to smile and laugh. Instead, she kept a straight face and her tone solemn. "Excellent choice."

22

Kit had to force himself not to speed all the way home that day.

This time it wasn't worry that made him impatient to get there—just the overwhelming desire to see his family.

And Lizzy.

Okay, yeah. He was definitely antsy to see Lizzy again. Even so, he had to make a quick stop for groceries before he headed home or else he'd have a couple hungry, cranky kids on his hands come dinnertime.

He raced into the store, waving to Edna behind the counter, and gathering up a cartload of necessities before heading to the line.

"Why, Kit Swanson, is that really you?" Bonnie teased. The brunette he'd shared more than a few drinks with over the years was beaming at him as she joined the line.

"Hey, Bonnie," he said. "Good to see you."

"I'll say." She tilted her head to the side and shifted so one hip was jutting out as she eyed him. "I haven't seen you around in ages."

He grinned, the same Cheshire cat grin he always wore

around ladies like Bonnie—the young, single, eligible ladies who understood that flirting was just flirting when it came to Kit Swanson.

"I've had my hands full," he said.

She tsked. "I heard your parents are away. Is there anything I can do to help?"

He hesitated for a moment, taken aback by the offer as much as by the shift in her gaze. Not quite so laughing and flirtatious as usual. Almost…serious.

He cleared his throat. "That's awfully nice of you, Bonnie."

She smiled. "Not at all. What are neighbors for, right?"

His own smile was starting to feel forced. "Right."

An awkward silence fell. She seemed to be waiting for him to speak—maybe to take her up on her offer. But he couldn't do it. And not just because with Lizzy in the picture he had his ducks in a row for a while. It was more than that. He had a hunch asking Bonnie for help with his kids would open a door he wasn't sure he wanted to open.

Not with Bonnie, at least. He'd never invited any of his female friends home to meet the kids. He'd kept his flirtations light and easy. No strings.

He wouldn't want his kids to get attached to someone unless he felt it had potential to be a serious relationship.

Bonnie arched her brows, leaning in toward him to run her long fingernails down his bicep. "Kit?"

"I'm doing all right," he said quickly. "But thanks for the offer."

She gave him a little pout, and he tried to ignore the unsettled sensation in his gut.

How come it was okay to ask Lizzy to watch his kids but not Bonnie?

He swallowed hard as the person before him moved up in line and he followed her.

It was because he knew she was leaving, that was why. He gave a short nod as he shifted the basket from one hand to another.

There was no risk of misunderstandings or having his kids get the wrong idea so long as Lizzy was planning to leave.

He eyed the tomato in his basket like it held the mysteries of the universe.

That was the only reason he'd asked Lizzy to step in rather than reaching out to another friend.

Right?

"Everything okay, hon?" Bonnie asked. She was eyeing him closely, and he forced another grin.

"Yeah, I'm fine. Just a long day at work."

"Long hours, huh?" She gave him a flirty smile. "Is that why you haven't been coming out at night to see me?"

His smile nearly faltered. *Yeah. That and the fact that I have two kids at home who need me, a demanding full-time job, and a house to buy.* "Got a lot on my plate is all."

He cast a glance toward the register, mentally willing Edna to hurry it up so he could get out of here to see his kids.

And Lizzy.

Man, he really couldn't wait to see Lizzy. Would she stay for dinner again? Would it be asking for too much if he invited her? She'd already spent hours taking care of his kids, but maybe if he—

"Wanna talk about it?" Bonnie asked.

Oh heck. For a second he'd forgotten she was there. "Uh…"

For a moment, he imagined explaining to Bonnie that

he had a crush on an out-of-towner who was currently taking care of his kids. "I don't think so."

She pouted again, and he felt like he was hurting her feelings by not confiding in her, so he shifted the basket and blurted, "I need to find a house."

She blinked in surprise, and then her whole face brightened. "Well, hon, why didn't you say so before?" She set her basket down and started rifling through her giant purse. "I can help with that."

He stared at her blankly until she handed over her card. "Real estate agent," he read aloud.

She beamed. "Don't tell me you forgot I got my license last year?"

"Oh, uh…" He had. Holding up the card, he widened his smile. "Good for you, Bonnie. Maybe you could give me a hand, then."

"Sure thing, sweetheart."

His smile felt too tight. "Sweetheart" was just one of her many terms of endearment. She was flirty like that, and it didn't mean anything.

His mind went blank as she launched into a monologue about the different types of homes on the market and all the mortgage options.

"…so what do you think?" she asked. "Do you know what you're looking for?"

No. The answer was no, plain and simple. "Just, uh… just something that will work for me and the kids."

She leaned in close, offering him a view of her cleavage along with a whiff of her cloying perfume. "And maybe your future wife?"

"Uh…" He leaned back so quickly he nearly bumped into the woman ahead of him in line.

Bonnie laughed. "Why don't you take a look at the listings? There are a few open houses this weekend that you could check out and get a better idea of what it is you're after."

She somehow made that sound flirty and followed it up with a wink.

Yup, she was definitely coming on to him.

He cleared his throat, relieved that the person ahead in line was now paying. "I'll surely do that," he promised, holding up her card. "I'll be in touch once I've figured it out."

"I look forward to hearing from you." She wiggled her eyebrows with a mischievous grin.

He chuckled as he turned to ring up his food. He'd never minded Bonnie's flirting before—heck, he'd usually given as good as he got. So why was he suddenly acting all weirded out by it?

A vision of Lizzy popped into his head, and all thoughts of Bonnie fled as he hurried through the checkout process to get back to her.

Only because he felt bad about leaving her alone with the twins any longer than necessary. Obviously.

He winced as he reached his truck because even he didn't believe that. He wanted to see her, plain and simple.

When he walked in, he was struck with the same overwhelming rush of emotions he'd felt the night before. The sight of his kids so happy, and Lizzy laughing at whatever Chloe had just said as they bent over some fabric together…

He had to stop and take a deep breath before calling out, "Fee fi fo fum—"

He'd barely gotten out 'fum' before he was being tackled at the knees. Laughing, he let them take him down to the ground, Lizzy standing over all three of them with an indulgent smile.

"Welcome home," she said.

"Thank you." He tickled Chloe while pulling a laughing Corbin in for a hug. "Thanks for watching these little monkeys."

"Hey, I'm not a monkey," Chloe called out.

"Of course you're not," Lizzy said easily. "You're a fairy princess."

"Fairy princess, huh?" he asked as he struggled to his feet, dragging the twins up with him as they laughed and tried to escape.

"That's my mood," Chloe informed him.

He shared a look with Lizzy, who was pressing her lips together hard in an admirable attempt to hold back a laugh.

Just like the night before, it was all so easy. So happy. This house was filled with warmth and a magic he and the twins had never known.

It was Lizzy. Obviously. Nothing else in their lives had changed.

Joy bubbled up inside him so fast and fierce, it took him by surprise.

"You want to stay for dinner?" The words just popped right out of his mouth even though he'd convinced himself on the drive home that he shouldn't even offer. He didn't want her to think he expected her to stick around until bedtime every night.

Still, he felt a flicker of disappointment when she winced with regret. "I better not. Emma's cooking my favorite meal, so..."

"Oh, sure. Right. Of course." He took off his cowboy hat and raked a hand through his hair. "Well, then, I guess, uh…" Oh heck, he was stalling. "I guess I'll let Cody know you're ready to head back?"

Stay.

There was that word again.

Stay.

Not just a word, a freakin' plea. He couldn't remember the last time he wanted anything so much. But it was selfish of him to ask for more than she was already giving. He was itching to spend more time with her. More time with him and his family and more time one-on-one.

Not that it could go anywhere, obviously. But would it be so wrong to enjoy one another's company while she was here? After all, she was already in their lives. And as long as his kids knew she was leaving, they couldn't be hurt when she was gone.

He scratched the back of his neck as he watched her laughing along with his kids.

It's a waste of time, he told himself. He'd always said he wouldn't get close to a woman unless there was a real chance for a future. He ought to be putting his focus on finding a new house.

An idea took hold as he watched her and Chloe carefully put away the fabric and sewing equipment, and then she told Corbin to shut off the TV and pick up his toys.

She clearly had good taste and an eye for design, and he was so out of his element when it came to home shopping.

She met his gaze with a smile, and he started to talk before he could stop himself. "Hey, Liz."

Her nose wrinkled, and she focused back on Chloe's dress.

"I mean Lizzy."

She grinned and looked back up at him.

He drew in a deep breath. "Can I ask you a really big favor?"

"Another one?" Her eyebrow arched, but there was a playful glint in her eyes.

He chuckled, picking up the groceries he'd dropped by the door and setting them on the table. "Hey, kids, can you both go wash up? I need some help with dinner, and those fingers need to be nice and clean."

They ran off, and he slipped his hands into his pockets. "Thing is, I know you have really good taste, and, uh…I was wondering if you could help me find a home."

She blinked in surprise. "A home?"

"I know it's not clothes shopping," he teased, hoping to lighten the atmosphere which suddenly seemed too serious, "but I could really use another set of eyes while I search for a place for myself and the kids. I'd like that to be wrapped up by the time my parents get back, so the clock is ticking."

He forced himself to clamp his mouth shut.

Lizzy stared at him for a moment, then gave him an understanding nod. "They told you it's time to move out, huh?"

"Something like that." He frowned, then ran a hand through his hair. "They're right. I've just been…" He shook his head, wishing like heck he didn't have to explain himself, but she probably thought it was weird that he was still living here, right?

Her smile grew, revealing two beautiful dimples. "Sounds like fun. I'd be happy to help."

His eyes widened. "Really?"

"Of course." She glanced past him toward the hallway, then leaned in close. "Have you told the kids that they'll be moving?"

"No, I'm still figuring out how to sell the idea to them. Chloe in particular will be heartbroken to leave Grammy's house."

Her eyes were filled with so much understanding, it almost hurt to hold her gaze.

"Well, just tell them it's a big adventure and that Aspire is pretty darn small, so Grammy will never be far away," she said.

He grinned at her. "You free this weekend?"

She laughed. "Of course I am."

23

That Friday afternoon, Lizzy had a day off from watching the kids since Kit was going to duck out of work early. But she still left the ranch, this time to meet Trina for coffee.

The coffee shop was cute, with modern art on the walls, a friendly barista, and surprisingly current music playing over the speakers. A group of old men sat at an outside table, sipping from white mugs and nattering away like a bunch of old ladies after church.

Lizzy had smiled at them when she walked through the door and was met with curious stares. She couldn't tell if she was being judged or figured out. Thankfully, Trina's sunny disposition had shaken the thought from her mind, and she was soon thoroughly engrossed in her favorite kind of talk—fashion.

Trina looked up from the notebook where she'd been jotting down notes based on their conversation. "I should hire you on the spot, Lizzy O'Sullivan. You are a gold mine of knowledge."

Lizzy blushed but had to laugh. As if she could stay in

Aspire long term. She was a city girl. Everybody knew that. But even so, the praise was welcome after so many bruises to her ego these past weeks.

"Glad I could help," she said. "And I can't wait to hear more about this fashion show you're planning for the fall festival."

Trina grinned. "It'll be Aspire's first fashion show, but I think they'll get into it. Hopefully we can get some of those hot ranchers to strut their stuff too." She wiggled her eyebrows

Lizzy giggled, her insides flushing as she pictured Kit walking along a catwalk.

I wonder what he'd look like in a suit, she mused. He'd be pretty darn hot in those dark navy Hugo Boss jeans they'd just been admiring in the catalogue.

Lizzy glanced at the iPad screen, hoping the heat flooding her body wasn't showing on her face.

"Jesse Jamieson would make a fine model." Trina made a sound of appreciation. "You know, I actually bid on him at the bachelor auction for the town festival, much to my husband's shock." Trina giggled. "I couldn't help it! He just looked so rugged, mountain man delicious. I couldn't stop my hand from shooting in the air."

Lizzy's eyes bulged, and she nearly choked on her sip of coffee. "JJ? Seriously?"

"Oh, yes please." Trina batted her eyelashes, and they laughed together. "My husband was very relieved when your sister won."

"What!" Lizzy gaped.

"She didn't tell you? I don't think she meant to win. She was just trying to raise the bids and got a little carried away. It was for charity."

Lizzy was still trying to absorb the news, surprised in

more ways than one. Emma usually told her things like that. Although, Lizzy hadn't really been herself lately. It was probably the last thing on Emma's mind and so trivial compared to the nightmare Lizzy had been facing.

"I doubt she'll go through with it. She's so loved-up on Nash, there's basically no other man on the planet. I wonder which lucky lady she'll give the date to."

Lizzy raised her eyebrows and shook her head, determined to tease her sister about this news the first chance she got.

"But I'll definitely ask JJ if he's willing to get involved." Trina started scribbling down names. Cody and Kit ended up on the list, but Lizzy didn't have a chance to comment before Trina started talking again. "Oh, and Ethan. He's with the fire department. Have you met him?"

"I don't think so."

"He's like Dwayne Johnson and Will Smith merged together. Believe me, he is *quite* the specimen."

Lizzy laughed. "Oh man, I wish I could be here to see it."

Trina stopped writing, her head snapping up to look at her. She opened her mouth like she was going to say something but obviously changed her mind. "I wish you could see it too."

Lizzy shifted in her seat. She suspected her new friend wanted to say more—ask questions at the very least—but she appreciated the woman's tact.

If she asked 'Why can't you stick around?' or 'What are your plans?' Lizzy would have come up woefully blank.

Really, at this point, all she knew was she couldn't stay here. She'd stick it out until Kit didn't need her anymore—she obviously wouldn't leave him stranded—but after that, there was nothing keeping her here.

There was nothing drawing her anywhere else either, but that was a topic for another time. She and Trina had been having such a fun conversation. She really didn't want to ruin it with tears now.

"I should get going," Lizzy said. JJ had driven her into town today because he'd had to run some errands for the ranch, but she didn't want to make him wait.

"Let's do it again sometime?" Trina said, her gaze sweetly hopeful.

"Definitely," Lizzy said.

She headed back to the ranch. JJ wasn't much of a talker, and right now Lizzy appreciated that more than ever. She didn't even have it in her to raise the whole bachelor auction thing. She'd gone from a giggling high in that café to a melancholy slump. What was wrong with her?

The sun was starting to set, and the view was spectacular as orange light spilled over the meadows, giving every barn and ranch house a romantic glow.

She found her mind wandering to Kit and the kids. She supposed they were getting on just fine without her. Which was good. It really was.

But she couldn't quite dismiss a pang of…something. Something bittersweet. A yearning. Almost like homesickness. But that was ridiculous because she knew very well that Kit's home was not her home, and his kids weren't hers either.

She turned her gaze out the window as JJ drove in silence beside her. She should really start to make plans to leave soon, because clearly the longer she stayed the more confused she'd become.

The sooner she got back to her real life and found herself a job and a new apartment the better.

Emma was busy in the kitchen when she and JJ arrived.

"You staying for dinner, JJ?" Emma asked.

"No, ma'am," he said as he tipped his hat with a slow smile. "But thank you kindly."

"Thank you for the ride, JJ," Lizzy called.

She got a tip of his hat in return as he strode out the door.

"He sure is a man of few words, isn't he?" Lizzy bulged her eyes as he left.

"That's putting it mildly." Emma wiped her hands on her apron. "The more I get to know him, though, the more he talks. But he's still not an open book." She arched her brows as she shot Lizzy a look. "Even Nash doesn't seem to know his story."

"That would drive me nuts if he were my friend," Lizzy said.

Emma laughed. "Right? That's what I said."

Seeing her sister eased the blues from the drive back, and Lizzy toyed with an impish grin as she leaned against the kitchen counter. "Maybe you could unravel some more when you go on your date together."

"What?" Emma's head shot up, her blue eyes blinking in surprise. "What date?"

"The bachelor auction?"

"Oh, that." Emma laughed, her shoulders instantly relaxing. "I really need to find someone to pass that along to. Can you think of anyone good?"

Lizzy grabbed an apple out of the fruit bowl and went to wash it. "I barely know anyone in this town."

"True, but it won't stay that way forever. How was your time with Trina?"

Lizzy chatted about the fall catalogue and the fashion show ideas while she munched on her apple and Emma kneaded the dough for dinner.

"Sounds like you had a lovely time."

"I did." Lizzy murmured to herself, like the idea of a good time in Aspire was truly mystifying. Maybe it was.

Maybe—

Emma's phone started ringing.

"Could you grab that?" she asked, her hands covered in flour.

"Sure." Lizzy threw the apple core away, then snatched the phone, frowning when she glanced at the screen. "I don't know the number. What if it's a telemarketer?"

Emma laughed at the horror in her voice. "Can you just answer it, please?"

Lizzy's eyebrows puckered, but she did what her sister asked. "Hello. Emma's phone, Lizzy speaking."

"Uh…hi. Um, this is… This is Rose." The woman's voice was soft and so unsure of itself.

Rose.

"Hi." Lizzy frowned. She recognized the name but struggled to place where she'd heard it before.

"Rose O'Sullivan."

Lizzy's eyes popped wide. "Oh, *Rose*."

Emma stopped what she was doing to turn and stare.

"Oh, of course! Rose!" Lizzy babbled. "You're one of the flower sisters."

Emma winced, but there was a very soft snicker, and Rose replied, "Yes, I suppose. My mother loved…she, uh, loves flowers."

Lizzy's belly tightened, and unexpected nerves took hold. *This is my sister.* Her palm was clammy as she clutched the phone tighter. "Well, I think Rose is a very pretty name. Just between you and me, it's my favorite flower of the three."

Rose let out a nervous titter, and Emma arched a brow,

wiping her hands off as she watched Lizzy with new intensity.

When the silence drew too long, Lizzy asked, "So, what can we help you with?"

Rose made a noise that was somewhere between clearing her throat and a squeak. "Oh, I was just wondering if there was any update on the sale."

She sounded so nervous, which only made Lizzy's nerves hitch up in response. Some part of her brain was trying to reconcile with the fact that the woman on the other end of the phone was a newfound sister.

She'd known she'd had half sisters for weeks now, but knowing about their existence and talking to one of them on the phone were two different things.

She gave Emma a panicky look as she focused on the question. *The sale. Right.* "Uh, not really. I mean, well, Emma still hasn't been able to track down Sierra, and April's a total no-show as well." Emma's stare was starting to freak her out, so Lizzy turned to face the window overlooking the front of the ranch. "Emma's started working too, so she's pretty busy."

"Oh." Rose went quiet. "Are you taking over for her, then?"

"Uh…" Lizzy whipped around to gaze at her sister, and they shared a look. Emma's brows arched in question. It was clearly killing her that she couldn't hear the full conversation.

Lizzy swallowed hard. She'd been dutifully calling April regularly and making half-hearted attempts to track down Sierra, but she hadn't done much to help Emma. In her mind it was still Emma's project.

She bit her lip as a surge of guilt flooded her. "Yeah, I

guess…I guess I am taking over handling the directions Frank O'Sullivan left behind."

Emma's arched brows arched even further in surprise at that.

Lizzy shrugged, a silent 'I'll explain later.'

"So, what's your decision?" Rose asked, her voice so soft that Lizzy pressed the phone against her ear to hear her better. "Are you going to sign?"

Lizzy opened her mouth to answer but then paused. "Actually, Emma and I think it's really important that every sister come see the ranch before they decide to sell. It just feels like the right thing to do."

Emma smiled at her, and the gratitude there only made Lizzy feel more guilty. Her sister had been dealing with this all on her own, and she was the only one who seemed to care about Frank O'Sullivan's wishes or this ranch.

That just didn't seem right.

There was a long silence before Rose said, "I don't think Dahlia will like that very much."

Lizzy gave a little huff of amusement. Emma had told her all about this Dahlia chick, and Lizzy wasn't here for anyone who was rude to sweet, angelic Emma. "Well, she'll just have to get over herself, because I'm not signing anything until my sister's wishes have been met. It's only fair."

Emma gave her a surprised and grateful smile now, and Lizzy winked in return before focusing back on the call. "So, Rose, when do you think you can come see the place?"

"Um…I'm not sure. I'll… I'll try to…plan…something. I'm not… I don't know."

Lizzy rolled her eyes at how uncertain the woman sounded. Emma giggled as she leaned against the counter.

She'd already talked to Rose once, so she must have known exactly what Lizzy was thinking. But she wondered if her kindhearted sister had the nerve to put this timid creature on the spot.

Probably not.

She took a deep breath. "Well, Rose, you let us know the dates, and we'll make sure we've got a room made up for you."

"You'd make up a room for me?" Rose's sweet voice was so surprised that Lizzy nearly laughed.

What did she expect them to do, make her sleep on the porch?

She curbed her tone and managed to politely say, "Of course. This house is big enough for everyone, and we'd love to have you stay."

"That's…really sweet."

Rose's soft reply made something in Lizzy's chest expand. This poor, timid sister was so surprised by the simple gesture of hospitality. What kind of life was she living to have a response like that?

"It's only right. It's…well, it's your home too." Lizzy didn't know what compelled her to say that, but she had an overwhelming urge to welcome this woman in.

Rose cleared her throat, her voice soft and trembling when she finally responded. "Yeah, I guess it is."

"So, you'll come stay?"

"Um…I'm not sure when, but maybe you're right. You know…about me…us…his daughters all seeing the place."

Lizzy smiled, happy with her agreement. She didn't want to battle any of them, but she would for the sake of Emma.

These newfound sisters might each have a unique personality, but they were all Frank O'Sullivan's daughters, and it was only right that they at least see what he'd left behind for them.

"I'll… I'll let you know." Rose's voice hitched like she was about to start crying.

Lizzy's chest ached a little more intensely. "Rose?" She frowned at Emma, whose eyes were soft with concern. "Rose, are you, uh…are you okay?"

"I'm fine," she squeaked, then quickly hung up without a goodbye.

Lizzy frowned at Emma's phone. "Weird."

"Yeah, she's quite…nervous, right?"

"That's one way of putting it," Lizzy scoffed. "She could barely get out a full sentence, and she was *so* surprised by my offer to let her stay. It was…" She shook her head, unsure how to even describe it, or what was up with this maternal throbbing in her rib cage.

Emma winced. "Poor thing. With a sister like Dahlia, I can only imagine the kind of life she's had."

Lizzy growled. She didn't know Rose at all, but her protective instincts rushed to the surface on her behalf. It was exactly how she felt whenever she suspected someone was taking advantage of Emma's kindness.

"I need to speak to this Dahlia chick," she muttered.

Emma patted her shoulder. "Do me a favor and put your armor on first. She's got a sharp tongue, and I don't think she's all bark and no bite."

Lizzy snickered but quickly turned serious. "Hey, Em. I'm sorry I didn't offer to take this on entirely when you started work. You shouldn't have to be stressing about this on top of a new job."

Emma smiled. "You've been going through a lot. It's okay."

"Well, I'm officially taking it on entirely now. Don't you

worry. We'll get all seven sisters here at some point." Leaning against the table, she crossed her arms and watched her sister carefully. "When they get here, how do you want me to sell this thing?"

"What do you mean?" Emma asked.

Lizzy took a deep breath. It was a conversation they'd both been avoiding, but she was done skirting the issue. "You want to keep this place, don't you?"

Emma gave her a hesitant smile, but then Nash walked in the door, and her entire face lit up like the sun.

"Hey, beautiful," he murmured as Emma headed toward him, drawn into his embrace like they were a couple of magnets who couldn't resist each other's pull.

Lizzy's smile faded to one more rueful as she turned away from the tender moment.

Oh yeah, Emma wanted to keep it all right. She didn't need to say it; it was written all over her face. She loved this home, the land, and everything else about this town.

Rose's question was still ringing in her ears.

Emma wanted this place, but what did she want?

"Maybe it's not always about what you want."

She let out a huff of amusement as she studiously ignored the happy couple and went to take over where Emma had left off. Funny how Kit's voice had gotten stuck in her head. He'd become her very own Jiminy Cricket.

The thought had her snickering under her breath as she kneaded the dough. She could only imagine what Kit's response would be if she told him that.

She started to laugh in earnest at the thought but sobered quickly when she realized what her conscience was trying to say.

Emma had always been there for her. Always. She'd

always been the one to comfort her, and look after her, and listen to her troubles.

For once, someone should put Emma first.

No, for once, *she* should put Emma first.

If she didn't get that windfall from the sale, she'd still survive. She'd have to go back to work no matter what, and finding another roommate wasn't the worst fate she could imagine. Heck, it would be preferable to living alone anyway.

With each toss of the dough, she felt more and more confident in her decision. She'd find her way no matter what, but Emma had already figured out what she loved. She'd made her choice.

And Lizzy would do everything in her power to make sure she got it.

24

Kit pointed to the pile of Legos that was still lying on the floor. "I thought I told you to pick those up," he told Corbin.

His son moved as slow as molasses to pack his toys away while Kit spun around to face Chloe. "Lovebug, you still have syrup all over your face. Go wash up. Lizzy will be here any minute."

As his kids launched into action, Kit tried to calm his nerves.

Nerves. What was even happening to him? He turned to eye his reflection in the hallway mirror. He made a face. Same shaggy hair, short scruffy beard, and stained T-shirt. Nothing Lizzy hadn't seen before, and it wasn't like this was a date or anything. She was helping him out, that was all. As a friend. Nothing more.

He drew in a deep breath as if that could squelch the topsy-turvy sensation in his gut. The thought of seeing Lizzy again was way too powerful.

This was just two friends hanging out. Just like they'd been two friends on Tuesday night when she'd made dinner with him, or Wednesday when she'd agreed to help him look at houses, or Thursday when she'd stuck around for family movie night and shared a pizza with them.

He groaned as his head fell back and he eyed the popcorn ceiling of his parents' den.

Just friends. Even though he couldn't stop thinking about kissing her again. And even though he felt more like himself around her than with anyone else he'd ever met.

Sure, he'd first thought of her as a judgy, snobby, entitled princess, but he'd been figuring out pretty quick that when he was real with her, she didn't judge him at all. In fact, she seemed to actually understand him.

Which wasn't nothing.

And yet it definitely couldn't be something since, as far as he knew, she was still set on leaving Aspire.

He might not have forgotten that brief, earth-shattering kiss a few weeks back, but he also hadn't forgotten the words she'd been spewing that had prompted him to cut her off with a kiss in the first place.

"I don't belong here."

That's what she'd said. And it was exactly what Natalie had said too. He'd learned his lesson by now that if a woman said she didn't want him—that he, or this town, or his children weren't where she belonged—then he should absolutely take her at her word.

"Ready, Daddy!" Chloe skipped out of the hallway with a clean face and a brilliant smile that was impossible not to return.

"Much better, pumpkin. Now go help Corbin so we can get out of here as soon as Lizzy arrives."

"I can't wait to show Lizzy my drawing from school," Corbin said.

"And she gets to see me wearing my new dress," Chloe added.

Kit grinned. "I know she's going to love them both."

And she would. Much as she'd said she didn't like kids, she was so dang good with them. He could feel his chest tightening, his thoughts struggling to reason and rationalize and give him hope.

He'd admitted to himself a while ago that he had a crush, and every second he spent with her, it only grew stronger.

But that didn't mean she felt the same. And even if she did, it didn't mean she'd have a change of heart about staying.

His traitorous, torturous brain called up the memory of her scowling as she realized that her decision not to have kids might not have been what she'd wanted.

Was it too much to hope that she might change her heart on Aspire too?

He thought of Natalie and all the time he'd wasted hoping her cutting little comments didn't really mean anything.

Yeah, it was probably total idiocy to hope a Gucci girl who loved city life would go falling for a cowboy and his twins.

And yet...

He couldn't quite make himself stop no matter how much his mind told him it was a lost cause.

He was still grappling with those thoughts when Nash's truck pulled into his driveway.

"She's here!" Corbin shouted.

"Uncle Nash is here too!" Chloe raced after her brother.

They were out the door in a flash, Kit following right behind. He nearly stumbled over his own boots when Lizzy slid down from the passenger seat, looking like sunshine on a rainy day in a cheerful little sundress and shoes not at all appropriate for…well, *anything.* The dang things looked like their function was to help you roll an ankle.

But gosh, did they make her legs look good.

It was her smile, though, that made his heart slam against his rib cage. It was brighter than her dress and sweeter than anything he'd ever seen. And the fact that her smile seemed to light up even more at the sight of his kids made his chest ache. And when she turned that brilliant smile on him, well…

Stick a fork in him, 'cause he was done. One smile and he was a goner.

All those reasons he'd been giving himself to steer clear of the Gucci girl flew out of his mind.

He swallowed hard as Nash came over to him and clapped a hand on his shoulder. "Can't believe you're actually looking to buy a house of your own, man," Nash said. "That's a pretty big step."

Kit shrugged, his eyes still on Lizzy. "Yeah, well…truth be told, I'm still not sure I feel ready, but it's time."

Nash nodded, his gaze darting back and forth between Kit and Lizzy. Thankfully, good, quiet, awesome friend he was, Nash didn't make any comments or ask any questions about why Kit had invited Lizzy along for the house-hunting trip.

Lizzy was laughing over something the twins had said when she came to join them in front of the porch steps.

"I guess that's the way it goes, huh?" Nash said. "You never really feel ready for the next big step. But you still take the leap anyway."

Kit nodded, and now it was his turn to eye his friend.

Nash had always shied away from talk of marriage and family, but right now Kit couldn't tell if that comment was meant for him or if Nash was talking to himself.

"That's why it's called a leap of faith, right?" Lizzy chimed in.

He and Nash both turned to look at her, and her cheeks pinkened in a way that was downright adorable.

"Sorry," she said. "Didn't mean to eavesdrop."

"What's an evil drop?" Corbin asked.

Nash chuckled as Lizzy mussed his hair. "You just wait until tickle torture time and I'll show you my evil-drop move," she teased.

Corbin's eyes widened with feigned fear as he and Chloe ran off screaming.

Kit laughed. "You got tickle moves I don't know about?"

She shrugged nonchalantly as she clasped her hands behind her and swayed sweetly from side to side. "A girl's got to keep her secrets, Kit." She then pointed at Nash. "Don't go asking Emma."

Nash arched a brow as he looked between them. They were flirting. Blatantly. Not even her ploy to draw him into the conversation could fool his best friend. Kit knew this was all very foolhardy—like serving his beating heart up on a platter and just waiting for it to be butchered—but he couldn't seem to stop. And Lizzy couldn't seem to help but flirt right back.

They were playing with fire. Some part of him was shouting 'Danger!' but he ignored it as he exchanged a goofy grin with Lizzy.

"All right, well," Nash said slowly. "If y'all are still thinking of coming to my parents' barbecue later today,

Kit, you can just bring Lizzy with you, and I'll take her home from there?"

He and Lizzy nodded.

"Sounds good to me," Lizzy said.

Kit arched a brow. "Another barbecue, huh?"

Nash laughed. "One last hurrah, my mama says. Before the weather turns."

Kit chuckled. "Just so long as your mama's making her famous peach cobbler, I wouldn't miss it for the world."

"See you there, then," Nash called as he headed to his truck. "And good luck with the house hunt."

As he drove off, Kit gathered the kids and got them into their car seats. He helped lift Lizzy into the passenger seat, trying and failing not to notice that clean, fresh scent that was so uniquely her.

When he was in his seat and the truck was in gear, she swiveled around to face the kids.

"Who's excited?" she asked, her voice filled with enthusiasm.

"Me! Me!" It was a loud chorus in the back.

"Our new house is going to be a big adventure," Corbin said proudly.

Lizzy shot Kit a knowing smile, and he winked. Yes, he'd totally sold it to them the way she'd suggested, and it had worked. They couldn't wait to find a new home.

"Then let's get this adventure started," she shouted, which brought on new cheers.

The first house he'd lined up a viewing for, with Bonnie's help, was in a newer development outside of town.

"This is nice," Lizzy said mildly as he helped her out.

Her tone was perfectly even, but he could tell by her lack

of enthusiasm that she wasn't smitten. Neither was he, for that matter. The house was new and an exact replica to the ones on either side, with little room in between for privacy.

Bonnie stepped out of her sedan a second later.

"Hey, y'all!" she called as she sashayed her way up the drive. She was in a pencil skirt that hugged her hips so tight, it strained the fabric at the front and pulled it up her thighs. Her bright red pumps clipped across the concrete—two red stop signs, which Kit was happy to abide by. He wasn't used to seeing her dressed up this way, and it kind of threw him.

Lizzy stiffened. "Who's this?"

"The realtor." He glanced down, surprised by Lizzy's tight expression. Where had that smile gone? "She set up the viewing."

"Oh." She nodded, but her posture didn't ease, and Kit watched her curiously from the corner of his eye.

"Hiya, hon." Bonnie grinned, reaching up to kiss his cheek. She even wrapped her arm around him and gave a little squeeze. It didn't exactly scream 'professional'—or even 'friend' for that matter,—but Kit tried to give her the benefit of the doubt. She was new at the whole realtor thing, right?

Maybe she was trying just a little *too* hard to make a good impression.

He eased her away gently but didn't miss Bonnie's gaze narrowing in on Lizzy. She tipped her head, her smile kind of freezing into place as she extended her hand. "And who's this?"

"Lizzy," she answered before Kit could, returning Bonnie's handshake.

"Oh right." Bonnie's gaze raked over Lizzy—a quick

assessment before plastering on a big smile. "The O'Sullivan girl."

"Grown woman, actually," Lizzy said, showing off her dimples. "And as of today, Kit's consultant." She shot him a wink that had him choking on a laugh.

"Oh. I see. I thought that was my job." Bonnie's laughter was high and plastic.

Lizzy let out a polite little sound of amusement. "Well, you're trying to sell him a house. I'm here to help him say yes to the right one."

"Oh, don't you worry. We'll find Kit the perfect home." She patted Kit's cheek before he saw it coming, and all he could do was stand there trying not to offend her while watching Lizzy's eyebrows dip together for a moment. "I am the expert, after all." Bonnie's voice was breezy. The white-knuckle grip on her sales binder was anything but.

Lizzy's lips twitched, but she kept a sweet smile in place and pointed to the house. "Please, lead the way."

Bonnie spun on her red heels and clipped past his children while Lizzy arched her right eyebrow at him.

His head jerked back as he tried to interpret the spark in her pretty green eyes.

It was almost like…

He had to swallow a laugh and squelch a smile as he followed Bonnie to the front door.

It was almost like *jealousy*.

He hated how much he loved that. But he couldn't let either lady get the wrong impression. It wasn't right. So, once Bonnie had conducted the initial tour, he turned to the bubbly realtor and quietly said, "Thanks for setting this up, Bonnie. Lizzy and I will just have one more look around together."

Bonnie's gaze dimmed with disappointment, but she

kept a smile on her face as she walked to the door and waited outside for them. They toured the place again, the kids running ahead, their shouts and giggles bouncing off the walls and echoing through the cavernous space.

When they reached the main living area again, Lizzy looked up at the high stud and murmured, "This isn't right for you."

For a second, he wondered if she was referring to the house or the woman waiting outside.

"There's something better out there. I can feel it." Lizzy winked at him and walked for the front door.

"Yes, ma'am."

She spun and shot him a withering glare.

He just grinned. "Sorry, darlin'."

As much as she tried, she couldn't stop a snicker, and they walked out of the house laughing. A sound that quickly died when Bonnie got back out of her car.

She crossed her arms and stared them down. Her tight smile fooled no one. "So, what'd you think?"

Kit winced and shook his head. "I'm not sold."

Her eyes darted to Lizzy like it was her fault, but it was a very fleeting glance, and Kit had to wonder if he just imagined it.

He cleared his throat to cut the weird vibe buzzing in the air, and Bonnie pulled her shoulders back, flipping open her file.

"It's not a problem. There are other places to check out. I'll give you a call in a couple days, and we'll line up something else." Her smile was back, bright and professional. "Y'all have a lovely day."

When Bonnie got back in her car, Lizzy's shoulders sagged with a quiet sigh.

Are you jealous?

The words were right there on the tip of his tongue, but he managed to hold them back. It did get him thinking though…

Was he the only one feeling this connection?

Was he the only one harboring a crush?

Or did she feel it too?

Does it matter whether she feels it or not if she's dead set on leaving?

That was probably the better question.

"Come on, let's go check out that private listing." Kit rested his hand on Lizzy's lower back and led the family to his truck like it was the most normal thing in the world.

He had to remind himself that it wasn't real, especially when they jumped out of the truck fifteen minutes later and Lizzy grabbed the children's hands so he could walk up and greet the owner with a handshake.

The second house was better, he thought, but he couldn't tell what Lizzy was thinking as they joined two other couples who were also interested. It felt homey, sort of, and he didn't mind the wallpaper and quite liked the large windows overlooking the backyard. The curtains in the kids' room would need changing, and the dark walls in the kitchen could use a fresh coat of paint.

Did he even like the kitchen? It was kind of small.

"What did you think?" Lizzy asked as soon as they reached the truck and could talk in private.

His brow furrowed. "Honestly?"

"No," she deadpanned. "I'd like for you to lie."

He huffed with amusement, and some of the tension that had been building in him during this last tour started to ease.

He nodded toward the passenger seat. "Need a hand?"

A hint of a blush stole into her cheeks, just the way it

had the last two times he helped her into the truck. Was he being too hopeful, or did she feel it too? Was there a spark whenever he laid his hands on her?

He sure felt it.

She gave a short nod, and he helped boost her into the seat as the kids chatted loudly in the back about the house's creepy basement.

To be fair, it *had* been creepy, complete with an antique doll collection and spiderwebs everywhere they'd turned.

"Well?" Lizzy said when he'd climbed in to join them. "What did you think of this one?"

He shrugged. "I really don't know."

Frustration gnawed at him. He was supposed to be leading this family onward and upward, but he'd never felt more out of his depth than he had this week. He cast a sidelong look in Lizzy's direction as he put the truck in gear.

He suspected some of that was due to the knockout blonde beside him. Every time he looked her way, he felt the ground shifting beneath his feet.

"You know what we need?" Lizzy stated.

"What's that?"

"Fuel." Her lips twitched, and a dimple flashed. "I don't know about you, but I'm starving."

"Me too!" Corbin chimed in.

Kit chuckled. "Fair enough. Let's get some lunch before the next stop." He arched a brow at Lizzy. "Mama's Kitchen all right?"

She shrugged. "Sure. I've never been, but I hear it's good."

Kit gaped. Even Chloe and Corbin fell silent as they stared at her.

"What?" She shifted in her seat, her tone defensive. "Why are you all staring at me like that?"

Kit dropped his voice and feigned seriousness as he met her gaze. "Mama's Kitchen is a national treasure, Lizzy. You don't know what you've been missing."

Her giggle was sweet and light. "Then by all means, let's go to Mama's Kitchen."

This was met with more cheers from the back seat, and Kit drove the short distance to the local favorite. Saturday afternoon was a busy time for Main Street—relatively speaking, at least. He suspected the crowds of pedestrians in front of Mama's Kitchen were nothing compared to downtown Chicago, but here it was a madhouse.

Not to mention, the moment the family and Lizzy all piled out of the truck, they were met with stares.

Lots of stares.

He recognized more than a few local busybodies who were gazing at Lizzy and whispering among themselves.

"Morning, Mrs. Donnelly," he said with a tip of his hat to one of the old biddies. "Mrs. Gardner."

"Why, Kit, those twins are getting big too fast," Mrs. Gardner said.

"Don't I know it," he agreed.

He put a hand on Lizzy's back and nearly pulled it away instantly as both women's gazes narrowed on the gesture.

"Correct me if I'm wrong," Lizzy said under her breath, her tone dripping with amusement, "but are we currently making front page news by showing up here together?"

Kit gave a short laugh as he herded the twins in front of them. "Yes, ma'am."

"Kit," she said warningly at his use of 'ma'am.'

He chuckled again, and he fought the urge to move his hand to her waist so he could tug her against his side. That would really give the old gossips something to talk about.

It would also be way too easy, and it was far too tempting.

"It's me, isn't it?" Lizzy murmured as they joined the line at the hostess station.

He turned to her in confusion, all while telling Corbin and Chloe to mind their manners as they fidgeted with impatience. "What are you talking about?"

Lizzy glanced back outside. "Everyone's talking about me, aren't they?" She wrinkled her nose. "I'm still that pathetic O'Sullivan sister who got left at the altar, and that's all anyone says about me."

He gave a short huff of amusement. He couldn't help it even though it had her pouting up at him.

Man, his arms were aching with the urge to draw her in close to comfort her. "Lizzy, it's not you they're whispering about. It's me."

Her brows drew together in clear disbelief.

He laughed. "All right, fine. It's us." He gestured to the twins. "All of us."

She hitched her lips to the side. "What do you mean?"

He smiled as he reached out to tuck a loose wave behind her ear. "Ever since Natalie left, this entire town has been waiting for me to find a…replacement."

Lizzy's brows arched. "A replacement? That's horrible. That makes it sound like any woman could just step in and replace your wife and the mother of your children."

He chuckled, loving her anger on his behalf. "I know, but there's a lot of old-school thinking around here. Not many people think a man like me could handle two kids on his own." He winced as he thought of the way his parents had been forced to step in. "And maybe they were right."

She shook her head. "Kit, I don't know anyone who could have taken on working full time and caring for two infants without a good deal of help. Man or woman."

His lips curved up again, and he wondered if she had any idea how much he'd needed to hear that. His heart was aching as he drew in a deep breath. "Maybe you're right. But that doesn't change the fact that any time I'm seen with a woman, tongues start wagging."

"Oh." Lizzy nibbled on her lower lip as she considered that. "I guess that makes sense."

He grinned. "That's why I'm normally good about not giving anyone the wrong impression. I wouldn't want to fuel the fire, if you know what I mean."

She nodded. "But you brought me here."

He watched closely as pink crept up her neck and into her cheeks. Her gaze darted away from his, and he…

Well, he swallowed down another wave of hope.

This crush was making him lose his senses. As much as he knew it was wrong, he was still hoping against hope that this woman was feeling it too. That this crush wasn't totally one-sided.

"Yeah, I brought you here," he agreed. And he left it at that because he had no good explanation for why he was breaking his own rules for her.

He wished he did.

She turned her head back to meet his gaze head-on. "I guess us being here together can't cause too much harm since everyone knows I'm leaving, right?"

That hope fell flat, right along with his insides. He struggled not to show it, forcing a Cheshire smile instead. "Right."

"Well," Lizzy said with a sigh, "what do you say we avoid giving them any more gossip and get this food to go?"

"Great idea." He grinned, and when they reached the front of the line, he placed a to-go order for enough burgers and fries to feed a small army.

By the time the foursome carried their food to a nearby park and settled in for a picnic, the disappointment from earlier had passed, along with any of the awkwardness.

Kit fetched a soccer ball out of the truck so the twins could play while Lizzy and him talked and picked at the last of the fries.

"So?" she said after they'd had a slow, leisurely conversation about their favorite games to play when they were kids. For Kit, it was roping with the older boys. For Lizzy, it was setting up fantastic Barbie fashion shows for Emma and their friends.

"So what?" he shot back.

She grinned and leaned back on her hands, her legs stretched before her like she was utterly relaxed, her head dropped back and her eyes closed.

He liked this side of her. A laid-back Lizzy just soaking up the sunshine. He could have watched her all day.

"You never did say what you thought about that last home. Did it have anything you wanted?"

He sighed, and that had her cracking her eyes open and turning her head to face him.

"That's the problem, Lizzy," he admitted. "I don't know what I want."

A line formed over the bridge of her nose as she gave that some thought. "I don't think that's true," she said slowly. "I think you just haven't been asking yourself the right questions."

He blinked. "And what questions would those be?"

Her lips quirked up in a small smile as her gaze met his. "What do you see when you picture the future?"

You.

For a second, the earth stopped spinning. The answer was on the tip of his tongue, and it threw him for a loop, knocking the ground out from under him. He cleared his throat and looked away.

Focus, he told himself.

He tried to picture the future, but that initial gut response was true. He kept picturing her. Lizzy in his arms. Lizzy laughing at the kitchen table. Lizzy playing with the twins.

He swallowed hard and Lizzy shifted, tucking her legs under her so she could face him. "Let's start with Thanksgiving."

"Thanksgiving?" he repeated, doubt in his tone.

She nodded. "Let's say you're in this new home by then, so you decide to host."

"Okay," he said slowly. "Can we just take a moment to feel sorry for my poor guests who have to suffer through my first Thanksgiving dinner?"

She burst out laughing. "Fine. Now, moving on. What do you see when you look around you?"

He stared at her. "What?"

She laughed again, this time a cute little giggle that made him want to tug her into his arms so he could kiss those pretty pink lips, then press his mouth against each dimple.

She surprised him by clapping a hand over his eyes.

"Now," she said again, "what do you see?"

He let out a sigh, but he couldn't stop smiling. Her touch made him ache all over, and his heart was beating so hard it felt like it was trying to escape his rib cage. He focused on her question.

What did he see?

Lizzy. Lizzy and the twins. His parents, of course. And beyond that…

"A fireplace," he said, surprising himself.

"Good." He could all but hear the smile in her voice. "What else?"

He smiled, getting into it now. "There's a big yard out back. Big enough for a trampoline and a chicken coop."

She laughed quietly. "I like it. What else?"

The game continued for a while. Long enough that by the time she dropped her hand, he saw it. Clear as day in his mind, he saw his dream home.

Also clear as day? Lizzy was in that home. Every single daydream had Lizzy in it right alongside his twins.

The thought left him dazed.

"There you have it," Lizzy said with a triumphant smile. "Now you know what you want."

He nodded. "So I need to give Bonnie that criteria, then."

"Yep." Lizzy's tone was suddenly clipped, and she angled her body to face out to the park.

His eyes narrowed as he watched her raised chin and ramrod posture. Hope flared like a bonfire. "You know there's nothing between Bonnie and me, right?"

Lizzy shrugged. "Why should I care? It's not my business."

He shifted for a better view of her. "I guess I just want you to know."

Her lips pressed together as her gaze narrowed, but she was still staring into the distance. Finally, she blurted, "Why?"

His lungs hitched at the flicker of vulnerability he heard in that one word, and perhaps against his better judgment, he told her the truth. "Because I like you."

She paused and then spun to face him, blinking her beautiful big eyes. Her lips parted in surprise, and the way she was looking at him...

Well, it wasn't a total confirmation that she felt the same, but she was temptation itself.

Unable to resist, he reached for her face and skimmed his knuckles down her cheek. She shivered, but she didn't pull away, so he leaned in and brushed his lips across hers.

They both pulled away then, and Kit was a little dazed. Had he really just done that? His gaze met hers, and he saw the same shock...but also the same desire. Her brilliant emerald eyes were dark and hooded, her lips still parted as her breathing grew ragged.

It might very well be a mistake, but he couldn't stop himself from diving in for a second kiss. This time he lingered, pressing his lips against hers like he could tell her everything he'd been dying to say in this one kiss.

After a moment she kissed him back, and soon their lips were clinging, gliding, tasting. Her breath was sweet and hot against his skin, and her taste was intoxicating. Her scent made his head spin. He was cupping her face in his hands still, and the feel of her skin was both a torture and a tease.

He wanted more. He ached to hold her closer, and yet—

"Ewww! What are you guys doing?" Corbin shouted right next to them.

They pulled away like kids busted by their parents, both their cheeks flaring with color.

Kit groaned. How had he totally forgotten his kids

were there? He'd always made sure to never kiss a lady in front of them, because he never wanted to get their hopes up or freak them out.

He saw both twins staring and his insides deflated.

He'd tried so hard, and now he'd just gone and blown it. When he dared a look at Chloe's face, she was absolutely beaming.

He could practically see her hope, nearly as bright as his own—and no doubt just as silly. There was no future here. He knew that. Lizzy knew that.

But Chloe?

All he could do was close his eyes and pray he hadn't just broken the poor girl's heart.

He shouldn't have kissed Lizzy. That was painfully obvious as she scooted away from him and made some excuse about how they were playing a game.

Gucci girls didn't stay in Aspire. He knew this better than anyone. City girls with big dreams and high class didn't fall for the likes of him.

They got bored and left on a whim.

25

Four weeks.

Four.

Lizzy didn't need any kind of landscape wall calendar to know just how much time had passed.

It'd been four weeks since Kit had told her he'd liked her. Four weeks since he'd flipped her world upside down with a kiss so heady it ought to have been illegal.

Lizzy sighed as she stirred the pot of white bean chili, the sounds of Chloe and Corbin laughing and playing outside providing the perfect soundtrack for her latest attempt at cooking.

She'd been getting better…she was pretty sure.

And this recipe Emma had given her was straightforward. She leaned over to give it a sniff and smiled with satisfaction.

It smelled good, at least.

If her cooking was improving, then at least one area of her life had been moving forward these past four weeks. Which was more than she could say about her sister search. Sierra was still a mystery, and April was steadfastly ignoring Lizzy's regular calls, emails, and texts.

Honestly, when it came to April, Lizzy was starting to feel like a stalker.

Which was only slightly better than feeling like a pest, which was how Dahlia had made her feel when she'd responded to her last email with a dismissive text that had clearly been meant to send her away.

Career plans? Forget it. She was no closer to knowing what she'd do when she returned to Chicago than she had been that day in the park when Kit had kissed her.

She stopped stirring, another sigh escaping.

And there it was. The memory that she could not forget no matter how hard she tried.

And she *had* tried. Especially once it became apparent that Kit wasn't about to kiss her again.

But why?

She took a break from stirring to peek out the window over the kitchen sink. Despite this annoying crush on Kit and all the questions that came with it, Lizzy couldn't help a grin at the sight of the twins chasing each other through the yard.

It was early October and the leaves were changing, giving the Swansons' fenced-in backyard a picturesque quality. In a little while, she'd call them inside so they could wash up and help set the table for dinner, but she and Kit had agreed that the more time they spent outside now, the better. Snow would be here soon enough, everyone was fond of reminding her.

She still wasn't sure she believed them that they'd get snowfall in October, but Nash and Kit had insisted on stocking her closet with snow boots and winter clothes just in case.

Her former coworkers would die laughing if they could see the frumpy, puffy clothes they expected her to wear.

Kit had teased her mercilessly when she'd come out of the hardware store dressing room wearing bibbed snow pants that puddled on the floor because they didn't have her size.

Her smile grew at the memory until she shook her head with an exasperated huff.

There she went again. Daydreaming about the man. It was getting to be really annoying, especially since he didn't seem to return her feelings.

"Because I like you."

She frowned at the memory.

Or...he didn't return her feelings any longer?

She was so confused. For a second there, it had seemed like he'd been suffering from the same silly infatuation. A dead-end relationship waiting to happen. So it was for the best that he'd had a change of heart.

At least, that was what she kept trying to convince herself. But it would be a lot easier to move on if she had any idea why he'd gotten over her so quickly.

She stabbed at the food in the pot.

Had the kiss been horrible?

No, most definitely not. It'd been electrifying.

But it must have been too much for Kit. He wanted a friendship and that was all. And if Lizzy was honest with herself, that was better.

She was heading back to Chicago after he found a home, right?

It was for the best.

The weeks had passed with her falling into a routine of picking up the kids when Marsha couldn't, then staying for dinner, because she was invited to every time. Sometimes Cody joined them before giving her a ride back to the ranch, and Lizzy got to see firsthand just how much the twins adored their playful, cheerful uncle—yes, the shy, quiet man came out of his shell around the twins in a way she didn't think was possible. She kept busy helping Kit house hunt on the weekends and even picking up a couple shifts working in Trina's store.

Between all that and spending some quality time with her sister and Nash on the ranch, Lizzy's days and weeks were full to bursting.

She was quite content with her life, although she knew it wasn't a permanent solution. She couldn't just *move* to Aspire. She was still healing, that was all. Healing took time, and this place was sheltering her while she tried to find the courage to return to her old life.

Once she felt strong enough to face her friends in Chicago, she'd return.

And she and Kit would remain friends.

Yup, that was for the best. She shouldn't even be—

A shrill scream from the backyard jarred her out of her thoughts and sent a cold shiver racing through. Flying into action, she threw open the back door, her heart surging into her throat at the sight of a wailing Corbin, lying on the ground, his face red with pain.

Chloe was standing next to him, wide-eyed and stricken.

"What happened?" Lizzy ran to his side, her stomach roiling at the sight of blood on the arm he cradled.

So. Much. Blood.

It was coating his fingers and smearing the little hairs on his arms.

Her head felt too light, but she took a deep, steadying

breath. Stroking Corbin's hair off his wet cheeks, she tried to see how badly he was hurt, but she was too afraid to move his arm to do much of an inspection.

What she wouldn't give to have Emma here right now. She always knew what to do. Or Kit. Or Nash. Or Cody. Or Marsha. Or…

Oh heck, anyone in the world would be more competent and useful in the face of an emergency.

But no one else was here. She closed her eyes to block out the blood and tried to think. He needed to get to the doctor ASAP. Luckily she'd borrowed Emma's SUV to watch the kids today, so she had a vehicle.

She used the calmest voice she could as she turned to Chloe. "Sweetie, I need you to get my keys and my purse from the entryway table, okay? Corbin and I will meet you at the car."

Chloe nodded before dashing off to do as she was told, and Lizzy crooned what she hoped were comforting words as she carefully got Corbin to his feet and into her arms with as little jostling of his wound as possible.

Racing back into the kitchen, she flicked off the stove and grabbed a clean dish towel. Corbin protested in panic while she tried to wrap the gash and stem the bleeding.

"You're hurting him!" Chloe danced on her toes, jittery and on the verge of tears herself.

Please don't start crying too! Lizzy silently begged her.

"We need to stop the blood and hold his arm together." Lizzy tried not to gag when she got a decent look at the wound. It was a long gash running from the middle of his outer forearm up to his elbow. She had no idea what he did to get it, but it was gross and looked extremely painful. She kissed Corbin's head when she rested his arm back against his chest. "I'm sorry, baby. Just hold it still and we'll get you to the doctor."

Corbin sniffled and cradled his arm while Lizzy scooped him up and carried him to Emma's SUV. She couldn't think about the spots of blood staining her beautiful white shirt with the burnt orange stripes. It was clothing. It could be replaced—Corbin's arm could not.

Her hands shook as she buckled Corbin into his booster. Chloe had started crying and couldn't manage her buckle either, so Lizzy leaned through the car and helped her, only to bump Corbin's arm and get a fresh wave of wails piercing her eardrums.

"It's gonna be okay. It's gonna be okay," she mumbled to herself, not believing a word of it.

The ride to the doctor's felt interminable. Frustration and anxiety had her chest tight after she'd left two messages for Kit with no response.

She called their doctor next, and thank heavens she got through. Nash's sister, Casey, was calm and bright on the phone, settling Lizzy's nerves enough to make it the rest of the way. The lovely nurse was waiting for them in the parking lot when they pulled up to the office.

Lizzy let out a breath of relief at the sight of her. She'd met Casey at a barbecue at Nash's parents' house a month ago and had run into her many times since. She was sweet, outgoing, and so very competent that Lizzy's legs were shaking with relief as Casey helped her get Corbin out of his carseat and into the doctor's office.

All three of them were crying by the time Casey got them settled into the exam room, Corbin on Lizzy's lap and Chloe huddled up to her side.

Lizzy tried to stop her own tears, but it was no use. They tickled her cheeks, but she didn't have a spare hand to brush them away. She rested her cheek on Chloe's head and kissed the little girl's blonde locks.

Dr. Dex arrived a second later, and his warm, unfazed demeanor was just as much of a relief as Casey's.

"So, I hear young Corbin has been trying to take on a tree?" He smiled like he wasn't facing down three tearstained faces. Crouching in front of the boy, his brown eyes warmed with a compassionate smile. "Can you tell me what happened?"

Corbin sniffed and proceeded to hiccup his way through the incident, with Chloe interjecting. He'd been climbing in the tree out back, and neither of them had noticed the nail which had started coming loose from the homemade ladder.

"Hmmm..." Dr. Dex put on gloves while he was listening, nodding and affirming their story. "So, your arm must have snagged the thing when you jumped down."

"Uh-huh." Corbin nodded, his lips wobbling before he buried his face in Lizzy's shoulder.

She kissed his forehead and crooned.

"Thankfully"—Dr. Dex gently pulled Corbin's arm away, removing the blood-soaked dish towel and inspecting the wound—"bodies are amazing at healing. All this arm needs is a good clean and some neat little stitches. You'll be back to new in no time."

"But I don't want stitches!" Corbin's protest was muffled by Lizzy's shirt.

She rubbed his back. "But stitches are cool, buddy. Everyone at school will think you're really brave."

"This is true." Dr. Dex shared a little smile with her. "Are you all right for me to proceed?"

Her eyebrows furrowed, but she gave a tentative nod.

"I haven't been able to reach Kit, but I'm sure he'd be fine with whatever you suggest."

"Cool." The doctor smiled again, then spun in his chair, calling Casey in and asking her to prepare the equipment. He had a young face for a doctor, but his demeanor somehow countered that. Lizzy definitely felt put at ease. He seemed to know exactly what he was doing. He was handsome too—in that baby face kind of way—and surprisingly single considering he was a young, handsome *doctor.* That was the extent of Lizzy's knowledge of the man, as they'd never actually met before.

She'd heard him mentioned, always spoken of in high regard, and Lizzy understood completely. Both he and Casey screamed competent and reassuring, while Lizzy couldn't stop obsessing over how she was going to explain to Kit that she'd totally failed him and his twins.

He should have known better than to leave her in charge. Emma should have told him what a useless wreck she was.

She could dress well and look pretty. That was it. The beginning and end of her life skills.

She deserved a guy like Connor. Sure, he'd only seen her as a trophy wife, but wasn't that what she was? What she was destined to be?

"So, here's what we're going to do..." Dr. Dex explained the procedure in a way Corbin could understand. He kept his voice light and calm, even telling a joke that made Chloe giggle before injecting the boy with a local anesthetic.

"What does ana-static mean?" Chloe asked, watching with fascination while Corbin squirmed on Lizzy's lap. She held him tight and kissed his head.

"It's a special medicine that numbs the pain so it won't hurt Corbin so much."

"Oh good!" Chloe gazed up at him, her eyes so wide and pleading that another little piece of Lizzy's heart was instantly claimed. "Can you give him a lot, because I don't want him to feel anything. No more pain for you, Corby."

Her brother sniffed, his lips obviously trying for a grateful smile, but all he managed was a little lip twitch.

"We'll give that just a minute and then get to work." Dr. Dex sat in front of them, starting up an easy conversation about school and how he loved playing with blocks. He'd try to build his tower higher than anybody else's.

As the pain meds kicked in, Corbin started to participate, and soon they were so absorbed in discussing tower building that the little boy didn't even notice Dex starting on the stitches.

Lizzy was more than impressed and couldn't help thinking that this lovely man should have been watching Kit's children. He would have noticed nails sticking out of boards in the tree. He would have no doubt checked the yard was safe before just sending them out there to get butchered.

Lizzy winced, wondering if the nail was rusty, imagining what could have happened if one of the wonky boards on the tree platform had given way and Corbin had plummeted to the ground. She should have been keeping a better eye on them. This never would have happened if Kit or Marsha had been in charge.

How had she let this happen?

As if he could read her mind, Dr. Dex addressed her in a low voice as he began covering up the wound with a special bandage. "Accidents happen all the time, Miss

O'Sullivan. You did the right thing by bringing him here right away."

She tried for a smile, but she was certain it fell flat.

Oh yeah, she'd been real responsible all right. Someone ought to give her an award for Babysitter of the Year.

"You holding up okay, buddy?" she whispered to Corbin.

He nodded, resting his head against his shoulder. "I want my daddy."

She lightly squeezed his uninjured arm. "I wish he were here too, bud."

That was the truth. He should be here with Corbin.

But also…

How on earth was she going to explain that she'd failed him and his twins?

She sighed as she fell back in her seat.

If he hadn't already gotten over his crush before, he definitely would today.

26

Cody made a joke.

JJ laughed.

Nash made some sort of comeback remark.

They were all heading home—Nash to the ranch house, and his brother and JJ to the bunkhouse where they stayed for most of the year. Kit had been joking and laughing right along with them as he headed toward his truck.

But then he'd gotten Lizzy's message.

Kit jerked to a stop.

Cody noticed immediately. "You all right, bro?"

Kit's breathing grew shallow as he listened to her panicked message. His babies were wailing in the background, and he'd never truly understood the meaning of the phrase 'his blood ran cold' until that very moment.

Ice was in his veins as he muttered, "Corbin's hurt."

"What?" Cody tensed beside him. "What happened? How bad?"

Kit shook his head as he broke into a run, his brother and friends close behind him.

"They're at Dr. Dex's," he shouted over his shoulder. "I have to get there."

"What can I do?" Cody asked.

Kit shook his head. "I don't know."

He didn't even know what *he* could do. Man, he'd never felt so helpless in his life. Prayers started running through his brain faster than he could utter them.

"Casey's working today," Nash said. "I'll call her and see what she knows."

Kit nodded, but he wasn't planning on sticking around long enough for a phone call. He was already at his truck.

"Let us know," Cody shouted.

Kit nodded, throwing them a wave as he revved the engine and took off toward town.

He wasn't sure he'd ever driven so fast in his life, and when he pulled into the driveway and saw Corbin and Chloe walking out of the doctor's office holding Lizzy's hands and sucking on lollipops, he was sure he'd taken a blow to the gut.

He sat in the truck for a full second, swamped with relief before darting out and heading straight to Corbin.

Corbin's lip wobbled, and when Kit scooped him into a hug, he clung to his Daddy's neck like it was a life preserver while Chloe latched on to his leg and Lizzy…

Aw heck, Lizzy burst out crying.

The sight nearly killed him, but he was too relieved to be holding his kids to do much more than offer her a smile.

Chloe and Corbin were talking over each other, their words indecipherable through the overlapping chatter and the lollipops that muffled their words, but Kit just held them both tight as he took them to his truck and got them in.

"Meet us at the house?" he asked Lizzy.

For a second he thought she might say no, but then she nodded, her expression oddly stoic, like she was waiting for a blow.

It wasn't until they were back at his home and were both watching the twins eat peanut butter and jelly sandwiches that he understood why.

"I'm so sorry, Kit." She turned to him with such a solemn look in her big eyes, it took his breath away.

"Sorry for what?" He reached out to brush her hair back. He couldn't help himself.

It had been torture to keep his hands to himself these past few weeks, and after the emotional turmoil of the last hour, he wasn't sure he had the willpower to keep his distance.

Her lower lip wobbled, and her throat worked as she swallowed. "I'm sorry I let this happen."

He frowned. "You let…" He trailed off with a shake of his head. "Lizzy, it was an accident. It could have happened to anyone. If anything, it's my fault for not checking the treehouse and ladder more regularly." He scratched the back of his neck, making a mental note to get up early in the morning and do a thorough check of the kids' play area.

Lizzy didn't respond, but her eyes said she didn't believe him.

Corbin's eyes, meanwhile…

"Lizzy, hold that thought, okay?" He gently squeezed her knee and stood. "These two look absolutely wrecked. I'm gonna get them to bed."

She nodded, her lips pressed together as he went about a very abbreviated nighttime schedule.

He knew for certain this day had worn them both out

when the twins were asleep just about as soon as their heads hit the pillows.

When he came back out to the living room, Lizzy was curled up in a ball on the end of the couch, hot cocoa in hand and one for him sitting on the coffee table.

"I should get going soon," she said. "But I know I owe you an explanation."

He arched his brows. "Lizzy, you don't owe me anything. I get it. Trust me. No matter how good of a guardian you are, there's no way you can protect them from everything." One side of his mouth hitched up. "Least of all themselves."

"Yes, but—"

He put a finger to her lips, and the moment he did, he knew it was a mistake. Her lips were soft and warm, her breath uneven.

"No buts," he whispered.

She swallowed.

When he dropped his hand, her eyes welled with tears. "Oh, Kit, there was just…" She sniffled. "There was so much *blood*."

He winced as he tugged her into his arms. "I can imagine."

"And I didn't know what to do, and I was trying to think clearly, but all I felt like doing was throwing up. I was panicking, and Corbin was so upset…"

She rattled on as he held her tight, stroking her arm softly because she clearly needed to let out her stress and fears. He kissed the top of her head while she spoke, inhaling the perfect, sweet scent that was so uniquely her and trying not to notice just how good she felt tucked against his side.

"…and I am just so sorry I let this happen," she ended,

her voice going high with a little wail that was equally funny and heartbreaking.

He kissed the top of her head as he squeezed her tight. "You didn't let it happen. This wasn't your fault."

"I should have checked on him more or something."

"Lizzy, have I ever told you about the time I turned away for one second and Chloe ate a crayon?"

She choked on a laugh. "No way."

He nodded. "Or the time I was put in charge of watching Cody when I was younger and managed to knock his tooth out."

"What?" She pulled out of his embrace to gape at him. "Really?"

"It was a baby tooth, but there was so much blood I was certain I'd killed him."

"Seriously?" Her lips were quivering with an almost smile.

"Then there was the time that Corbin fell off the bed while my dad was changing Chloe's diaper. Or the time we were sure they'd gotten lost at the hardware store, and—"

She burst out in a laugh that made his heart soar.

"I like that sound." His voice got a little mushy as he brushed away the last of her tears. "I love watching you laugh."

Her smile was shaky, and her eyes were still wet—glimmering, vibrant emeralds that mesmerized him. "I was worried you'd be annoyed with me. I should have known you'd be understanding."

Lizzy snuggled into him, and it felt so right he could barely breathe for a moment. She fit against him perfectly, like the final piece of a puzzle, and all the effort to resist her suddenly felt paper thin.

She looked up at him with her tear-streaked face. "You're a good man, Kit."

His chest ached with emotion as his gaze fell to her lips. "And you're a beautiful woman, Lizzy. So very beautiful."

His comment made her smile falter just a little, but he kissed her anyway, gently brushing his lips across hers before adding more pressure. She hesitated for a brief moment, then leaned in, kissing him back with a power that sent lightning bolts skittering throughout the room. Their spark was both inspiring and terrifying.

This, his heart seemed to say as it thudded wildly in his chest. This was what he'd been missing this past month. He'd missed it so desperately it scared him.

But he shoved aside those thoughts as her lips parted for him, welcoming him as he deepened the kiss.

She made a soft noise in the back of her throat, and he groaned in return.

Did she feel it too? The rightness of this moment? The connection that felt so bone-deep and so overwhelmingly perfect that it made him feel like he'd finally come home after years away at sea?

27

"I think we're about to win some sort of award," Lizzy gasped when Kit came up for air.

They were next to Emma's SUV, and Lizzy's knees were so weak from all this blissful kissing that she couldn't stand on her own two feet.

Luckily Kit seemed all too happy to hold her close so she didn't fall.

He moved his lips to her neck. "An award for kissing?" he teased. "Do they give those out in Chicago? Maybe the big city does have something going for it after all."

She giggled as she wrapped her arms tighter around his neck. "I meant an award for the longest goodbye ever," she clarified.

It was true. She'd said she had to get going an hour ago, but actually peeling themselves away from each other had been a monumental task. One they were failing epically.

She left in small stages. Finally getting off the couch only to make out at the door, then walking onto the porch only to make out against the railing, then finally down to the truck only to kiss against the door.

He pulled back with the smuggest smile she'd ever seen.

It was exactly the sort of smile that would have made her itching mad for no good reason when they'd first met, but right now it just made her want to fling herself into his arms all over again and beg him to never let go.

She took a deep breath as she pulled away.

That right there was exactly why she had to leave. Her heart had been put through the ringer today, and all this kissing had her head spinning. After four weeks of keeping careful distance between them, talking and laughing like friends but not venturing into anything physical, this sudden change was confusing. She didn't know what it meant.

Her body seemed to, but her heart and head were in turmoil.

What did she even want this to mean?

"I really should go," she whispered.

He let out a resigned exhale before kissing her forehead gently. "Drive safe, all right?"

She nodded, and he pulled back so she could get in the SUV.

It was weirdly painful to wave goodbye, like she was leaving her heart behind.

"Stupid romantic heart," she muttered.

The whole drive home, she tried to find some clarity. Her head and her heart seemed to be heading in two different directions at once, and she was left no closer to an understanding of where things stood by the time she pulled up to the ranch.

All she really knew was their emotions had been

running high. Between adrenaline and relief and fear…

Was it any wonder they'd acted a little crazy?

It didn't necessarily mean anything. He'd just been trying to make her feel better after she'd let him down. That was the only reason he'd kissed her.

"And you're a beautiful woman, Lizzy. So very beautiful."

And because she was beautiful, she amended as she climbed out of the SUV. So very beautiful.

She shook her head. It was silly that such a pretty compliment had her feeling so unsettled.

He was attracted to her. That was a good thing, right?

She frowned as she collected her things and walked inside.

Of course it was. She was just being overly sensitive, that was all. She just needed to clear her head. It was nothing a nice warm bath and a good night's sleep couldn't cure.

But when she walked through the front door of the ranch house, she stopped short. "Mom? Dad?"

"Surprise!" They laughed and hugged her.

She squeezed them back, all those earlier tears threatening to return at such an unexpected sight. "What are you guys doing here?"

"We just had to come see our girls," her mother said. "It's only a quick visit. We're heading back late Sunday night. We're going to spend the day with you and Emma tomorrow. She's dying to show us around the ranch, and then we're going to a dinner party at Nash's parents' house."

Derek was beaming. "We're so happy for our Emmy girl." He leaned in and lowered his voice. "And guess what? Nash just asked our permission to marry her."

He put a finger to his lips, and Lizzy's eyebrows rose in

surprise.

"Of course we said yes." Her mother's laughter was merry. "One evening with those two and I can tell they're meant for each other." She grinned some more, then seemed to notice her youngest daughter for the first time. "Oh, sweetie, is this too upsetting for you? Still too soon after what happened?"

"No, I'm fine." She forced a grin, punching down her emotions. "I'm really happy for Em."

That was the truth. No one in the world deserved true love and a lifetime of happiness as much as Emma.

Her mother held her cheeks. "What's up, kiddo?"

"I just had a rough afternoon." Her eyes filled with tears, and she told her parents what happened with Corbin.

Their sympathetic murmurs were comforting as they sat on either side of her in the living room.

She could hear Emma and Nash laughing in the kitchen as they made hot drinks for the travelers, and while she didn't relish repeating the story, she was grateful to have a moment alone with her parents.

"I really shouldn't be looking after them." Her voice wobbled with unshed tears when she finally admitted the truth out loud. The truth Kit had been too nice to acknowledge. "I'm not cut out for it. I should just stay in fashion. That's all I'm good for, right?"

"Lizzy," her mom chided. "You're worth so much more than that."

"But I'm beautiful." She blinked. "That's all I really am. Born to decorate the world...and that's about it."

"Not true." Derek's voice was firm as he shook his head. "You are a talented, amazing woman. You just haven't tried to expand your horizons before."

She frowned. Was that true?

Her mother nodded. "You'd been living a safe, comfortable life up until that Connor disaster. Much as I hate that you had your heart broken, I am glad it forced you to spread your wings."

She let out a broken laugh and shook her head. "I don't feel amazing or talented. I just… I feel…"

"You feel what, honey?" Derek asked.

"Lost," she choked. "I don't know where I belong right now."

Her mother's sympathetic wince was kind, but it made Lizzy's insides turn. "Is it time to come home?"

That wince had said she'd take care of Lizzy. Derek would too. She knew that. And Lizzy was beyond grateful for that support, that safety net she'd always had, and never really appreciated.

She was grateful for it now…but she didn't want it.

She didn't want to be someone else's burden any longer. She didn't want people taking care of her like *she* was the child.

"Why don't you come home with us?" Derek added as if her silence was an agreement.

"I want to go home," she said slowly, trying to put her wayward thoughts and spiraling emotions into words. "It's just…I don't know where home is." She shrugged and buried her face in her hands.

That sounded even more pathetic when she said it aloud.

Her mother rubbed her back but didn't say anything, and Lizzy could just imagine that she was sharing a look with Derek. The same way she shared looks with Kit over the dinner table when the kids said something cute.

Her chest ached at the thought. Her heart seemed to

swell even as her rib cage tightened and her mind drew up the image of Kit across the table, Chloe and Corbin laughing on either side of her. Kit sharing a grin with her that seemed to say they were in this together.

Those moments were so perfect. So precious. So intimate and…

Oh no.

Closing her eyes, she acknowledged the truth she'd been so desperately trying to avoid.

She was in love.

For the first time in her life, she was really, truly, genuinely in love. And not just with one person but three. She'd gone and fallen for Kit and his two perfect children.

But was she even worthy of them?

Today's disaster wasn't exactly a rousing yes. And what did she even have to offer?

No career. No plans.

She was beautiful, that was about it. And that was all Kit seemed to notice right now.

But if she were to stick around… If they were to give this a shot…

She sighed as she sank into the warm comfort of her parents' embrace.

He hadn't wanted to give it a shot before, even when he'd admitted he'd liked her. He'd known just as she had that it wouldn't last.

And did she even want to stick around?

She sniffled in their arms.

What would that even look like?

She didn't belong here.

And how was she supposed to fit into a place where she didn't belong?

28

Nash's parents didn't know how to do anything small. A 'little get-together' at the Donahues' almost always meant a giant party thanks to the size of their extended family and the number of people they counted as their closest friends.

Kit was fortunate enough to be among the latter, thanks to nearly a lifetime of holding the status of Nash's best friend. If his parents weren't half a world away, they'd be here too. They called this morning, their voices high with excitement. They were loving every second of the cruise, and their weekly check-ins were always filled with stories of fun and adventure. Kit was really happy for them, and now that Lizzy was filling a gap in Chloe's life, saying goodbye to Grammy's face on-screen wasn't eliciting tears anymore.

Lizzy.

He scanned the room for her. His eyes wouldn't let him do anything else. She'd walked with him in his dreams and had been his first thought when he opened his eyes. His heart couldn't do anything but seek her out.

There were no signs of the stunning beauty, but he did catch his kids darting away. He wasn't worried, as he counted nearly everyone in this house among their extended family as well. His kids might not have a mama, but they had more honorary aunts and uncles than most every other kid combined.

He'd just finished making the rounds of small talk with Nash's aunts and uncles—his gaze drifting constantly toward the front door for any sign of Lizzy's arrival—when he spotted Corbin and Chloe standing with Casey and her new husband, Ryan.

Casey was regaling that whole side of the expansive, high-ceilinged living room with tales of Corbin's heroics as he'd nobly withstood the pain and agony of stitches. Chloe was also being touted for her bravery, and between the two of them, their smiles were bright enough to light the entire town during a blackout.

"Proud as peacocks," he muttered to Nash, who was standing nearby.

"Hmm?" Nash looked over, his demeanor distracted as his gaze shot to the doorway. "What? Oh yeah. Right." He laughed. "Those two had quite a day."

"Did Lizzy tell you about it last night?" Kit asked.

Why? He didn't even know. He was just jonesing for some word of her. If he couldn't see her or hear her or touch her, he at least wanted to talk about her.

He hadn't been able to get her off his mind for the last twenty-four hours. Heck, the last four weeks. But this was different, because now…

Well, now he knew.

It was useless to fight his feelings. Four weeks of distance, and what had it accomplished? Nothing.

"Uh, sorry, what?" Nash asked. He was dragging his

gaze back to his best friend. Kit wasn't sure he'd ever seen Nash so distracted in his life.

"You okay, man?"

Nash nodded, letting out a rueful chuckle. "Sorry. Just... This is a big day."

"Yeah, I bet," Kit said. "Your folks meeting Emma's. That's a huge deal."

Nash blinked like he didn't understand, and then he gave Kit a cryptic grin as he clapped a hand on Kit's shoulder. "Yeah, that too."

Then Nash was heading toward the door—a man on a mission. Which meant...

They were here.

She was here.

Kit's heart instantly started to race with anticipation. It was crazy. He'd just seen her last night. He saw her all the time.

But after their epic kisses, he woke up feeling like everything was different.

The battle had been lost. He was waving the white flag of surrender in the face of these overwhelming feelings. He couldn't shut them off, and he was helpless to ignore them.

So that left only one option. He was embracing it, plain and simple. Did he know what the future held? No. But he liked her, and he was almost certain she liked him. That had to count for something, right?

Maybe they didn't have to have all the answers right now. She didn't seem to be in any hurry to leave, and he wasn't ready to rush into anything either. So why not relax and go with it? See where things go and—

His gaze caught on Chloe just as Lizzy and her parents

entered, along with a beaming Emma, who headed straight into Nash's arms.

Chloe's smile said it all, and then she and Corbin veered right to Lizzy, barreling into her waiting arms as her parents looked on with delight.

A pang of doubt caught at his chest.

Did he really have the luxury of thinking that way?

What? He'd see where things went and just pray his kids didn't get hurt if he was making a mistake?

Lizzy spotted him just as the doubts were firing through his brain, and her smile faltered, almost like she could sense his trepidation. Or maybe she felt it too. But then she straightened and he moved toward her, greeting her parents and making introductions.

Her parents were friendly and kind, not to mention good with kids. Not surprising, really, since they'd raised Emma and Lizzy.

After a good amount of small talk, Nash's parents stole Emma and Lizzy's mom and stepdad to introduce them to the entire family.

Kit, meanwhile, saw his opportunity to steal Lizzy away.

He tugged on her hand while Corbin and Chloe were distracted by Nash and Emma. She giggled as she followed him into an empty hallway that led to the Donahues' master bedroom. "Where are you taking me?"

His answer was to spin around, gather her against him, and kiss those luscious lips. She sank into him on a sigh, and he felt it all over again.

Home.

Sweet, perfect home.

That was what she tasted like. That was what she felt like when he pulled her into his arms. That was what she looked like when she smiled up at him, one dimple peeking out.

"We'll get in trouble," she whispered teasingly.

He chuckled, but then he caught it.

She didn't seem unhappy to be here with him. Not by any means. But there was a hesitance in her eyes. A wariness that made him tense in return.

"What's the matter?" he asked.

"Nothing." She smiled, but it didn't quite reach her eyes.

His gut churned with wariness.

He'd been so over the moon these past twenty-four hours, it hadn't occurred to him that she might regret it.

They jumped apart when they heard someone coming.

It was Nash.

His eyes widened as he looked between them. "Oh, uh...sorry. I didn't mean to interrupt." He started backing away, but Lizzy beat him to it, edging out of the hallway.

"Oh no, you didn't interrupt. I'd really better find my parents. They're probably overwhelmed by all the new names and faces."

Kit watched her flee. She'd been talking too quickly, her actions and her voice almost nervous, which she never was around him. So...what did that mean?

He'd say it was a good sign if her nervousness wasn't also matched with wariness.

This was not the giddy nerves of that uncertain stage in a new relationship, it was something else.

Something that made Kit's stomach pool with dread.

Nash was frowning as he watched Lizzy run away. Despite her excuses, that was exactly what she was doing, and Nash and Kit both knew it.

"She okay?" Nash asked.

Kit shrugged. "Did she seem all right to you last night?"

Nash's gaze was fixed elsewhere. On Emma, it seemed, and Kit watched his friend take a few deep breaths as he shoved his hands into his pockets.

It was clear he'd forgotten all about Kit and didn't even appear to have heard his question.

As Nash walked away, Kit was left shaking his head. *What on earth is wrong with everyone tonight?*

Nash's mother called everyone into their dining room for supper a little while later, and Kit tried to tell himself he was being paranoid when Lizzy didn't so much as look his way.

She was concentrating on her parents, that was all. She was being a good daughter, not actively trying to avoid him.

But even so, his spirits were low when he and the twins found a seat at the far end of the table, opposite Lizzy and her parents, who were whispering among themselves as everyone was seated.

After grace, Patrick Donahue, Nash's father, informed everyone that they needed to pipe down because Nash had something to say.

Kit straightened, but he saw Lizzy flash her parents the most adorable grin.

What the…?

And then it clicked as Nash, looking more nervous and emotional than Kit had ever seen him, turned to face Emma.

He was going to propose.

No sooner had Kit thought it, Nash dropped down to one knee, eliciting squeals of excitement and sappy "Awws" from their families gathered around the table.

Kit's heart swelled with happiness for his friend. Nash deserved this, and so did Emma. They were so right for each other. Such a perfect fit with common goals and shared dreams.

His gaze flickered over to Lizzy, who clapped a hand over her mouth, her eyes wet with unshed tears as Nash started in on a speech about how much Emma had changed his life.

"...you make me want to think about the future," he was saying. "You make me want to be the best man I can be. You inspire me with your big heart, you dazzle me with your brilliant smile, and I love you more than I ever thought possible."

Emma was crying, her smile wide as she let out a little sob that had half the women at the table dabbing at their eyes. Some of the men too.

Kit looked over to see Lizzy crying. Happy tears, he was sure. But he couldn't help wondering if this was stirring up other emotions for her as well.

Worry for her nearly distracted him from the critical moment.

Nash pulled a ring box out of his pocket, which made the guests at the table gasp and whisper. "Emma O'Sullivan, keeper of my heart, will you do me the honor of being my wife?"

"Yes!" She said it so quickly she spoke over top of him, throwing her arms around him and burying her face in his neck as the room exploded with cheers and shouts of congratulations.

Kit was clapping and shouting right along with them, his heart fairly bursting with happiness for his friend. But after a little while, when the excitement calmed down and the happy couple got back to their meal, along with the rest of the table, Kit looked over to see Lizzy had disappeared.

"You behave," he said to Chloe and Corbin. "I'll be right back."

He slipped out of the room, concern for Lizzy giving his steps urgency as he poked his head into the sprawling ranch home's many rooms and hallways.

He couldn't find her.

She was gone.

The thought made him stop still in his tracks in the hallway just outside the dining room.

She was gone. Maybe just outside, or to some room he hadn't checked. But it was like a bellowing statement: she was gone.

An impending warning: she was gone.

And it reminded him of the truth. She *would* be gone soon enough.

It all made sense now. That wariness in her gaze, the hesitancy of her smile.

His heart fell. He very nearly heard it go splat on the floor at his feet.

He was such an idiot!

Here he'd been so sure that their night of kissing and touching and holding and laughing had meant something more. He'd been so certain of it, it never even occurred to him that she might have had the exact opposite response.

She might have been frightened off.

She'd never asked for more than friendship. She'd never made any promises to stay. She'd never so much as hinted that she wanted to be his girlfriend, let alone…

Let alone his wife. The mother of his kids.

He shut his eyes tight against a wave of pain.

That was what he wanted. Needed.

If they continued down this path, marriage was the ultimate goal. The long-term plan. He knew it like he knew he needed air to breathe.

Watching Nash propose to Emma, it had been almost frighteningly easy to picture himself in Nash's position. To imagine Lizzy smiling as she said yes.

His head fell back against the wall with a thud that seemed to echo in his hollow chest.

He was such a fool. Because he knew better. He knew better than anyone what that wariness meant. She wasn't playing hard to get, she was trying to keep her distance, because she didn't want what he had to offer.

She never had.

She never would.

Only an idiot would knowingly make the same mistake twice. He wouldn't put himself through that again. And he certainly wouldn't let his kids suffer that heartbreak.

They deserved better. They all did.

29

Lizzy had never seen her sister happier. Holding Emma's hand, she gazed at the stunning engagement ring—a square-cut diamond nestled atop woven white gold. The intricate metalwork was so detailed and gave the ring a splash of uniqueness that Lizzy instantly loved.

But what she loved even more was the look on her sister's face.

"You are absolutely glowing," she gushed in Emma's ear as she hugged her tightly after coffee and desserts were served. "Have I told you how happy I am for you yet?"

Emma laughed as she patted Lizzy's back. "Only a couple hundred times."

Lizzy's eyes welled with tears. Again. "Well, I am."

Emma drew back and eyed her with a look of concern that Lizzy was all too familiar with. "Lizzy, are you sure you're okay? I know this can't be easy for you–"

"Uh uh uh." Lizzy shook her head and wagged a finger in Emma's face, so close she nearly booped her nose. "No more of that. It is possible for me to be happy for others, you know, even if my own life isn't exactly stellar."

Emma looked like she was about to interrupt, but Lizzy wasn't having it.

"I'm serious," she said. "I know I have a tendency to be a little…" She hitched her lips to the side as she thought of how to finish that. "Self-absorbed," she finally admitted.

Emma tilted her head with a rueful little grin, like she wanted to argue but couldn't.

Lizzy straightened her shoulders. "But I'm working on that. Actually…" She forced a smile, trying desperately not to look over toward Kit and the kids. "I'm working on a lot of things."

"I know you are," Emma said as she squeezed her hand. "And I'm proud of you."

Nash came over and wrapped an arm around Emma's waist. Lizzy ignored the pang of jealousy and focused on how grateful she was that Emma had found someone who saw her for who she truly was and appreciated every bit of her.

She wouldn't be jealous, she decided right then and there. She'd use her sister as inspiration. When Lizzy fell in love again, she'd make sure it was the real deal. She wouldn't settle for anything less than what Emma had with Nash.

Her chest ached, and it took physical effort not to seek out Kit and the kids. Tonight wasn't about them, and it certainly wasn't about her. She made a show of reaching for Emma's hand yet again and tugging it in her direction.

Lizzy studied the ring from every angle and nodded at Nash with a smile. "You did good, brother."

He grinned. "Thanks, *sis*."

She leaned over to kiss his cheek and then Emma's one

more time. "Congratulations, you guys. I'm seriously so happy for you."

His aunts were heading their way, so Lizzy took the opportunity to slip away. Unfortunately, her escape was far from graceful, because she rounded a corner and bumped right into Kit.

They shared an awkward glance, like neither of them knew what to do with themselves. It was weird.

And it was her fault.

She winced at the memory of her awkwardness when they'd first arrived. It was just that after everything she'd shared with her parents last night, and with all that had transpired between them the night before, she felt like one big raw nerve where Kit was concerned.

And in her defense, she'd thought the dinner tonight was going to be Nash's and Emma's families only—although in hindsight, she should have realized that Nash's best friend counted as family as far as the Donahues were concerned.

"That was some speech, huh?" she offered.

"Yeah. Real nice." He shifted from one foot to the other. His gaze wasn't quite meeting hers, and there was a tension in his jaw that put her on edge.

This silence sucked. Even more so because conversation usually flowed so easily between them.

She racked her brain trying to think of anything to say. But words weren't coming. Her mind was blank. Her body, on the other hand…

She was torn right down the middle between wanting to kiss him senseless and turning tail to flee.

Flee where? That was the question. She could run away with her parents, head back to Chicago. But Chicago didn't feel safe either. It didn't feel right. Chicago felt like taking a step backward, but no matter how hard she tried she couldn't see which way was forward.

Kit scrubbed the back of his neck, looking more uncomfortable than she'd ever seen him. "So, I have another house to check out after church tomorrow. You want to come?"

"Uh..." She shifted in place. "I need to hang out with my parents while they're in town."

"Oh, yeah, of course."

"I'll probably drive them to the airport and see them off," she added.

"Makes sense." He nodded. "Are you still good to pick up the kids on Monday after school?"

"Yeah." She opened her mouth to say more and drew a blank. She pressed her lips together, and there was no end to the awkwardness of the silence that followed.

He cleared his throat. "Thank you so much for that."

"It's no problem," she said quickly. "And send me pics of the house. I'll give you my opinion." She added a big smile, but she was pretty sure it fooled no one.

"Okay," he said. "Well, I'd better..." He trailed off with a gesture over his shoulder that said absolutely nothing.

"Yeah, and I'd better..." She nodded toward the front entrance.

"Right."

"Okay, then," she added.

"Good night, Lizzy."

Her forced smile faltered. Why did 'goodnight' sound so much like 'goodbye'? "Goodnight."

She turned and fled, but not to Chicago, just the ranch house. The ranch house that Emma called home.

But it wasn't Lizzy's home.

And in less than twenty-four hours, she'd be taking her parents to the airport so they could go to their home.

But that wasn't her home either.

Lizzy let herself into the house and found herself wandering around like she had over a month ago when she'd finally come out of hiding in her bedroom.

It felt far more familiar now than it had then, but she was still living in someone else's house. Not hers, even if her name was technically on the deed.

Hers and six others'. She shook her head. It still caught her off guard, the whole "you have more siblings than you knew about" thing. Seven sisters. *Seven.*

That Frank O'Sullivan sure was a player.

Lizzy found herself exploring his room and April's too. Not that she was looking for anything in particular. Except maybe answers.

But the questions were too big to ponder. They felt unwieldy, and trying to nail down the answers felt like trying to pin down a cloud.

What did she really want from this life?

What truly made her happy?

She didn't know the answers, and all she found while wandering the empty house were the remnants of a family she'd never known.

Or maybe…

Maybe she did know the answers but she didn't want to face them.

She stopped in front of the floor-to-ceiling window overlooking the ranch. It was dark out there now, but the moon cast the meadow before her with a strip of light. It was pretty, really.

Pretty but terrifying. All sorts of creatures lived out

there. All kinds of dangers. She leaned forward until her forehead rested against the glass.

Emma had always been the one to face dangers head-on. Well, dangers in the sense of real-life problems. The old Lizzy—the one who believed that all life's problems could be solved if she married a rich, handsome man who spoiled her—wouldn't have even admitted she was scared.

But now?

Lizzy breathed out so heavily that the window fogged over. Well, now she could admit she was afraid.

Not of the questions she was facing but of the answers.

What if she lost it all again?

She gave her head a shake. Kit would never cheat on her. She knew that. But he could hurt her.

He could hurt her so much worse than Connor had ever been able to. Because Kit was good and kind and thoughtful and funny. He was understanding and sweet and…and *perfect.*

And she was so…not.

She was pretty, and she knew fashion. But what did she know about real relationships?

Apparently nothing, if her failure of an engagement with Connor was anything to go by.

And families?

Her belly erupted into butterflies at the thought of being a mom. Not just a babysitter but an actual mother.

She'd never planned on that. And she wasn't some natural caregiver like Emma.

But she was getting way ahead of herself. Because maybe…

Maybe it wasn't just about what she wanted.

Kit hadn't exactly proposed. He'd just kissed her. Many

times. But after a full month of keeping his distance. And he'd said she was beautiful, that was all. He hadn't said he'd liked her again. He hadn't asked for some commitment.

And what if this was just attraction for him? What if he got tired of her, or grew to know her better and realized she was just a pretty face? One day she'd grow old and wrinkled, and what would he think of her then?

Beauty took work, and it wasn't necessarily a quality that lasted forever.

Kit deserved someone with more substance!

She pulled away from the window with a sigh, because even through the pitch-black view outside she could see clearly.

Kit might like her looks, and sure, they had some fun, but she was no one's idea of the perfect partner or mother. She'd never fit into his life here. Not truly. And if he didn't see that now, he'd figure it out quickly.

Lizzy turned away from the window and headed back down to her own room.

She already had her answers, all right.

She just didn't like them.

30

Bonnie was beaming at him as she waved toward the kitchen in a Vanna White move. "And don't you just love that tile?"

Kit gave a grunt and a nod, hoping that said enough.

Who loved tile? Was tile something people actually got excited about?

He glanced over at Bonnie, who was still grinning ear to ear.

Clearly this woman got excited about kitchen flooring.

He peered at the ground, as if concentration could help him form some sort of opinion about the plain white floor.

What would Lizzy think?

He inwardly cursed as that thought popped up.

Again. For the fiftieth time since they'd arrived here today, and for probably the millionth time all weekend. The house yesterday had been a bust. He hadn't needed any second opinions to know it was far off the mark.

Today's showing was…perfect. On paper, at least.

"Did you see the second bedroom?" Cody asked as he

strode into the kitchen, acting like he wasn't aware he had a twin sitting on each foot.

Chloe and Corbin were giggling hysterically at their uncle's antics. They had been all morning. For that alone, he was grateful Cody had agreed to join them on this viewing after church let out. And now here they all were, in their Sunday best.

At least his kids were having fun, because Kit was definitely not.

"Well? What do you think?" Bonnie asked, her gaze frighteningly hopeful.

Kit scratched an eyebrow as he winced. "I don't think this is the one, Bonnie. Sorry."

Her face fell, but she didn't try to sway him. She also hadn't flirted with him once since they'd arrived. Cody, yes. Kit, no. He found himself wondering what the gossips had been saying about him and Lizzy if Bonnie had gotten the hint to back off.

"Are you sure, bro?" Cody asked. "This place checks all the boxes."

Kit nodded. "Yeah, it just… It doesn't feel right."

Cody looked like he was smothering a smile. "You sure that's not because a certain new *friend* isn't here by your side?"

Kit shot his brother a glare. Cody had been teasing him about his friendship with Lizzy for weeks now. JJ and Nash too. He'd kept insisting they were just friends, as unlikely as that might seem.

It didn't take a genius to see that they didn't have much in common.

Kit glared at the white tile Bonnie thought he should love.

"This isn't the house for us," he said firmly.

Bonnie nodded. "Fair enough." With a sigh, she unlocked her iPad and started scrolling, then let out a delighted gasp. "Of course! The old Murphy property just went up for sale. I'm hosting a viewing tomorrow, if you can make it."

Kit pinched the bridge of his nose. A headache was forming, and his children's loud squeals and laughter weren't helping.

"Cody," he growled.

"Sorry." Cody stopped tickling them, but the grin he shot Kit was far from apologetic.

"No offense, Bonnie, but I think I need a break from house hunting."

She put a hand on his arm, her expression sympathetic. "I know it's a lot. But just check out the Murphy house tomorrow before you call it quits. I have a really good feeling about this one."

Cody was nodding beside her, and Kit knew he was outnumbered. "Okay. But just that one." He sighed.

As Cody chased the twins out of the house, racing them back to the truck, Kit finished up with Bonnie, getting the details for the next viewing. On his way out, he pulled his phone from his back pocket.

No messages.

Not that he'd been expecting any, really. He and Lizzy had ended their last conversation badly. It had been awkward to the extreme.

Which probably meant she regretted those kisses.

His fingers tapped against the screen, scrolling through old text messages with Lizzy as if he could decipher something from her cute, flirty little texts and the ridiculous overabundance of emojis that accompanied them.

He felt a smile tugging at his lips as his gaze fell on the

last one, when she'd texted to let him know she'd gotten home safe and sound after he'd kissed her senseless. A chuckle rose up in him at the string of emojis. What did two dancing girls even mean?

He shook his head with a sigh, and before he could stop himself, he was texting her.

Hope you had fun with your parents. Any chance you could check out a house with me tomorrow?

He held his breath, stopping in the walkway as he waited for an answer, listening with half an ear as Cody wrangled Chloe and Corbin into their seats.

His heart felt like it was lodged in his throat. After a few seconds passed, he already started to jump to the worst-case scenario.

She was going to ignore him. It was clear she didn't want to pursue whatever it was they'd started, and now she was going to give him the cold shoulder.

Kit forced himself to shove his phone into his back pocket. He couldn't stand here all day waiting for a response. Taking off his hat, he scrubbed the back of his neck. His palms were sweating with nerves as he put the hat back on and strode toward his brother.

Was he pathetic for asking her to keep helping him with the house hunt when she was clearly trying to keep her distance?

Maybe. But it wasn't the same checking out houses without her. She always knew what questions to ask and had such a different way of looking at the world.

He'd teased her the last time they'd viewed a house

together, saying they might be standing side by side but they were clearly living in two different dimensions. All he'd seen was a house. She'd seen what it would look like as a home.

"You guys ready?" Kit asked as he forced a smile for his kids' sake.

"Yes, Daddy!" Chloe called out.

She was wearing that dress again. The one she claimed made her a fairy princess, just like Corbin was now convinced that the friendship bracelet Lizzy helped him make was his foolproof lucky charm when it came to making new friends at school.

And he *had* made friends, because that charm had given him the confidence to make the first move.

Lizzy had done that. She'd quite literally brought magic into his kids' lives.

Kit's chest ached as he leaned in to ruffle Corbin's hair before shutting the back door and climbing into the driver's side.

He pulled out his phone one more time, just to make sure the sound was on so he wouldn't miss the text alert.

He ignored Cody's knowing smirk as he set it down under the dashboard.

It wasn't pathetic to reach out to a friend to ask for a second opinion. He just needed her help, that was all.

But even as he tried to tell himself that, a voice in his head called him out as a liar. He'd texted her because he missed her. There were no two ways about it. He'd felt her absence like a hole in his chest, and it'd only been a day.

"All right, spill," Cody said as Kit put the truck in Reverse and pulled away from the house. "What's eating you?"

Kit kept his eyes on the road in front of him. "Nothing."

Cody scoffed. "It's something."

Kit rolled his eyes. "I'm fine."

"Lies," Cody muttered teasingly. "All lies."

Kit refused to respond to that. Was it a lie? Yeah. But everyone was allowed to have a bad day every once in a while. Didn't mean he had to spill his guts to his little brother.

"If you don't tell me, I'm gonna tell Mom and Dad that you're not doing okay next time they call."

Kit glanced over in horror. "You wouldn't."

Cody crossed his arms, leaning back in his seat with a stubborn set to his jaw. "I would. And it would be a shame too. They'd probably call their trip short and run right home—"

"That's enough," Kit interrupted with an exasperated sigh.

Cody wore a triumphant smirk.

Pulling in a breath, Kit tried to remain calm, aware the kids were in the back seat, but they were chattering away and not really listening. "Just finding this house-hunting thing hard, that's all."

"Well, maybe you'll feel better when Lizzy's there with you." Cody smirked, and Kit gripped the wheel a little tighter.

He shrugged, trying to play it down as his gaze darted to the still black screen of his phone. "She's good at this stuff. She helps me see things I don't notice."

His tone was too defensive, and he knew it.

Cody snickered. "The fact that she makes you so dang happy probably doesn't hurt either, now does it?"

Clenching his jaw, Kit kept his eyes on the road.

A long silence passed as Kit drove them all back to his house. Cody was sticking around for dinner, which meant it was fun uncle day and Kit could actually prepare them a Sunday meal in peace.

Cody broke the silence first. "You should probably tell Lizzy that sometime."

Kit stiffened. "Tell her what?"

"Don't play dumb," Cody shot back. "Tell her that she makes you happy. That she makes your life better. Tell her that you've smiled more since she's been in town than you ever have. Tell her that you can't stop thinking about her, that she owns your heart."

Kit whipped around to look at his brother, his heart kicking like an untamed colt.

Cody just grinned. "You know I speak the truth."

Kit's chest deflated. "She's a city girl. She doesn't want to be here."

Cody winced. "Is that what she said? Sorry, man. No wonder you're so grumpy."

Kit shifted in his seat as he turned onto their street. "Well, she didn't actually say it, but I know."

Cody had the nerve to laugh. "Oh really? And since when did you become an expert on reading women's minds?"

He threw his brother a glare.

"I'm serious. Just talk to her," Cody said. "Ask her outright, because you won't really know what she wants until you do. And yeah, she might say exactly what you're already thinking, but she might not. Either way, you'll know, and that's a darn sight better than being blindsided."

He was talking about Natalie, and the reminder made Kit's insides twist in a sickening manner.

"Look, man," Cody continued, his voice softer than before. "You've been through a lot. You and the kids. It's only natural that you'd want to protect yourself and them from getting hurt."

Kit parked the truck but made no move to get out. Cody didn't either.

"But at some point, you've got to move on, right?" Cody continued. "Moving out is great, but when are you going to let yourself move on with another woman?"

Kit didn't answer, and Cody sighed as he opened the door and got out, helping the kids out of their carseats while Kit sat there like a lump, his head spinning too fast for him to keep up.

Cody's words ate at his gut. He wasn't sure what to make of them other than the fact that they were true. Natalie had blindsided him, and maybe because he'd never really taken the time to talk to her. He definitely hadn't listened to her when she'd tried to tell him what she wanted…and what she didn't.

And then, after the twins were born, he could sense she was unhappy, but he hadn't wanted to delve into an unpleasant conversation. Like some coward, he'd dodged honesty and then been cut off at the knees.

His hands gripped the steering wheel hard. Had he learned nothing from that experience?

Clearly not, because he'd been avoiding the truth with Lizzy too. For all their talking this past month, for all their laughter and even their kisses, he hadn't had the guts to straight out tell her that he wanted her. And he hadn't asked her what she wanted either.

He ran a hand over his face, the sound of Corbin and Chloe's laughter reaching him as Cody led them into the house.

Cody was right. And Kit knew what he had to do.

Yeah, it was terrifying, but Lizzy had to know what was going on in his head and heart or he just might regret it forever.

The next day, he had his chance.

Or he would have if Lizzy hadn't arrived at the viewing a few minutes late.

"Sorry." She dashed out of Emma's SUV, looking slightly pale and maybe a little flustered. "Because of the time change, I arranged for the kids to go to Trina's. I mean, I know you said I could bring them, but they'd be bored, and this way we can concentrate on the house."

"Yeah, sorry about that. I should have arranged it in advance, but I was rushing to try and get things done at the ranch before I had to leave."

"It's no problem. Chloe was ecstatic to have a playdate with Maddie, and Trina can watch the kids until five thirty, so we're all good."

Kit studied her carefully, wondering how annoyed she was, but she caught his eye and put on a bright smile. "Come on." She pointed at the house. "We don't want to miss the start of the tour."

Bonnie was already in the house, along with a couple other potential buyers, and Kit wasn't sure how or when he'd have time to talk to Lizzy alone.

They walked into the house together, Kit resisting the urge to rest his hand on her lower back like she was his for keeps. "How was your visit with your parents?" He tried to keep his voice casual, friendly.

Was the tension he was nearly vibrating with starting to show?

"Great," Lizzy sighed, oblivious to his thrumming heart. "It was so nice to have a taste of home, you know?"

He nodded, a niggle of fear making itself known. *Is Chicago still home?*

He so desperately wanted to ask, but not in front of an audience.

"Lizzy," Bonnie called in a cheerful greeting. "Glad you could make it."

Lizzy smiled and waved.

Any prior tension seemed to be gone. Kit found himself hoping that was just because Bonnie had moved on and not because Lizzy had.

"You ready to do this?" Lizzy's tone was light, her smile bright. But there was a spark missing in her eyes.

As they toured the house, he waited for her to chatter away about all the pros and cons, but she was unusually quiet. He was hoping for some enthusiasm about the size of the kitchen, which opened into a large family and dining room area. The Murphys had obviously done some big renovations, knocking down walls and reshaping the living space. Bonnie described it all to the group, waxing eloquent about the polished wood flooring and the copious amounts of light streaming in from the added skylights above them.

The upstairs was bright and airy as well, the master bedroom plenty big enough with an en suite bathroom that had been refurbished as well. Kit liked the curtains and carpet, the finishes in the main bathroom and the size of the closet and storage space.

His favorite part of the house, though, was the sunroom. It'd been added on to extend the living area but had a sliding door to make it a separate space. The tinted glass tempered the afternoon sunlight but didn't hinder the view of the spacious backyard. Kit crossed his arms, gazing around the room and picturing himself sitting in an armchair with a cold beer and Lizzy on his knee, sipping a Chardonnay while they watched the twins play outside.

Bonnie was in the middle of telling them how great this space was when she was called away by one of the other couples to answer a question about the kitchen. Kit stayed put, eyeing Lizzy where she stood by the wall of glass.

Nerves ate at him. He was desperate to know what she thought and was about to ask her when she spun and walked back to his side.

"Well?" she prompted.

He tried to read her expression as he gave her his initial thoughts and then ended with a surprised snicker. "To be honest…it's kinda perfect."

She was nodding in agreement before he even finished speaking. "This is the one, all right."

"So, you like it?"

"Yeah." She looked away from him and brushed a hand over her forehead. "It'll be perfect for you and the kids."

He tried not to let the comment bother him. He was seconds away from asking again if *she* liked it, because it was important that the house was perfect for *her* and the kids.

"I'm serious, Kit. This place is the best we've seen, and for me, the main selling point is this sunroom. How great will it be to sit out here, sipping a cold one and watching your kids play?"

His smile grew a mile wide.

He wasn't sure if it was nerves, fear, or excitement that had him choking on a laugh. "Am I really about to do this?"

She turned back to smile up at him, a dimple appearing, and he realized he'd missed the heck out of that dimple. "You'd better go talk to Bonnie and put in an offer before you miss out."

He nodded. She was right. But also…

"Lizzy, I wanted to say—"

"Go." She gave him a little push toward the door, her smile faltering but then pulling back up into full beam. "I've got to go get the kids. Trina's due to go out at five thirty, and I don't want to keep her waiting. You deal with Bonnie, and we'll hear all about it when you get home."

He swallowed and nodded. Now was not the time. Not for what he'd been about to say. He needed privacy if he meant to tell this woman that he'd been able to see this place as a home for all of them.

Now he just had to convince her of that.

31

Lizzy's stomach turned when she went to go into downward-facing dog. She flopped over with a thud as she watched the twins go up on their hands and feet, their cute little butts sticking up in the air.

"Lizzy, you're not doing it right," Corbin chided.

She gave them a half-hearted laugh, turning her attention to the YouTube video all three of them had been following. It was a yoga channel for kids, and Lizzy had been promising them they'd try it ever since she'd discovered they'd never even heard of yoga before.

"I want to watch you guys." She pressed her lips together and swallowed.

Her stomach did an unpleasant flip-flop, and her head fell back with an internal moan. *What is wrong with me?* She'd been feeling off all afternoon, ever since she'd made herself lunch.

Maybe she'd eaten too quickly.

She certainly didn't want to eat anything else. Trying to sit there while the kids devoured grilled cheese sandwiches—it was all she could manage—made her want to throw up. She'd bitten her lips together and concentrated on not breathing through her nose. By some miracle, she survived the dinner, but she was failing at yoga.

"Watch me, Lizzy," Chloe said. "I'm a tree in the forest."

Lizzy chuckled, despite her discomfort, as the kids went up on tiptoes to act out the next part of the story adventure the narrator was leading them on, using yoga poses for each new twist in the tale.

She almost wished Kit would get home sooner to watch them. But last he'd texted, he was still filling out a mountain of paperwork back at the realtor's office where Bonnie worked. The back-and-forth negotiations had motored along with the buyers responding quick smart. It sounded like the Murphys could potentially be accepting Kit's final offer before the day was done.

Lizzy was so happy for him. The house was perfect. Ticked all the right boxes. It was just the fact that she'd kept envisioning herself living there with them that had been the problem.

Her stomach roiled, and she put a hand to her belly.

Well, that and the fact that she'd felt queasy throughout the entire tour. She did her best to hide it with bright smiles, not wanting to burden Kit with her woes when he was trying to make life-changing decisions.

The moment she'd sailed down that road just out of town, drinking in the fields and then that beautiful elm tree guarding the entrance to the Murphys' home, she had a good feeling about the place.

She didn't want to do anything to stop Kit from getting it, especially as they toured the lovely home and she grew more and more certain that it was right for Kit and his family.

She kept her lips sealed, wanting him to make his own decision and not be swayed by her. She'd been ecstatic when he told her how perfect it was, but she couldn't muster the energy to really show him.

The video came to an end, and Lizzy pulled herself to her feet and shut it off. "All right, you two. Next stop, your beds. A deal was a deal."

They grumbled but did as they were told, rushing through their teeth brushing and getting into pajamas as Lizzy herded them along.

When they were tightly tucked into bed, bedtime prayers said, she pulled out the two books they'd chosen. Her head was starting to pound, her muscles were achey, and paranoia was starting to set in.

It wasn't flu season yet, was it?

Lizzy said a silent prayer that she wasn't contagious. She'd feel horrible if the twins got sick because of her. She tried her best to be enthusiastic and use all the voices and accents they liked, but her hands were shaking by the time she was done.

Corbin was fast asleep when she set the second book down.

Chloe, on the other hand, seemed to be wide awake and started peppering Lizzy with questions about the new house her daddy was currently buying.

Lizzy had tried earlier to explain that he was only making an offer—there were still a lot of stages to go before it was a done deal—but that had all seemed to go over their heads.

"Chloe, sweetheart," she said as she knelt down beside the little girl's bed. "I know you're excited, and I'm sure your daddy will tell you all about it in the morning. But right now you need to get some sleep."

Please, she begged silently. *Please let me lie down on the couch in silence.*

Her headache was growing worse by the second.

"But I'm not sleepy," Chloe pouted, then grinned. "I'm too excited."

"Mmm," Lizzy murmured in understanding. "That used to happen to me too, when I was a kid."

"It did?"

Lizzy nodded. "Oh yeah. I'd get myself so excited about what I was looking forward to that I couldn't so much as shut my eyes."

Chloe's eyes widened as she nodded. "Me too."

Lizzy smiled. "Do you know what my mother did to help me sleep?"

"What?" Chloe turned on her side and curled up in a ball.

"She'd sing me a lullaby, like this one." Quietly, so as not to wake Corbin, she sang "You Are My Sunshine," which had always been her mom's favorite.

Chloe's eyelids were drooping by the time she was finished, but they were filled with sadness too.

"I don't have a mama to sing to me." Her voice was so pained it made Lizzy's heart splinter. Before she could respond, Chloe added, "And if we move away from here, I won't have a grammy either."

"Oh, sweetie, just because you move doesn't mean you're not going to see your grammy." Lizzy ran her finger along the edge of Chloe's hairline. "You two will probably be closer than ever."

"Really?"

"She'll come visit all the time, and you can have sleepovers in this house. It's going to be so fun. And she'll love the new house."

Chloe met her gaze evenly. "Do you think my mom ever thinks about me?"

The question, said with such sweet sincerity, broke Lizzy's heart. Swallowing, she blinked and fought a few tears. "Well, my dad left me when I was little. I can't remember him, but I know he thought about me, because he'd send me birthday and Christmas cards. See? So even when your parents can't be with you, they're still thinking about you."

The little girl's eyebrows pulled together. "But I don't get anything from my mommy."

Lizzy nodded, her throat choked. "I know, kiddo. But you know what? If I was your mom, I'd be thinking about you all the time."

Chloe smiled, but she still looked sad.

Lizzy ached for her in a way she never thought possible.

Tucking a stray curl behind Chloe's ear, she softly said, "I'm so sorry she's not here, sweet girl. But you know, when things like that are taken out of our lives, God always finds a way to fill the spaces." As Lizzy said the words her mother always used to say, they sank into her, and she felt like she was speaking to herself as well. For the first time, she wasn't just hearing the words, she was understanding them.

Losing her father, losing Connor…it might have hurt, but her life had been filled with so many blessings in the wake of those disasters. She'd had the father of a lifetime in Derek, and her world had opened up in a way she'd never expected after losing Connor.

Her eyes glassed over as she reached out to stroke Chloe's hair. Her life had been filled with so many new and wonderful people since her broken engagement, and she found she couldn't regret a single thing of how she ended up here, because she was *here.*

Chloe seemed to be considering her words. "God fills the spaces?"

Lizzy nodded. "God's brought people into your life to fill the hole your mommy left behind, like Grammy and Gramps, and Aunt Marsha and your dad, who is...*so* amazing. He's like two parents in one."

Chloe giggled. "And Miss Emma. And Uncle Cody. And you." She smiled. "God's given me you."

Lizzy's heart melted in her chest. She forgot all about her raging headache and the worrisome queasiness as her entire body flooded with love and gratitude.

"I love you, Lizzy," Chloe whispered.

Lizzy swallowed hard, willing the tears at bay. How could she ever walk away from this girl? From her brother? From their father? From this life?

Pressing her lips against Chloe's forehead, she whispered the truth she'd been holding so tightly inside. "I love you too, Chloe. I love you and your family so very much."

32

Kit was flying high when he pulled up in front of his parents' house.

His head was still reeling from the enormity of what he'd just done, but it had felt right, so there were no doubts. Only hope.

He reached for the bag from Mama's Kitchen before climbing out of the truck.

Lizzy had no doubt eaten with the kids, but he'd picked up some pie, along with some candles. He let out a sharp exhale. No way was he going to let nerves stop him tonight.

He wasn't going to let anything hold him back from telling Lizzy how he felt. Because seeing that house? He'd known it would be his new home; he'd known it deep down in his gut. Just like he'd known it wouldn't be a true home without Lizzy by his side.

She was part of their family in a way he'd never known a woman could be. She fit with them like a missing puzzle piece. She made his family feel whole.

He couldn't imagine a future without her, and he needed her to know it.

It might take some coaxing. He knew that. She wasn't totally sold on Aspire, let alone him. It was clear as day that she had her hesitations. But he was Kit Swanson, dang it. He didn't run from a challenge, and he sure as heck didn't turn tail and hide when the woman he loved was standing right in front of him.

She might not know it yet, but she was meant for him, and he for her.

He paused before the front door and took a deep, steadying breath before letting himself inside.

The quiet spoke volumes, telling him the kids were already asleep. He nodded with a grin.

Thank you, Lord. This is exactly what I needed.

Some quiet time to tell Lizzy the truth.

He walked into the den to find Lizzy sitting up with a frown.

He paused, surprised. "Did I wake you?"

She shook her head, but her smile was weak. "Just resting. How'd it go?"

"Great." He grinned, his earlier excitement back in force as he filled her in on the process. "Bonnie talked to the sellers, and she thinks it's as good as done, assuming the inspections go well."

"That's great, Kit," she said. "I'm really happy for you. And the twins. You chose well."

Her usual exuberance was gone, and he tried not to take that to heart.

She seemed tired, that was all.

And besides, he'd already decided that nothing in the world was going to keep him from telling Lizzy exactly how he felt.

"I should get going," she said, her gaze on the door as she shuffled toward him.

"Wait." He blocked her path, and she looked up with brows arched in surprise. He held up the bag he was carrying. "Celebrate with me?"

She blinked.

"I know you probably ate dinner already, but Mama's Kitchen makes a mean blueberry pie, and I was hoping maybe we could..."

He trailed off because she didn't just look unenthusiastic. She looked repulsed. The blood drained from her face, and she turned her head away with a hard swallow.

"Can I take a rain check?" She crossed her arms over her chest.

He took a step closer so he had a better view of her, and this time when she looked up at him, his heart stuttered with alarm.

Her eyes were flat, her gaze distant. It was like she wasn't even here. She already had one foot out the door. She couldn't even pretend to care anymore.

The thought made his chest ache. Was he too late?

Snagging her arm, he led them toward the kitchen. He'd already decided, dang it. Come what may, he was going to tell this woman how he felt.

Cody was right. He couldn't keep assuming he knew her mind, and they both deserved to know the truth. No more avoiding it, even if her truth was that she was sick of him and his company and had booked the next flight to Chicago.

"Kit, I really need to get going," she murmured but didn't try to pull out of his grip. She followed him into the kitchen, leaning against the counter as he unloaded the bag filled with Mama's Kitchen containers.

"Lizzy, there's actually something else I want to talk to you about." He took a deep breath, focusing on the boxes he was laying on the counter. When he lifted his head again, he saw her staring at the food, her brow pinched and furrowed.

He cleared his throat and straightened. "Just share some dessert with me," he said. *Man, am I begging right now? Yeah. Maybe I am.*

Her response was not at all heartening, but he wasn't about to quit.

"Kit—"

"Just for a few minutes, Lizzy. Please." He pulled out two cake forks, but she didn't move to take the one he was offering. Her expression grew even more pinched, and she winced.

His heart catapulted into his throat, a voice in his head telling him to save himself and stop now before he forced her to reject him outright.

He ignored the voice.

"I've been wanting to talk to you for a while now, actually." He steeled himself, reaching into the cupboard for two plates. "I thought maybe tonight–"

He stopped when Lizzy let out a weird sound. It took him less than a second to figure out she was retching, and he spun just in time—to be puked on. Wet sick hit him with a splatter, and he didn't even have time to think. All he could do was react, reaching for Lizzy and tugging her over to the sink.

She bent over the stainless steel, and he held back her hair with one hand while rubbing her back with the other. She finished vomiting and let out a pitiful moan.

Kit murmured comforting words, just like he would if it were one of the kids. Worry on her behalf was overwhelming, but there was also a voice of reason that was clicking all the pieces together and calling him every name in the book.

What an idiot.

How had he not noticed she was sick? He'd been so quick to see rejection and any sign of her pulling away that he hadn't spotted the telltale signs that she was ill.

When she was done heaving and weakly hanging over the sink, he lifted a hand to feel her forehead. "You've got a fever, darlin'."

"I'm sorry," she said, her voice high and pitiful as he scooped her into his arms.

"Why should you be sorry?" he said, kissing the top of her head. "You didn't ask to be sick, did you?"

"I hope I didn't get the kids sick," she whispered.

His heart gave a tug. She was worrying about them while she looked like death warmed over.

"Even if they get it, they'll survive," he said. "Let's just focus on you."

"I need to go home," she said, shifting like she was trying to wiggle out of his arms.

He tightened his grip. "Whoa, whoa. Easy, love. You're not driving anywhere in this condition."

She went limp in his arms, and his chest tightened with worry as her head flopped against his shoulder.

"I'm so sorry," she moaned.

He held her tightly, as if he could give her comfort through sheer force alone. "There's nothing to apologize for, sweetheart. Now just rest and let me take care of you."

"I…I…" Her voice was watery and small. "I puked on you."

She started crying in earnest then, and a little huff of amusement escaped. It was true, she'd hurled on his boots and some splattered on his jeans, but he wasn't worried about that.

"That's what's upsetting you?" he asked.

Her sniffles seemed to be a yes, and he sighed as he brushed his lips over her burning forehead.

Setting her gently on the edge of his bed, he lifted her chin so her gaze met his directly. "Lizzy, you do know I have two small children, right? It'd take a whole lot more than a little throw-up to freak me out."

Her lower lip wobbled with her next hiccupy sob.

"And don't forget, I work on a ranch," he said, gently pushing her back against the pillows. "I muck out stalls and deal with cattle and livestock. There's really not much you could do to faze me."

She reached for his hand when he went to walk away. "Where are you going?"

He stilled, his heart thudding painfully at the sight of her there in his bed, so pale and fragile, it took everything in him not to spill his guts right then and there and tell her just how much he loved her.

He wanted to be her man. The one who made her laugh, who lifted her spirits when she was down…and the man who took care of her when she was sick.

"I'm just going to get you something more comfortable to wear," he said.

"I can't stay here—"

"You can, and you will," he said, his tone gentle but firm. "I'll tell Emma where you are, and I won't leave your side until you're well." He met her gaze evenly. "Understand?"

Her lower lip wobbled again as she nodded. Then she flinched and her hand came to her belly.

"I'll be right back with a bucket too," he added.

A little while later, he had a cold wet rag on her forehead, and she was decked out in one of his T-shirts that was so long on her it came down to her knees.

"I think I'm dying," she moaned.

She'd just finished throwing up again, and Kit's worry was through the roof. But he wouldn't let her see that.

"Shh," he said as he eased her back against the pillows. "You'll feel better come morning, I guarantee it."

"Promises, promises," she mumbled.

He felt a smile tugging at his lips. It was sheer relief that she was at least well enough to make a joke.

Tomorrow, she'd be feeling better. He hoped. And if she was, he was going to tell her what was in his heart.

That she was his, and he didn't want to ever let her go.

Her eyelids fluttered shut, and he hoped like heck she could find some sleep. She'd need rest to recuperate, and she deserved whatever reprieve she could get from the pain.

He quietly changed out of his dirty clothes before snagging the spare blanket from the closet. He made himself comfortable in an armchair in the corner so he could be there next time she woke.

It was going to be a long night, but as soon as she was well again they'd be on their way to a new beginning.

33

At some point in the night, Lizzy had clearly died. She knew as much because when she woke up the next day, she found herself in hell.

She groaned as she registered the light hitting her eyelids. Her temples were throbbing, and her mouth tasted like a garbage disposal. She wrinkled her nose as she tentatively stretched her arms and legs—still aching, but she was no longer chilled to the bone.

Also, she finally didn't feel like hurling. Hooray for minor miracles.

She lifted her head slightly and then let it fall back against the pillow with a thud. Nope, still not enough energy to get up, but at least she didn't feel like her insides were trying to revolt.

She'd take the win.

"Morning, sleepyhead."

Kit's warm voice beside her had her eyes popping open, and she turned her head to find him sitting on a chair by the bed.

By his bed.

In his bedroom.

She groaned again as memories from the night before came back to her in agonizing clarity. She threw up on him. He carried her in his arms. And then came a seemingly endless string of incidents throughout the night, each more disgusting and humiliating than the last. But through it all, she remembered his soothing voice, his calming touch, the way he'd dabbed her forehead with a wet rag and given her sips of water when she was done.

Oh yes, this was definitely hell.

She squeezed her eyes shut tightly.

The hottest man she'd ever met, the man she'd gone and fallen in love with...and he'd seen her at the lowest moment of her whole dang life.

Lizzy clapped both hands over her face as other memories surfaced. *"Morning, sleepyhead."* That was what he'd said when she'd first come out of her room at the ranch. The day he'd first kissed her because she'd been rambling on about how pathetic and useless she was.

She made an embarrassing little squeaking noise in her throat as she swallowed a sob.

She'd been wrong. He'd seen her at her lowest, all right. *Twice.*

Apparently it was her fate in life to be humbled before the man she hoped would love her back.

"Lizzy?"

She could hear him shifting, moving closer.

"You need anything?" he asked, concern clear in his voice. "I've got some water here for you—"

"The kids," she said, finally swallowing down her own misery and humiliation enough to think clearly. She dropped her hands and opened her eyes. "Where are the kids?"

"At school."

"Are they sick?" She couldn't hide the panic from her voice. It was bad enough that she'd gone through that, but to think of the twins suffering the same fate actually made her ache all over again.

His expression shifted, his smile so affectionate it made her heart hurt.

"No, ma'am," he teased.

She was too tired to manage anything more than a minor frown. "How long have I been sleeping?"

"Well, you stopped throwing up around 6:00 a.m., and you've been in and out ever since. How are you feeling?"

She groaned, and he let out a soft chuckle.

"Work?" she asked.

"I took the day off. I had a patient to look after." He knelt down by her bed. "I've spoken to Dr. Dex. Went through all your symptoms, and he's pretty sure it's food poisoning. We have to keep your fluids up, and you can start nibbling on plain carbs when you feel up to it."

She closed her eyes and swallowed. Her stomach was no longer roiling dangerously, but the thought of eating made her uneasy.

"Food poisoning," she repeated. She'd only eaten at the ranch earlier the day before.

"I've already talked to Emma. She threw out anything you might have used for breakfast and lunch, just to be safe."

She nodded, sighing with relief. "That's good. And the kids are all right?"

"They're fine." There was that smile again.

She swallowed hard. "I think I'll take that water now."

He hurried into action, grabbing her water and then helping her into the bathroom so she could brush her teeth and splash some water on her face. By the time she came back out again, her legs were shaky and weak, but Kit was there to scoop her up and place her back in his bed.

He'd done that the night before too, she remembered. And now he was sitting on the edge of the bed beside her, feeling her forehead and fussing over her comfort like her very own nursemaid.

And he was smiling. But it was different.

This smile was new. Not at all like his smug smirk or his laughing grin. This was something else. Something…alarming.

Nice but unnerving.

She didn't know what it meant, but it made her heart feel too heavy in her chest, and her blood felt like it was turning to lava. This smile crinkled his eyes at the corners and made his gaze soft. His look was so tender and so affectionate, it had her pulse skyrocketing as he held the water glass to her lips once more and then set it down.

Finally, she couldn't take it any longer. "Kit, why are you looking at me like that?"

He reached over to brush some hair out of her face, trailing his fingers down her cheek to her jaw. "Just admiring the view."

She wrinkled her nose. "Not so beautiful now, huh?"

"Lizzy, you are always beautiful." His brows knit together.

She scoffed. "Even when I'm throwing up on you?"

"Even then." He let out a breathy snicker.

She blinked, because he looked utterly sincere as he said it. "But I look awful. And don't try to tell me I don't. No mirror is required right now. I *know* I look terrible."

He leaned over her, his arms caging her in as his

expression turned more serious than she'd ever seen it. "It's not your looks that make you so beautiful."

She glanced at him, her heart freezing in her chest. The look on his face right now was so honest, so sincere.

"That's not why I love you." He started playing with her hair, brushing it back off her forehead.

Love.

Her heart slammed back into action at the sound of that word coming out of his mouth.

Had she heard him right?

"Love?" she whispered.

He didn't acknowledge that, continuing on as he toyed with her hair, then trailing his fingers over her jaw and neck. Almost like he couldn't stop touching her now that he'd started.

"What makes you so beautiful is the way you can light up a room with your smile, and the way you can walk down a street so confidently, like the world is yours to play with." His lips curved up at the corners. "You can turn anything into fun. The way you put a spin on things. Happy carrots." He chuckled to himself. His gaze met hers again. "I love that after being so sick, your first thought was for the twins. I love the way you read to my kids using those voices and the way you sew and make Chloe pretty dresses. I love that you see the world so differently, and you make it come alive with magic and beauty that I'd have missed if you didn't point it out. I love your sense of humor." He grinned outright. "And you snort when you laugh. That's the best sound in the world right there."

A watery laugh bubbled up as tears filled her eyes. "No, it's really not."

His expression turned tender again, and there was that

smile. *Her* smile. Like it was reserved for her alone. She wasn't sure how she knew it, but she did.

And she loved it.

"I love how your face gets all flushed when you're piping mad," he continued softly. "And how your eyes go all soft and gooey when you're looking at me."

Her heart was doing funny things in her chest, buzzing with this giddy joy she'd never felt before. Reaching up, she ran her fingers over the stubble on his jaw. "Like right now."

"Yeah," he whispered, brushing the tips of their noses together, then kissing her forehead. "I love you, Lizzy O'Sullivan. And I know I've got no right to ask it, but I want you to stay here with us. I want Aspire to be your home, because…well, you feel like part of the family." He reached for her free hand that was trapped between them, clasped it in his, and held it over his heart. "I want you to be part of my family."

She couldn't help crying as she touched his face, swimming in the beauty of his words and how much she loved hearing them.

A home. A family. His heart. He was offering her everything, and her soul felt like it might explode with happiness.

Her mind, however, was struggling to keep up. "So… are you actually going to ask me to stay?"

His face rose with hope. "Do you want to stay?"

She sniffed and paused to really think about it, then started nodding. Her heart had already made the decision, but she was starting to understand that in a weird way, it made sense.

Was this the future Lizzy had always dreamed of for herself growing up? No. Definitely not. But that was only because she'd been a child when she'd come up with those dreams for herself. She hadn't known the difference between looking happy and being happy. She never could have guessed that her Prince Charming would come in the form of a cocky cowboy, and she never would have dreamed that her happily ever after would come in the form of two precious kindergarteners in a blink-and-you'd-miss it town.

But that was before. Now she knew better.

Now she knew exactly where home was, and it wasn't Chicago. It wasn't even Aspire. It was with Kit and the twins. Wherever they were, she'd be home.

Her silence lasted too long, and she felt a pang of guilt at the tension starting to mar Kit's gorgeous smile.

"I want to stay," Lizzy whispered with a smile, not wanting to torture him any longer. And the moment the words came out, she knew precisely how true they were. Something inside her seemed to settle, like she'd finally found the missing pieces of a lifelong puzzle.

"Really?" Kit's brows hitched up, his eyes shining with hope.

She nodded. "As much as it scares me, yeah, I do. I never thought I could belong in a place like this, but you make it all so easy. Your kids are amazing, and I love being with them. I love hanging out with you, talking to you, kissing you." Her lower lip quivered with a surge of affection as memories from the night before hit her right in the chest. "And you carried me and looked after me even though I puked on your pants. You stayed with me all night and cleaned up every one of my messes."

He arched a brow, a smile of amusement on his lips. "Of course I did. And I'd do it again." He wrapped his hand around hers and kissed her wrist. When he lifted his head, he was grinning down. "Are you telling me that's all it took to convince you? Kinda wish you'd puked on me a month ago."

She giggled even as a tear trickled down her cheek.

Kit gently wiped it away.

"No, I just mean…" Her throat felt too tight. "I always thought that all I had to offer was my looks." Heat crept into her cheeks. "That sounds egotistical, doesn't it?"

He shook his head, his gaze thoughtful. "It sounds honest. And I love your honesty."

She swallowed hard. She wasn't sure she'd ever get enough of hearing the L-word coming out of his mouth. "I love the fact that when you look at me, you see me," she said, her voice choked. "Not just my looks or my fashion sense, and not how I'd look on your arm if you took me out on the town."

He chuckled. "I'm afraid taking you out on the town here means Mama's Kitchen."

She laughed. "I know, I just… I guess I'm just trying to say that I love the way you see me." She wet her lips. "I love the way you've challenged me from the very first day I met you. I love that you expect more from me. I love that you trust me with your kids and—" She pressed a hand to his chest. "—and with your heart."

He growled low in his throat as he leaned over until his nose brushed hers. "I love you so much, Lizzy O'Sullivan."

"Kit." She whispered his name like it tasted sweet.

He smiled down at her.

"How did I go and fall in love with a scruffy cowboy like you?"

His smile turned into a beam, joy lighting his eyes. "I

don't know, darlin', but I'm sure glad you did." He leaned down to kiss her, but she shook her head quickly.

"Not after what came out of there last night. You don't need to be kissing my lips right now."

He snickered. "Okay, fine, but just know I'll be making up for it as soon as you're better."

She laughed as she nodded. "Deal."

His concerned gaze flickered over her face. "You still look tired, sweetheart."

She winced. "I still feel tired." Her nose wrinkled. "Actually, I kinda feel like I was hit by a truck."

He murmured something soft and soothing as he kissed her forehead. "You get some rest. We have all the time in the world for talking."

"And laughing," she added. "And teasing, and kissing, and playing with the kids..."

He chuckled, brushing a hand over her hair so tenderly and so soothingly that it had her eyes fluttering shut again.

"We have time for all of it," he murmured.

She was already starting to fall asleep, a smile still curling her lips.

But she was awake enough to hear him say, "We have the rest of our lives, my love."

34

Nearly a month later, Kit was finally moving into his own home with his new family. Well, all but one of them. Lizzy had found a place in town. Much as he ached to call her his wife and move her into this house where she belonged, she'd been adamant about taking things slowly.

Lizzy stood at the top of the staircase, directing Cody and JJ, who were carrying an armchair. "That way, please."

"Yes, ma'am," Cody teased.

She shot him a cute scowl that had his little brother laughing.

Even if they weren't rushing into marriage, it was understood that this would be her home too, and he was pretty sure she'd already decorated the place in her mind's eye.

The thought made him grin, and when he reached the top of the stairs, his arms full of boxes, he couldn't resist stopping to kiss the self-appointed interior decorator.

"Tell me, darlin'," he said in a low voice when he pulled back. "Where'd you get that pretty outfit?"

She laughed, glancing down at the overalls he'd bought for her on her very first day in Aspire.

"Oh, these old things?" she teased. "Some cowboy I know thought it'd be a funny joke to see me in them."

He laughed too. "Just wanted to make you comfortable in your new home."

Love radiated from her, warming him more thoroughly than the sun ever could. "And that you did. You showed me what home truly means."

They shared a sappy smile that made Cody and JJ groan in unison as they passed by on their way back down to grab another load.

"Exactly how long does this honeymoon phase last?" Cody loudly feigned exasperation.

JJ chuckled. "Don't ask me, man. But Nash is still acting like a moron, so I wouldn't hold your breath."

"Are we that bad?" Lizzy asked through her laughter once their friends were out of earshot.

"I reckon so," Kit drawled, setting the boxes down so he could pull her into his arms. His nose grazed hers. "I love that you wore those today. It feels like we've come full circle."

She nodded, slipping her arms around his neck. "It has been quite a journey. And I will admit—" She glanced down. "—they are awfully good at protecting the clothes underneath."

"See?" He kissed the tip of her nose. "Told you."

"Bet you didn't think I could make them look so good." She wiggled her eyebrows, a sparkle in her eyes.

Kit chuckled as he took in the newly altered overalls, which were tucked in at the waist and sported girly embellishments on top. "I never doubted it for a second, my love."

They shared a soft, sweet kiss that spoke of promises for the future. Being here with her in his new home—it was perfect. He couldn't wait until she was living there full-time…as his wife.

But he'd swore to give her time to stand on her own two feet, and he'd respect that. Even if everything in him wanted to scoop her into his arms and take care of her.

It was important for her to know she was fully capable of taking care of herself first before she became a mother and a wife.

He didn't just respect that, he adored it.

Even if not having her under his roof yet was killing him.

At least she owned a car now and could pop over whenever she wanted. They went shopping for it last weekend. Kit drove her to the nearest city while his parents watched the twins. It was a date that lasted all day, and they'd had a blast together. Kit couldn't remember the last time he'd had so much fun.

They spent the morning strolling through car lots. After lunch in a fancy restaurant, they made out in the back of a movie theater before going back to collect her new car. Finally, as the sun set on the horizon, they drove home in two cars, their phones on speaker so they could talk the entire way. Lizzy couldn't stop going on about how much she loved her red Subaru Impreza, which she'd named Cherry before they even left the lot.

Lizzy glanced in the direction Cody and JJ had just left. They could hear Nash's voice on the ground floor as he helped Kit's father with some of the boxes.

"I sure hope you guys don't wear yourselves out too much before next week," she said.

He arched a brow. "Just how much stuff do you have to move into your new apartment?"

Her parents were sending all the contents from her storage unit in Chicago to help furnish her new spot, which was a second-floor apartment near Trina's boutique, where she'd been working part-time, and close to the school, where she still helped to pick up the kids.

She trailed her fingers over his biceps as she peeked up at him through her lashes. "Let's just say my wardrobe consists of a whole lot more than yours."

He gave a little huff of amusement. "I don't doubt it."

"Speaking of…" She reached for his hand and dragged him into the master bedroom. She pointed toward the walk-in closet. "Let me show you how I organized everything."

He shook his head as he came up behind her and wrapped his arms around her waist. "You do know you're going to have to reorganize everything soon enough, don't you?"

"Why, whatever do you mean?" Lizzy teased.

He growled and tightened his grip, making her laugh out loud. "I mean, I love the sight of you in my bedroom, Lizzy."

She adopted a schoolmarm tone as she playfully smacked his forearm, which was still tight around her waist. "Behave yourself, Mr. Swanson."

"I just can't wait, that's all." He kissed the top of her head.

She sighed sweetly. "Me too." She turned in his arms. "But I appreciate that you're letting me do this my way."

He nodded. "Truth be told, it's probably smart for me too. I was burned so badly before. I know I still have some issues of my own to work out before we take the next step."

She leaned in until her cheek was pressed to his chest, her ear right over his heart. He was sure she could hear what she did to him just by being near.

"I love you, Kit," she whispered.

"I know," he said teasingly, using his best cocky voice.

When she pulled back and saw his Cheshire cat grin, she laughed so hard she snorted.

Man, he loved that laugh.

"And I love you too, sweetheart," he added, pulling her in close and kissing her with all the passion that was in his heart.

She sighed against his lips before pulling back, her eyes deliciously dazed. "We're supposed to be working, not making out."

"I've still got kisses you owe me." His lips trailed down her jawline, then dropped to her neck before she squirmed out of his arms with a laugh.

"That was a month ago," she said primly. "I have definitely made it up to you."

He grabbed her around the waist again. "When it comes to you, I don't think too much is ever enough."

She sighed dreamily and sank back into his arms. His lips touched hers and she was lost all over again until…

"Found 'em, Grammy!" Corbin yelled. "They're doing it again!"

Chloe raced in after him and slapped a hand over her eyes, as she was prone to do whenever she caught them kissing.

Lizzy and Kit broke apart with a laugh. Kit grabbed his son, tipping him upside down and making him giggle. Kit's mom appeared with a grin, leaning against the doorframe and watching with a delighted gleam in her eyes. She'd fallen for Lizzy before she'd even met her in person. Kit had been kind of nervous to tell his parents the big news—he'd fallen in love with a city girl. They were surprised at first, but then Lizzy took it upon herself to call his parents and say hi. Two hours later, they were asking him when he was going to propose. Since they'd returned from their cruise, they'd shared several meals together, and Lizzy was now one of the Swanson clan, even if it wasn't yet official.

Chloe's laughter bounced off the walls as she raced around Kit in a circle, Lizzy chasing her. "I'm gonna get you!"

Chloe's screams of delight were soon muffled against Lizzy's shirt as she wrapped his daughter in a bear hug. Glancing at his mother, he caught her happy wink, and that was the moment Kit knew without a doubt that he was the luckiest man on the planet.

He was also the happiest he'd ever been.

35

Emma was fussing as she poured Lizzy a cup of coffee. "And you're sure the new apartment is working out? You know there's always room for you here—"

Lizzy cut her off with a hand on her arm. "I'm sure, Em. The apartment is perfect."

"You're not too lonely living by yourself?" Emma asked.

Lizzy smiled. It seemed she wasn't the only one adjusting to the new and improved Lizzy. Emma wasn't quite sure how to deal with a sister who didn't need to be taken care of.

Luckily for everyone, Lizzy suspected Emma would have her hands full with a family of her own in the very near future.

"How could I be lonely?" she asked with a laugh. "I'm almost always either working at Trina's, hanging out with my little munchkins, or chatting with you." She couldn't stop a huge smile from spreading as a warm fuzzy feeling took over her chest. "Besides, you know I spend most every evening and weekend day with Kit and the twins."

Emma laughed. "That's true. It's just… I worry about you. Old habits are hard to break, I guess."

Lizzy nodded. "I know. But I'm not that woman anymore."

Emma's smile turned maternal and sappy. "I'm so proud of you, Lizzy."

Lizzy sniffed back tears. "Thanks, Em. And honestly? I'm pretty proud of myself." She glanced down at the table as she looked for the words. "It's like for the first time in my life, I really love who I see when I look in the mirror." She gave Emma a wry grin. "Even if my hair isn't perfect and my makeup is smeared."

Emma nodded in understanding. "That's great, Lizzy. I'm so happy for you."

Lizzy smiled, leaning over to grab her tablet. "Thanks, but today isn't about me. Or did you forget?"

Emma laughed, sipping her coffee. "How could I forget our first official wedding planning meeting?" She smiled sweetly. "Have I mentioned how much I appreciate you helping me with this?"

"Are you kidding? It's my pleasure." Lizzy started scrolling through her Pinterest lists so she could show Emma some ideas. "I love this stuff."

"I know you do," Emma said. "And I can't wait until you finally get to have the wedding of your dreams."

Lizzy's lips lifted with a fleeting smile, but she didn't say anything.

"Oh, sorry," Emma said quickly. "I know you two are moving slowly. I didn't mean to—"

"No, no, it's not that," Lizzy interrupted softly. "It's just…" A smile tugged at her lips as she opened her mouth to explain but then changed her mind. Shaking her head, she shifted the topic back to her sister. "This is your planning session, not mine."

Emma arched her brows in surprise.

"Don't look at me like that." She lightly slapped her sister's hand. "Everything does not always have to be about me. I get that now."

Emma's eyes started to glisten as she rested her hand over Lizzy's. "You're the best sister. I love you so much."

Lizzy sniffed and let out a wobbly giggle. "You're gonna make me cry. Can we start talking about pretty dresses now, please?"

Emma nodded, slashing a finger under her eye. "Of course. It's one of the most important parts of the wedding, right?"

Lizzy snorted. "Oh, definitely."

They both burst out laughing, and then Lizzy launched into all her ideas for Emma's wedding.

They were interrupted when the back door opened and JJ walked in with Chloe clutching his arm. The twins had been playing in the stables with Cody, Kit, and Nash last time Lizzy had gone to check on them, and she arched a brow at the quiet mountain man in a silent question.

He kept a serious expression on his face as he explained, "I've been tasked with escorting Her Highness inside for her royal tea party."

Emma choked on her coffee, and Lizzy struggled to keep a smile off her face. "How kind of you, good sir."

He dipped his head and bowed to Chloe. "Your Highness."

Chloe turned to look up at him with big eyes. "I'm a fairy princess," she whispered. "Not a real one. You don't have to bow."

"Very good, miss," he murmured before taking his leave.

Emma's shoulders were shaking, but she kept quiet, leaning over to whisper, "I had no idea JJ was such a sucker for kids."

Lizzy snorted with laughter as she held out a hand to Chloe. "It's time?"

Chloe nodded eagerly, and Emma went into action, taking Lizzy's coffee cup and dumping the contents as she spluttered in protest.

"It's tea time," Emma explained, "not coffee time."

Lizzy opened her mouth to protest again but relented with a sigh at the sight of Chloe's eager nods.

They had agreed that today would be a ladies' day, which for Chloe meant a tea party. She'd made this very clear. There was no use fighting it now.

Even if Lizzy did hate the taste of tea.

Emma held up a plate of 'everything' cookies, which were basically cookies that contained every kind of candy imaginable, plus a plate of frosted sponge cake. "Tea and pastries."

Lizzy laughed as she helped Chloe into her seat for their very proper tea time. "Okay, now *that* I can get behind."

Chloe was abuzz with excitement as the conversation turned back to wedding planning for Emma. All three were discussing the pros and cons of a winter wedding when the men came in.

"Daddy!" Chloe threw herself at Kit, who lifted her easily and settled her on his hip as Corbin trailed in behind him.

Nash came over to kiss the top of Emma's head. "You guys talking wedding plans?"

"We are, and the more we talk the more excited I get!" Emma beamed.

The smile they shared was enough to heat the entire kitchen. And when Kit came over to put a hand on Lizzy's shoulder, she was struck by the fact that her favorite people were surrounding her and…

Well, there was no place she'd rather be.

Contentment filled her from her head to her toes. Kit seemed to read her mind, lowering Chloe to the floor then planting a swift kiss on Lizzy's lips, before reaching for the cookies. He handed one to Corbin, then munched through his own in three swift bites. Lizzy wrinkled her nose and shook her head. "Such a caveman."

He let out a playful growl, nuzzling her neck and making her laugh.

She was only broken out of her revelry when Corbin interrupted them with his loud question. "When are you and Daddy getting married?"

Kit jumped back from her, making a choking sound as Nash burst out in a boisterous laugh that had Lizzy blushing.

Emma smacked his arm, but she was clearly trying not to laugh too.

Kit leaned down to whisper in Lizzy's ear. "Out of the mouth of babes," he teased.

Lizzy dipped her head with a grin. He'd made it abundantly clear over the past month or so that he was in it to win it. He'd been talking about their eventual marriage and maybe even more kids since day one.

But he'd also been respectful of the fact that she needed time.

Although now…

Maybe it was the wedding planning, or just the joy that

overtook her every time she was surrounded by Kit and the kids, but she found herself feeling just as impatient as Emma to have her wedding. But more importantly, the marriage and the life that followed. She wanted to move in with Kit, wake up beside him, see these darling children each morning when she got out of bed.

With an adoring smile, she brushed the cookie crumbs off Corbin's shirt.

"Well?" Chloe demanded, not seeming to notice the amusement going on around her at this line of questioning. "When do I get to be a flower girl?"

Emma stepped in. "Tell you what, Miss Chloe. Until Lizzy and your daddy make it official, how about you be my flower girl?"

Lizzy shot her sister a grateful smile as Chloe jumped up and down with a squeal of excitement. She turned to Nash with wide eyes. "Is that okay, Uncle Nash?"

He picked her up and gave her a big hug. "Of course, sweetheart. We wouldn't have it any other way." He arched a brow at Corbin. "How would you feel about being my ring bearer?"

Corbin's shoulders straightened. "I'd be honored, sir."

Kit's eyes were shining with laughter and joy when Lizzy looked up at him. He squeezed her shoulder, and his gaze seemed to say so much without him having to utter a word.

"Still didn't answer my question, though," Corbin muttered.

Lizzy snickered as she sipped her tea.

"Well?" Chloe persisted.

Lizzy shot Kit a mischievous smile. "Well, your daddy would have to ask me first."

He arched his brows, his gaze accusing. She'd been the

one to put the brakes on wedding talk, not him, and they both knew it.

Chloe pouted and then turned to Lizzy. "Couldn't you just ask him?"

A silence followed as Lizzy's eyes widened. Her gaze collided with Kit's again, and she was almost certain he could read her mind, because his smile was nothing short of triumphant.

"Yeah," she said slowly. "I suppose I could."

Because when it came to Kit and his family, she didn't need tradition. She didn't even want it. Their family would always be unique, and she wouldn't have it any other way.

A knock on the door interrupted them all. Emma got up to see who it was, Nash trailing closely behind her. Chloe and Corbin decided it was their responsibility to investigate too. Lizzy hampered a laugh as she stood and prepared herself. It wasn't every day the ranch got an unexpected visitor.

With a moment alone in the kitchen, Kit wrapped his arms around her and kissed her lips. "So, when should I be expecting my proposal?" He wiggled his eyebrows.

She laughed. "Now, if I told you, it wouldn't be a surprise."

His gaze grew serious for a moment, and he held her face. "Don't make me wait too long."

A thrill raced through her, and she went up on her tiptoes to kiss him properly. "I won't. I promise."

They were interrupted by Emma's voice from the entry. "Rose?"

Lizzy stiffened, her wide eyes meeting Kit's. "Rose is here?"

They both hurried into the entryway to find a slim,

petite blonde on the doorstep, her eyes too big in her pale face.

"I'm sorry I didn't call." Her voice was so small it was hard to hear.

Rose.

Lizzy blinked, her hand instinctively clasping Kit's.

Her sister.

"No, no, come on in," Emma was saying as she shooed everyone aside to lead Rose into the kitchen. The whole family followed.

Rose moved slowly; her entire body seemed to be trembling and her energy waned before she even reached the kitchen. Resting her hand on her stomach, she stopped and leaned against the archway leading into the kitchen.

"Rose?" Emma asked. "Are you okay?"

Rose's attempt at a smile was feeble. Her face was gaunt, and there were dark shadows under her eyes. "Just car sickness. It's a long way from New York."

"You drove here?" Lizzy cast a shocked look in Emma's direction.

Emma was frowning in concern.

"I think I need to lie down." Rose blinked, touching her forehead and looking ready to keel over. "If that's okay."

Kit jumped forward to catch her, but she shied away from his touch. Lizzy stepped into his place, worry swarming her.

"Your old room," Nash said in a low voice.

Lizzy nodded and helped Rose to the hallway, murmuring quietly to her all the while. Rose seemed okay with Lizzy's company and leaned into her, mumbling apologies as she went.

"Kids, stay in the kitchen for me, okay?" Kit directed the twins.

Lizzy glanced over her shoulder and saw Emma following her with a glass of water and some crackers.

"Here we go." She spoke softly, directing Rose as if she were a nurse or mother. Tucking her into bed, she rested her hand on Rose's forehead. "You don't have a fever."

"It's just car sickness," Rose murmured, but Lizzy wasn't sure she believed her.

"We'll get you a bucket, just in case." Lizzy hadn't even finished speaking before Kit appeared in the doorway with a large stainless steel bowl.

"Perfect, thanks." She set it up next to the bed while Emma shut the curtains.

Rose was already drifting off to sleep.

On tiptoe, Lizzy and Emma left the room and closed the door behind them, then followed the men back into the kitchen.

"Okay, that's weird, right?" Lizzy frowned. "Did you even know she was coming?"

Emma shook her head, concern creasing her brow. "No, but you turned up out of the blue, so maybe it's an O'Sullivan thing."

Lizzy gave her sister an impish grin and shook her head. "Call me if you need anything, okay?"

"Will do." Emma leaned forward to kiss her cheek, and Nash gave her a hug goodbye.

Kit led her and the kids down to his truck and helped the twins get buckled in.

"Is the lady going to be okay?" Chloe asked from the back.

Lizzy turned to face her with a smile. "She'll be just fine, sweetie."

"Was it like what you had?"

Lizzy frowned. She certainly hoped not. "Maybe. Or

maybe she's just really tired. Sometimes people feel sick when they're overtired, and she drove a really long way."

She tried to keep her voice light, but a quick glance at Kit showed he shared her concerns.

"I hope she's all right," Corbin said.

"She will be." Lizzy turned to reassure him. Whether Rose knew it or not, she was surrounded by family now. She was surrounded by love. The thought had Lizzy smiling over at Kit. "This place has a way of making people all better."

Kit grinned at her, taking her hand and kissing the inside of her wrist. The love in his gaze was enough to fill Lizzy's heart to overflowing.

She'd found her home here in Aspire, all right.

She'd found her heart too.

EPILOGUE

"Shhh," Lizzy whispered to the twins. "Just stay low. We don't want him to see us."

Chloe giggled into her hand, and Corbin nibbled on his lip, peeking out around the furniture while they listened to Kit walk into the house.

"Hello? Is anybody home?"

Lizzy's heart trilled as she struggled to keep quiet. She'd been planning this surprise for three weeks and didn't want to jump the gun now. She and the kids had worked too hard.

"Hel-lo!" Kit drew out the word. His tone was playful, which Lizzy was grateful for. She didn't want him worrying. Any second now he'd see—

Kit's laughter boomed from the kitchen.

"He's found it!" Chloe whispered excitedly.

Lizzy winked at the little girl, barely able to contain her excitement.

"To Cowboy Charming," Kit read the note aloud, obviously loving this game. Lizzy wished she could see him, but she didn't want to spoil the surprise. This was a big deal, and she couldn't let her impatience ruin it.

Kit continued with the note, following the first clue up to the bathroom, where he was instructed to take a two-minute shower and put on the new cologne Lizzy had bought him. He'd smell divine, and yes, it'd be a struggle to keep her lips off him.

While he was showering, they raced to put the next clue in the hallway, where he was directed to his bedroom and a nice-looking suit. The three were back in hiding, Chloe vibrating with excitement, when his laughter rang down the hallway.

"He likes it!" she whisper-shouted.

"I know," Lizzy mouthed, running her hand down the sleeve of Chloe's new princess dress. They'd finished making two this week, and Chloe had picked the pale pink one for this occasion. Corbin was decked out in a suit as well. It was so cute seeing him dressed like a little man, but he insisted that if his father was dressing up, then so was he.

Kit's footsteps echoed off the wooden floors as he came back down the stairs. He reached the bottom and found the string they'd set up, chuckling softly as he followed it to the sunroom.

The second he stepped inside, they jumped out of hiding and shouted, "Surprise!"

The look on Kit's face was enough to melt Lizzy's heart. Nerves tore through her, competing with the giddy butterflies dancing from her stomach to her chest.

"What is going on?" Kit took in the champagne flutes and specially made food laid out on the table. "It's not my birthday."

"Nope, but it's a super-special day!" Corbin rocked back on his heels and shared a secret smile with Lizzy.

She winked at her boyfriend and told him to take a seat.

He sat down, smoothing his tie and looking oh so handsome.

As much as she loved her rugged cowboy, seeing him decked out in a suit and smelling this divine, well, she was struggling to control herself.

Chloe skipped around her, slipping her little hand inside Lizzy's before approaching her father.

"We've got something important to ask you."

"O-kay." Kit gave Lizzy a curious look. She was surprised he hadn't worked it out already.

"You know how we love you?" Corbin asked.

"I sure do." Kit grinned. "I love you guys too."

"Exactly!" Chloe jumped to her tiptoes and clapped her hands. "So, we want to know if it's okay for Lizzy to move in with us."

"Oh really?" Kit leaned back with an elated smile. "Well, I guess that's up to Lizzy, now isn't it?"

"Exactly," Lizzy whispered, her legs trembling as she walked to his side and knelt down in front of him.

Kit jerked up in his seat, his eyes wide and hopeful.

She grinned, pulling a box out from under his chair and holding it up. "Kit Swanson."

"Yes?" he choked, his eyes already starting to glisten.

"I love you. I love your children, your family, this home. I want to become a permanent part of it."

He blinked, his eyes starting to shine even more.

"Would you do me the honor of becoming my husband?"

Resting the pads of his fingers on her cheek, he touched her like she was a delicate petal.

"I love you so much." His voice trembled. "Of course I'll marry you."

She laughed, joy firing through her like rockets.

"Yay!" Chloe started jumping up and down. "Show him the ring! Show him!"

Lizzy giggled and popped the box open. Leaning forward, Kit looked at the stunning emerald ring and burst out laughing.

"I'm saving you the trouble of having to pick something for me," she explained.

With a delighted grin, Kit plucked the ring from the box and slid it onto her finger. "My future bride." He beamed, cupping her face and kissing her slow and sweet.

The twins tolerated it, up to a point, then got antsy and wanted to celebrate with champagne.

Lizzy poured Sprite into two flutes while Kit popped the cork on the real stuff.

Once they were all sitting around the table, Corbin raised his glass. "To our new family!" he toasted, and they gently clinked their glasses together before each taking a sip and sealing the deal.

Kit ran his hand along Lizzy's thigh, snuggling her closer on his lap as they sipped coffee and watched the kids run around the backyard. Chloe's princess dress hung down below her jacket, the hem already wet from the light sprinkling of snow that had fallen overnight. She'd insisted on sleeping in the dress, and Kit didn't have the heart to stop her. After their euphoric evening, he didn't want to get into a silly argument over pajamas.

Lizzy had stayed the night too. As much as he'd wanted her in his bed, they'd behaved themselves, and she'd slept in the spare room.

Seeing her tousled hair and sleepy smile this morning had been enough for him to want to drive to city hall as soon as breakfast was over.

"So, when are we getting married?" He fingered the emerald ring she'd had made. It was beautiful, and he loved the fact that it wasn't a traditional diamond engagement ring. She'd picked green to match her eyes.

"That's what I would have chosen," he'd said when she was telling him the story.

"I know." She'd kissed him. "That's why I went for an emerald."

She glanced down at their connected hands, the dimples in her cheeks appearing quickly. "I don't know. When do you want to get married?"

"Right now." He chuckled. "But I know these things take time to plan. There's a lot to arrange, and I want you to have a beautiful wedding. Everything you want." He dropped a kiss on her shoulder. "Everything you missed out on."

She went quiet, and he studied the side of her face.

"What are you thinking?" he whispered.

"I don't want to get in the way of Emma's big day, and with everything Rose is going through right now... She's still not better, and Emma's thinking we might just have to force her to see Dr. Dex." She shook her head, then placed her coffee mug down and turned to face him. Resting her hand lightly on his neck, she brushed her thumb along his jawline and smiled. "You know what? I don't need a big wedding. I don't want fancy. I just… I want you." She swallowed and blinked at the onset of tears. "With Connor, it was all about the show. I was consumed with the big day. My chance to be the star. To have everyone admiring me. I was so wrong." Her face bunched, and Kit ran his hand down her back, wanting to erase the unhappy memories for her. "I realize now that it's not even about the wedding. It's about all the days after it. It's about marriage, being a couple, raising these beautiful children and being a family."

Kit's heart swelled bigger than he thought it ever could.

"I love you, cowboy. You're my home, and I don't need some fancy-pants wedding. I just want to be your wife."

They were the most beautiful words he'd ever heard. Leaning forward, he pressed his lips to hers, quickly deepening the kiss and promising her a lifetime of love.

Finally pulling back, she rested her forehead against his and whispered, "Fancy a trip to city hall?"

His lips parted. "Are you serious?"

"You call your parents and Cody. I'll call Emma and Nash. My parents can phone in and watch on-screen." She giggled. "Kit, we could be married before the sun sets tonight."

He jumped up so fast that she toppled off his knee and he had to catch her before she hit the ground. She was laughing so hard as he swooped her into his arms and carried her to the glass door. Sliding it open, he called into the backyard, "Kids! Time to come in. Let's go marry Lizzy!"

"Really?" Chloe jumped off the half-constructed fort and raced for the door. "Let me go put my other new dress on!"

As she raced up the stairs, Corbin ran inside and pulled off his winter jacket, revealing the rumpled suit he'd slept in. "I'm good to go!"

Lizzy burst out laughing. "This is going to be a day to remember."

Kit beamed at her, kissing her lips, unwilling to put her down until they'd reached the top of the stairs. Lizzy walked to the spare room to put her dress from last night back on while he went for his suit and tie.

Excitement made his hands shake, but as he got dressed, making phone calls on speaker and inviting a bunch of surprised, excited people to his wedding, he couldn't have been happier if he'd tried.

Tonight, he'd be lying in his bed next to the Gucci girl of his dreams.

I hope you loved this ending. I couldn't finish the book without knowing these two were going to tie the knot.

But what's up with Rose?
How sick is she? And can Dr. Dex find a cure?

Keep reading to uncover the story of the next O'Sullivan sister and a kindhearted doctor who might just be able to heal her heart as well.

This kind country doctor might be able to treat Rose's health, but can he mend her injured heart?

Dex might be young for a doctor, but the small town of Aspire trusts him with their lives. It's an honor and a privilege to care for his community, even if his uber successful siblings and parents think he's nuts for choosing a tiny clinic in the mountains of Montana over a bustling emergency room in the big city.

Despite the town's overabundance of nosy neighbors who'd love to find a match for the handsome, eligible doctor, he's always put his reputation as a professional first. Dr. Dex is careful to keep a professional distance from his female patients. Until now. Until Rose...

Alone and on the run from a past best left behind, Rose is sure she's made a mistake coming to Aspire. Showing up on a ranch in the middle of nowhere to live with two half sisters she's never even met before? Yeah, Rose has definitely lost her marbles…along with the contents of her stomach.

Her illness has her newfound family worried, but one visit with the town's charming, kindhearted young doctor, and Rose knows it's not just her life at stake… it's her heart.

AVAILABLE IN MARCH 2022

ACKNOWLEDGMENTS

Dear reader,

Thank you so much for reading *Gucci Girls Don't Date Cowboys*. I loved working with Lizzy and Kit. They made me laugh, but also gave me the big feels. Their romance was fun and exciting, and Lizzy's character growth made me very happy.

If you enjoyed the book, I'd like to encourage you to leave a review on Amazon and/or Goodreads. Reviews and ratings help to validate the book. They also assist other readers in making a choice over whether to purchase or not. You honest review is a huge help to everyone.

And speaking of help, no book is complete without a team of people, so I'd like to thank Deborah for this beautiful cover, my eagle-eye proofreaders who caught those extra mistakes I'd missed and my amazing reviewers who have helped promote the book and left reviews that inspired me.

Thank you to every reader who has entered into this world of Aspire. I can't wait to provide more stories in this series for you.

And just before I go, I'd like to thank my creator. Thank you for love and the way it can transform and empower. You are an awesome God.

xo, Sophia

ABOUT THE AUTHOR

Sophia Quinn is the pen-name of writing buddies Maggie Dallen and Melissa Pearl Guyan (Forever Love Publishing Ltd). Between them, they have been writing romance for 10 years and have published over 200 novels. They are having so much fun writing sweet small-town romance together and have a large collection of stories they are looking forward to producing. Get ready for idyllic small towns, characters you can fall in love with and romance that will capture your heart.

www.foreverlovepublishing/sophiaquinn

Made in the USA
Middletown, DE
11 April 2022